Home for the Howlidays

Edited by

M.L.D. Curelas

HOME FOR THE HOWLIDAYS

EDITED BY

M.L.D. CURELAS

TYCHE BOOKS LTD.

Home for the Howlidays
Edited by M.L.D. Curelas
Copyright © 2021

Published by Tyche Books Ltd.
Calgary, Alberta, Canada
www.TycheBooks.com

Cover Design and Layout by Elona Bezooshko
Interior Art: Illustration 202668408 © Relato |
Dreamstime.com
Interior Layout by Ryah Deines
Editorial by M.L.D. Curelas

First Tyche Books Ltd Edition 2021
Print ISBN: 978-1-989407-35-6
Ebook ISBN: 978-1-989407-36-3

This book was funded in part by a grant from the Alberta Media Fund.

Alberta
Government

For my pack

TABLE OF CONTENTS

INTRODUCTION

IT STARTED LAST winter. Our family had had a rough year, not entirely due to the pandemic, and our upcoming holiday celebrations were going to be small—just our household, plus one friend who lives alone. No large parties, no carolling, no in-person gift exchanges . . . the overall mood was subdued at our house. We needed something to cheer us up. *I* needed something to cheer me up.

And then I saw the cover.

Wolves howling at a glowing Christmas ornament moon, framed by snow-covered fir trees.

Perfect.

I bought it. I didn't have a title or a concept, but I bought that cover because it made me nostalgic and happy and hopeful. Within a few days, I had both title and concept and quickly announced that an anthology call would be opening up in the new year. Because, ultimately, what I wanted was to read a lot of stories about friends and family coming together for the holidays. With wolves. (Or werewolves, because Tyche Books publishes speculative fiction, natch.) The call expanded quickly to include canids of all sorts, both supernatural and not, because lots of good doggos aren't slavering beasts during the full moon.

So here we are. *Home for the Howlidays* contains all sorts of dogs and wolves. Werewolves, obviously, but "normal" dogs too! Hellhounds. Ghostly dogs. Dogs with AI enhancements. Magical, mythical creatures.

You'll also find fellowship. Families forging or renewing bonds over large, festive meals. Communities coming together through adversity. Gifts of love, peace, and friendship.

Working on this anthology has been a balm for me over the past year, and I hope it brings you joy as well.

Happy howlidays,

M.L.D. Curelas
Calgary, AB
August, 2021

A Furtastic Gathering

Angèle Gougeon

"WE NEED MORE blood."

Lisa glared at the lone bottle of A-negative sitting on the skinny side-table, amongst the juice, wine, eggnog, and red plastic cups. Marie raced by, shrieking, setting the table wobbling and wearing her older cousin's winter boot on her head. A pack of little feet stampeded after her, howling at the top of their lungs. Daniel was already half-naked, legs stripped bare and showing off his bright red and blue superhero underpants; Eddie had found the festive Christmas cookies hidden in the hallway pantry, crumbs on his face and icing on his white dress shirt. He stopped to give Lisa a sweet smile, hiding his half-eaten Santa Claus behind his back.

"Love you, Grand-auntie Lisa!" he said.

"Thank you, sweetheart." With that, Eddie lunged out the kitchen doorway, smearing more icing, and shoving the rest of the shortbread into his mouth.

Will snorted, setting the second leaf of the kitchen table into place. His thick forearms corded attractively and Lisa took a moment to appreciate the sight. "Oh, gross," said David as he carried a load of chairs into the room.

"What?" Jack followed, five more stacked in his arms.

"Mom's ogling Dad again."

3

"Gross."

"And the world wonders why romance is dead," Will huffed, leaning past their boys to peck his wife on the lips.

"There's no romance allowed once you reach a certain age," David said. "It's cruel and unusual punishment."

"I'll show you punishment." Will snarled, flashing yellow eyes, and both boys squeaked and escaped from the room with a flurry of tripping feet and shoving shoulders. The wall quaked with a falling body, then footsteps joined the stampede headed down the basement stairs, several tiny voices squealing in delight.

Lisa sighed and moved one of the old wooden chairs into place. "You've scared away our help, darling."

"That was rather the point." Will grinned and leaned close, trapping her with his large hands on her waist. His thumbs curled into the dips of her hips, fingers nestling around the cord of her apron. "We'll be fine. Stop worrying about the blood. What's done is done, and besides, the stores are all closed by now."

"But what if it's no good? It could taste horrible. Maybe he prefers a certain blood type. And can he even eat the turkey? Is it insulting to not have more vintages? I just want things to be perfect."

"Honey," Will pulled his wife into his chest and rested his stubbled chin down on the crown of her greying head, "when have any of our Christmases gone perfectly?"

"Oh, don't even start," Lisa grouched, sliding her small hands over the worn cotton of his shirt. "This is the first time Karen's brought a boyfriend home for the holidays. I don't want her to be disappointed. Look at this madhouse."

Will chuckled a puff of air, nosing into the curls at her temple and big shoulders curling inward. "I'm just hoping no one phones the police this year."

"Oh God damn it, Will," Lisa pulled back with a scowl. "Now you've jinxed us."

Bridget, Lisa's sister-in-law, fair-haired and freckled, poked her head through the kitchen entrance. "Do you guys need any help? I heard the brats escaping. With all the noise they were making, you'd think a cat magically appeared."

Lisa straightened her reindeer-patterned apron and glanced at the timer over the stove. "Can you and my brother go corral the boys?"

"The kids are all in the basement."

"Well, bring up the older ones. You know who I mean—the ones that are somehow all grown-up but have yet to act like it." Will threw a poinsettia-patterned tablecloth over the not-quite-large-enough kitchen table. The platter of pickles and butter and the basket of buns sat ready on the old stained counter. A packet of candles stood nearby. Lisa was tempted to put them back in the cupboard—fire seemed like it was tempting fate. "As a matter of fact," she called out, hearing Bridget pause in the living room, "the turkey's just about done. Why don't we get everyone up here? I think we all need one last . . . *family discussion* . . . before Karen and her date arrives."

Will's shoulders shook as Bridget hurried towards the basement stairs, and Lisa glared at his wide back. "Don't you dare laugh when they get in here, Will," she told him. "You know you'll just encourage them."

"Honey," he smirked, "you're fighting a losing battle."

"WHY DO I feel like I'm in trouble?" David muttered as the family spread out in neat lines across the centre of the living room, in front of the plastic evergreen tree with its lopsided lights, homemade ornaments, and shiny Christmas star. Jack's daughter, Marie, now without her boot hat, muffled a giggle into the palms of her hands from the front row. Jack gave his twin a wide-eyed look of agreement and patted his pup on her head, messing up her riotous dark curls further. Rebecca, David's wife, elbowed him in the side with just enough strength to stagger him sideways.

Facing them, Will stood beside Lisa, silent and arms crossed over the red, white, and green Christmas sweater he'd slipped back over his head, one that had no right to be as ugly as it was— Lisa had hid it in the back of the basement closet and she honestly had no idea how he'd found the thing again, damn it all. Laurie, Alex, and Ellie kept arguing whether it was supposed to be an elf or a reindeer.

"Where's John?" Lisa asked.

"He's late." Harry leaned forward to hold Eddie in place, stealing another Christmas cookie he'd pilfered, a snowman this time, and popping it into his own mouth.

"Daaad!" he yelled.

Lisa glowered at her nephew, then pinned Eddie in place with a firm glare. "No more cookies until after supper."

"Cookies?" Marie perked up.

"No," Lisa said, and her granddaughter scowled.

In the corner, in his well-worn armchair, great-grandpa Wilson let out a snuffling snore. Someone had perched a rumpled Santa hat upon his sparse head. Tiny little hand-prints of icing crawling up his dress-shirt gave clues to the culprit.

"I want to make this very clear," Lisa said, making sure to catch every single eye. Her brother Mike threw her a grin with a wink, scratching at the uneven patch of skin on his jawline. "This year, there will be no fighting. There will be no baseball or soccer or hockey in the living room. No one will knock over the Christmas tree. No one will scream through Christmas dinner." She pinned her eyes on nine-year-old Daniel. "If someone doesn't like their food, they will spit it into their napkin. They will not chuck it across the room." Daniel made a face at the ground between his toes. There were already holes in both of his red-striped socks. He was also still half-naked. "No one will put bad werewolf movies on the television—it is no longer Halloween. No one will sneak outside and *jump* off the roof."

"I was eleven," Ellie muttered mutinously. "I'm a whole year older now. I *know* better." She mirrored her granduncle, crossing arms and glaring at Lisa. Her little sister, Alex, patted her shoulder in commiseration, just glad Grandaunt's attention wasn't on *her*.

"No one will put hockey on this year. And no one will be making bets! You know it always ends in a fight."

Andy, Jack's husband, made a disappointed sound, but drooped when his mother-in-law's gaze turned to him.

"When Karen gets here," she continued, "no one will interrogate her or her boyfriend. Especially before they even get inside the doorway. No one will even *mention* the words bloodsucker, leech, or ghoul, or I will have you doing dishes the rest of the evening while everyone else gets to open their presents and eat dessert."

"Worth it," David whispered, like everyone couldn't hear him.

"Mom should've been a dragon instead of a wolf," Jack

whispered back to his twin, and Lisa took a moment to breathe. She shared a look with her nephew Harry's wife, Sera, farthest down the row of adults, at the back of the room. At least the grandkids and grand-nephews and -nieces had the sense to squirm in the face of her outrage.

"No one," Lisa said again, "will ruin Christmas."

"*Grandma looks mad,*" Marie whispered.

"It's fine," Rebecca patted her head. "She's mostly talking to your dad."

"*Hey,*" Jack complained, while Andy looked as though he didn't know whether he should be insulted as well.

"Dumbasses," Sera muttered under her breath, making Alex gasp, scandalized.

"*Mommy,* you said a bad word."

"What's a dumb-ass?" Eddie asked.

Beside Lisa, Will began to laugh. Again.

That was when the doorbell rang.

Shit, thought Lisa. *This is going to be a disaster.* "Remember, no interrogating him!"

"But how will I know if he's good enough for our little sister if I don't threaten him a little?" David asked, heading for the door before Lisa could cut him off. She silently debated whether it was worth tackling him. *No.* There were too many little impressionable eyes around.

"I heard vampires can bench press a bus," said Harry as he escaped to the kitchen to move the platter of sliced ham to the table. Mike followed to help finish setting up the chairs at the other tiny table shoved against the wall for the kids.

"David can't even bench press a broom," Jack laughed, bringing up the rear with the bowl of gravy. He almost tripped on Daniel, who had followed them. The boy stuck out his ankle and growled.

"My daddy's a superhero," he yelled. "Bet he's stronger than you!"

Karen and her vampire boyfriend stepped into the madness, and Lisa pretended she wasn't rearranging the drink table so that she could stare openly. He was shorter than she had expected, dark-haired and dressed in dark jeans and a nice cobalt button-up. But he was just as pale as she thought he'd be. And when he smiled at her idiot son, two tiny fangs peeked out from the corners of his pallid lips.

"Can I get you something to drink?" she heard David ask, gesturing like an imbecile. "A Bloody Mary, perhaps?"

God damn it. She should have taken puns off the table, too.

Rebecca raced by with Daniel's pants, eyes a little wild and hair a little frazzled, and a tiny hand tugged on Lisa's floury Christmas apron.

"Grandma," Marie whispered, blue eyes big in her round face.

"Yes, sweetheart?"

"I have to poop."

LISA SET THE hot bowl of mashed potatoes down on an empty corkboard coaster and subtly looked around the packed kitchen table. An uncomfortable silence had settled once the roasted carrots, turkey, and meat pie had finished the rounds. A knife scraped too loud against a ceramic plate, and Andy coughed into the tension. A large glass of A-negative sat before Karen's date, Adrian. To Lisa's relief, he'd piled food high onto his plate as the platters swept by. He sat, buttering a warm roll, pretending not to notice how David leaned into his space to study his fangs.

The six kids sat at the small folding table in the corner, whispering and squashed against one another, elbows already starting to poke and prod for more space. The family had gotten larger over the years, but the kitchen had unfortunately stayed the same—more chairs stuffed around already full tables. Half the salads hadn't made it off the kitchen counters, and her family of meat-eaters were doing their very unsubtle best to ignore them.

Will handed a glass of red wine to great-grandpa Wilson, then sat down next to Lisa, who was still fretting that John was late, eyeing their daughter as she became quietly more and more furious with David from Adrian's other side. "So," Will cleared his throat, tugging his ugly sweater flat, for once trying to avert disaster, "we haven't heard much about you, Adrian. What is it that you do?"

"How did you guys meet?" David added, and Rebecca tugged him back into his chair.

"Adrian works at the bank." Karen ignored her brother and

started slicing her turkey into tiny little pieces with a grip on her knife that indicated she was about to stab someone.

"Ah," said Jack, and Lisa desperately grabbed her wine with a sinking feeling. *Don't*, she thought, trying to send the message with her eyes. "Of course," Jack said. "At the blood bank."

An amused curl lifted Adrian's lips. A dark eyebrow rose in an elegant arch. "No," he said, "just the regular kind." He picked up his glass of A-negative, and Daniel turned with laser focus from the kids table to watch, open-mouthed.

"I didn't know vampires could eat," Mike interjected, before David could open his mouth again, and Lisa turned incredulous eyes to her brother. What was he doing? That wasn't on the list of approved questions. The adults were supposed to be together on this. *Together.*

"We can't. Not really." Adrian's grin grew, lips already flushed pink from his long sip. His fangs were actually quite large. "Not to be crass, but . . . I will be expelling it later. That doesn't mean I can't enjoy a wonderful home-cooked meal in the meantime. It's very tasty, Mrs. Walker. Quite a treat from my usual fare."

"Just call me Lisa," she said, faintly to her own ears.

"What's *expel* mean?" Eddie whispered. But he was six, so it was more like shouting and everyone heard.

"He's going to chuck it up," Karen said plainly from the main table, smirking as multiple adults groaned. Andy made a face at his mashed potatoes and gravy and ate some ham instead.

"*Oh,* gross!" Laurie and Ellie shrieked, jostling Alex's arm, who still didn't seem to understand. Jack laughed, snorting into his white wine, then squealed when it went up his nose.

Karen laughed back at him obnoxiously, "Nice going, Jackyboo."

"Bite me, Kare-bear," he said, but his snarl wasn't very effective with his napkin held over his face.

"Only Adrian gets to do that," she replied.

David leaned around Karen's date to scowl at her. "None of us want to know that, Sis." Harry snorted something from the other end of the table, and suddenly he and David, Jack and Karen were all bickering. Andy got up to keep Marie from spilling gravy all the way down the front of her red and gold Christmas dress. Daniel loudly asked if he could see Adrian's fangs—and if the vampire had ever killed anyone with them. Will rolled his eyes fondly when great-grandpa Wilson began to nod off over his plate and reached down to squeeze Lisa's hand. For a moment, she thought that maybe, just maybe, for once everything might end up okay.

EVERYTHING WAS NOT okay.

Marie stood in the middle of the living room, shrieking. Adrian looked impressed at her pitch.

She'd been telling them all about the letter she'd gotten last Tuesday from Santa Claus when Daniel huffed, starting to say, "Santa Claus isn't re—" and Alex growled, leapt across the room, and bowled him over.

"Don't ruin the magic," she screamed, fur starting to sprout.

Lisa hurried toward them, then heard Harry saying, "We should go carolling," and took a hard left.

"We can't go carolling," Sera told her husband.

"Why not? We could—"

Lisa gripped his elbow, pressing tight. "No carolling," she hissed.

"What? But Aunty—"

Good. Will had gotten to the children. Daniel and Alex were both in the corner, being scolded. Marie hiccupped into her dad's shirt that no one was listening to her. She'd been *talking*. It was *her* turn to talk, Daddy.

Sera leaned closer to them and lowered her voice. "Last year those asshole cat-shifters on Gallier Lane called the cops on us, remember? We *can't* go carolling again. They said they'd arrest us if they found us out there again this year."

"What? How are they going to know it's us? Like no other werewolves ever Christmas-carol. Just because those furballs can't appreciate some good music doesn't mean we shouldn't—"

"We're the only pack in the area," Lisa interrupted her nephew again.

"We literally howl at the moon," said Sera.

They shared another look. "No carolling," Lisa reiterated.

"I don't want to hand out presents!" Laurie yelled. "Get Eddie to do it."

"Eddie can't read all the labels yet," Rebecca sighed, and David started making his way across the room to help. *Right,* Lisa thought, *multiple meltdowns imminent.* Christmas was right on track.

"I want to hand out the presents," Alex said, tugging at her aunt Rebecca's sweater sleeve.

"Why is it always me?" Laurie shouted, face turning red. "It's always *me*, Dad! God, Mom, why do you all hate me?"

"*Laurie—*"

"I want to hand out presents!"

Bridget nudged Lisa's elbow. "I put brandy in the eggnog," she whispered and handed her a cup. It was one of the extra-large coffee mugs that had been hidden in the upper cabinets, and Lisa gripped it with desperation.

Daniel had inched his way up beside Adrian again. He tugged on Karen's blouse. "Aunty Kare-bear?" he asked, and she sighed, deeply.

"Yes, Danny-wanny?"

"Can I see your boyfriend's teeth?"

"Whhhhy?" she asked, drawing the word out with suspicion.

"I want to know if they're bigger than Daddy's."

Karen went to reply, but Adrian smiled, showing off his fangs. "I assure you, mine are much bigger."

Daniel glowered, but he tugged on the vampire's button-up, urging him down low. He narrowed his brown eyes, pursing his lips in thought. "I think you're right," he finally said with disappointment. "Daddy!" he screamed across the room, to where his mom and dad were finally calming their burgeoning teenager down. "His fangs are bigger than yours! He's a better superhero than you!"

David looked gutted and Lisa snorted into her eggnog. Karen cackled and ruffled her favourite nephew's hair until it was even more of a mess. At least he still had his pants on.

"I want to hand out presents!" Alex shrieked at the top of her lungs, rivalling Marie, and Rebecca nearly flung her hands into the air, cracking her neck to the side and grimacing at the ceiling.

"That's fine. You do that," Sera told her daughter. "Let the others help out."

"There's brandy in the eggnog," Bridget told her.

"Thank fuck."

"Mom's saying bad words again," Eddie informed the nearest

adult, which happened to be a sleeping great-grandpa Wilson. And great-grandpa Wilson didn't seem too bothered, so Eddie headed over to the tree where Marie had already grabbed a gift that wasn't hers and tore off the paper.

"You can hand out this one," Alex told him solemnly, sending him back towards Grandma with a green-wrapped package almost as big as he was.

"This one's mine!" Daniel said, reaching under the tree.

"We have to take turns!" Alex shouted at him. "Put that back!"

"No!" Daniel held the wrapped rectangle to his chest. The large blue bow nearly poked him in the eye. "It's mine. It says so."

"It's not your turn!" Alex did a rather good impression of her older cousin, scowling and moody, and tried to rip the present out of Daniel's hands. He made a sound halfway between a yell and a growl, then a furious grey-furred pup sank its teeth into Alex's left hand. Alex yowled, then erupted into a similar ball of fur. Then two pups tumbled across the well-worn brown carpet, snarling with tiny razor-sharp teeth, and rolled toward the tree.

Damn it, thought Lisa as the tree slammed into the living room window, ornaments tinkling, then drank more of her eggnog as Harry, David, and Rebecca rushed over to the kids. Sera just sighed and looked heavenwards. Eddie had finally made his way over to their corner of the room, puffing and red-faced. "This one's yours," he said, letting the present thump to the floor by his grandma Bridget's feet.

"Thank you, sweetheart," she said, and ran a well-manicured hand through his sweaty curls.

He sniffed, wiping an arm across his face, then frowned as one of the Christmas baubles rolled past his feet. "Are they gonna go in the time-out corner?" he asked his mom.

Sera nodded. "Sure are."

"Are we still gonna open presents?" he asked.

"Well . . ."

"*I* didn't knock the tree over," he said.

Over by the knocked-over tree, and over the sound of crunching glass and plastic, David had gotten one pup in one hand, and one in the other, held by the scruffs of their necks as they frantically wiggled, trying to escape.

"They remind me of us," said Mike, as he sidled up to Lisa's side.

"Excuse me?"

"I still have a bare patch that won't grow back when I shift. And I still have a scar on my right thumb, too. Remember when you nearly bit it in half?"

Lisa frantically looked around. But, other than Sera and Bridget, no one was paying attention. "Don't say things like that," she growled under her breath, slapping her brother's arm. "Jack and David might be grown men, but don't give them any ideas. Before you know it, we'll have two hairless wolves running around looking like they've got mange."

"I once tore open my brother's ear so badly that my parents had to take him to the emergency room," Bridget offered, not having the decency to look even a little embarrassed. Or to lower her voice.

"You were twenty-five when that happened," said Mike. He smiled at his wife, then stepped around Lisa to lean into her side.

"And he never tried to tell me who to date again."

"Lucky me."

Lisa watched as the three adults across the room scolded the kids, then looked toward Karen and Adrian. At least their guest looked entertained. Still, Lisa felt obligated to wander over and apologize to him. "I'm sure this isn't how you expected the evening to go," she said. She would have explained that this wasn't how family holidays usually ended, but she didn't know how well vampires could hear lies.

"This is nothing," Adrian shrugged one thin shoulder. His button-up still hung impeccably off his frame, not one wrinkle in sight. "You should see Yule with my family. Literally a bloodbath."

"Right." Lisa hoped that was a euphemism, but her daughter looked rather shifty, so she expected it wasn't. She hoped her flat look expressed her desire for explanations later, and Karen gave her a thin, plastic smile.

In the end, they shoved the broken Christmas tree into the corner and swept the broken ornaments into a black garbage bag, then opened presents with kids of all ages sitting sullenly on the floor during a temporary period of silence. Soon, Ellie and Laurie were back to giggling in the corner, probably about the boys they'd both discovered the past year, much to the dismay of their fathers. Marie crawled on top of great-grandpa Wilson, tucking herself beneath his chin to share in on his nap, and Alex and Eddie and Daniel had curled up where the Christmas tree had once sat, tails to noses and half on top of one another.

Well, thought Lisa, as she and Will brought out the whisky, *that wasn't so bad.* Nothing had been set on fire. No one was dead (well, deader than they had started the evening, in any case). No one had begun a food fight. No blood had been spilled, on the carpet or otherwise.

Everything was just fine.

The door to the front porch opened with a rusted squeal.

"Hi, Mom!" John's voice called into the house, followed by the stomp of snow-covered feet. "Sorry we're late. The airport was a nightmare."

His dark-ruffled head popped around the corner, followed by his date's. Across the room, Adrian made a sound that not even a wolf could produce.

God damn it. Lisa clutched the whisky bottle tight as two sets of eyes immediately set to glaring.

"Holy shit," said Sera.

John had brought home a demon.

Will stepped out from the kitchen with his pile of glass tumblers, took one look, and let out a laugh.

ƳULE ᗰOON

Sarah Hersman

AT THE TAIL end of the storm, the wind howled through the winter forest, fierce as the local wolf pack, filling the sky with sound and carrying snowflakes in its wake. As it passed, the forest settled into silence. Until a cold, wet nose poked out of a burrow and sniffed the air. There was a flurry of activity within the burrow, with snow and dirt alike spraying out as the inhabitants tussled out of sight.

Some time later, a middle-aged man squirmed out of the hole, stared down at his old-fashioned suit, and brushed the snow and dirt from its faded threads. His hand flexed and opened, the nails flat and smooth. He extended the hand and pulled a woman from the hole.

She wore a long grey dress hemmed in a pale fur, and her hair was pulled back in a silver braid. Her cold-kissed cheeks warmed in the late afternoon light glittering through the forest's icicles.

A squeal of laughter erupted from within, and as quick as shadows, three children tumbled from the hole into the soft new snow.

"Mama, winter is so *cold*," the first said, her teeth chattering dramatically.

"What a waste of words," the second replied. He followed this with a more dramatic sigh. "At least use your Change day for something useful. I plan to talk about cars, and see one if I can."

"Winter is cold without fur," the third and youngest corrected. They looked particularly pleased with the conclusion.

A wolf leaped out of the hole next in a spray of snow, and more squeals erupted from the children. The girl watched the wolf shake off the snow and rub up against her until she stroked its thick, winter coat. "It's not fair," the girl said under her breath. "He gets to stay himself. The clothes are like pine needles. I miss my fur."

"Children," the father said. His voice rumbled like a glacier.

"Follow," the mother said. She sniffed the air, beckoned stiffly with one hand, and began walking through the snow, carrying the pack of supplies over one shoulder.

The wolf trotted happily, bounding forward and nosing through the snow to the burrows beneath. The two adults and the three children set out, trudging through snow wearing unfamiliar boots and unfamiliar faces. The boy folded and unfolded his fingers, fascinated. The girl breathed into her hands, trying to warm them. The youngest stared at the forest with new eyes, sharper than their old ones, each snow sculpture of each tree visible in stark relief against the grey sky.

"That one!" the youngest called, pointing to a pine tree three times as tall as they were, with wide branches that stretched many feet from the bough.

"Good," the father said. He smiled at the mother and ran towards the tree, lowering his shoulder at the last moment to ram the trunk.

The tree shook itself like a dog, and snow cascaded to the ground, covering the father from head to foot.

"You're a snow-man!" the boy said.

All three children laughed uproariously. The father tried to shake himself and succeeded only in getting the snow into every nook and cranny of his attire. He shook harder but to no avail.

The mother laughed, then covered her mouth, her eyes wide.

The father tackled her and they went down in a puff of snow. They tumbled until the father grunted in pain. The mother backed up a step as the father rotated his shoulder, the old wound aggravated by the tussle. When he braced his body for play, she gently pinned him under her and planted a kiss on his brow. The children cheered, all the louder to cover the echoes of their father's weakness.

After they had shaken off their snow, the mother opened the pack.

The kids crowded around and pulled from the bag. They gathered the sprigs of holly, and dried apples, and garlands of white baby's breath, and cleaned skulls of mice, and coloured plastic bags, and strange seed pods, and the other bits that they'd found throughout the year and brought back, proudly clutched in their teeth. They used their wonderful, magical little fingers to decorate the evergreen tree, reaching as high as they could. Their parents handled the upper boughs.

The wolf ran back and forth at their feet, whining and nipping at their heels.

"Hey," the girl said after the third time this happened. "So, you don't get fingers. So what? Stop being so annoying."

"Being able to transform isn't that great," the boy added. His joy at tucking in the mouse skulls so that they stared out of the tree with empty eyes detracted from his words.

The wolf took off in a loping run, away from the happy voice of his brother and his own lack of fingers, into the forest where his thick fur and sharp nose were just right.

He heard voices, and slowed, creeping toward them with ears flicked forward.

Two human females spoke in a clearing, with offspring at their feet. This human pack had sheep at the edge of their territory. The hunting had been good this year, and the sheep had been left alone again. But he could remember how the sheep flesh had tasted, beneath their fluffy, white clothing, from when he was a cub, many years ago.

"This is unwise," the female thin as an aspen said. "We can't trust them. Not even today."

"It's Yule," the larger female, broad as an oak, insisted. "And they're our neighbours. We should at least try."

"But the children—" Aspen said.

"This is for the children," Oak insisted. "They need to know."

"Don't they know enough?" Aspen said. She lifted her arm, where an old scar snaked out from under her human clothes.

Oak wrapped her hands around Aspen's arm and kissed it. "That was then," she said. "A new way might be possible. And it's Yule. They'll be safe."

The wolf smelled Aspen's unease, like the rotten, bitter smell of the hot bubbling water deep in the mountains. He left, trotting back toward the tree and the familiar scents of his pack, unsure of what he'd seen.

"Children," the mother said. "Time."

"I'll make a space!" the littlest said. They grabbed a branch and swept back and forth over a fallen log until there was a clear place to sit.

"Nice," the girl said. She reached out and wrapped an arm around her sibling and squeezed. "Let's stay close to stay warm."

"We don't need to cuddle," the boy scoffed. "We can make fire. Or had you forgotten?"

"Fire," the father agreed. "Wood?"

"On it," the boy said. He jogged into the forest.

The boy had returned, and he and his mother were building the fire, when a voice called out from the edge of the clearing. "Hello?" it said.

The family froze, and their invisible hackles rose. These noses were dull, and these ears were packed with snow, and they hadn't noticed the humans' approach. There were two females. The sheep females. Behind them were many offspring with curious eyes. The wolf whined, uncertain what their presence here meant.

Aspen whispered, "Wolf." Her eyes were wide with fear.

The mother tilted her head at the trees, and the wolf obeyed, retreating from the strange gathering.

Oak stepped forward. She gave a little wave. "Sorry to bother you. But we've seen the fire on Yule. We know what you are, and it's all right. The past is past, and our sheep are safely boarded up at home, besides. This is a night of fellowship. We wanted to celebrate with you, if you'd be amenable."

The children had fanned out behind their parents, keeping their own canines hidden because the adults hadn't shown further signs of alarm. Their brother, who couldn't transform, stayed where their mother had directed him, almost in the trees. The father stepped forward. He cleared his throat. "Fellowship. Friendship?" he asked carefully.

Oak took a step back at the growl of his voice. "Yes," she said. "Friendship."

The father's brow furrowed. He remembered weapons,

though none were visible. He glanced at the mother.

The mother tilted her head at the two females who resembled trees. She did not see their weapons, either. And hers were hidden, deep inside the Change. They and the humans were frozen in place, trapped by winter and by the past.

"Your hair's so soft," a high voice said.

Everyone stared at the little human girl who was petting the sister's hair.

"Softer in my other form," the sister bragged. But her voice was pleased.

The thaw was immediate. "Friendship," the mother said definitively.

"Wonderful! We brought food," Oak said quickly. "We're normally vegetarian but we figured tonight should be an exception."

"We're vegetarian too," the brother said. "We only eat vegetarians."

Both of the women's eyes grew wide.

"He's messing with you," the sister said. "Thanks for the food. Mama and Papa don't talk as much but they understand everything."

"Have you seen our tree?" the littlest one squealed. "Let me show you!"

They dragged a cluster of the smallest human children toward the tree, while the girl and boy engaged the older human children in tug-of-war over a fallen stick. It ended with everyone on their butts in the snow, which is tug-of-war's best-case scenario.

By the time they finished, the adults had gotten the fire going and were warming up the food the humans had brought: mutton and venison and game hen, with spices and sauces and even delicious vegetables. The family whined at the smell, dim as it was through their current noses. The humans thought this peculiar but chose not to comment.

When the food was almost ready, the humans reached into their pack with a smile on their faces. "A tradition you might not know," Oak said, "is that Yule also has exchanging gifts."

"Gift now?" the mother said.

"Yes," Oak said, "and ours is—"

The mother let out a high yip. The two women flinched. And flinched again as the wolf trotted up dragging a dead deer. He let it fall at their feet and panted, his bloodstained lips pulling back into a wide grin.

"Gift now," the mother said proudly.

"Ah," Oak said. "Th-thank you."

"Yeah, nice one," the boy said appreciatively.

The wolf woofed and trotted over to curl up by the fire.

The mother looked at Oak expectantly.

"Yes, as I was saying," she said, her voice higher than before. "Ours is something we thought we could all enjoy together."

"Is it a car?" the boy said excitedly. "I've seen them go zipping by, almost as fast as I can run."

"It's not a car," Oak said sadly.

"Is it gloves?" the girl asked hopefully.

"Oh, I didn't think . . . no, it's not gloves. Sorry."

"Is it a wish?" the youngest asked.

Aspen spoke, her voice warm as the fire. "It's our wish, yes, that this will continue. That we two families can come back here next year, after we've become a part of each other's traditions."

"That's not a gift," the boy pointed out.

"This is," Oak promised. "Kids?"

The children of the two women reached into the bag and drew out a shimmering ribbon of pure sunlight. Or moonlight, bright as the familiar orb that glowed in the clear sky above? It was hard to tell, with how fast the children whipped it from the bag and wrapped it around the tree. The decorations, which had become indistinct as the night had risen around the group, were illuminated in a soft glow unlike anything the family had ever seen. The two women placed a glowing star atop the tree, and the winding ribbon seemed a flickering tail left in the wake of the star's passage.

"How?" the mother asked.

"Batteries," Aspen explained, in a way that was no explanation at all.

"It's magic," the girl said. She wanted to lick the lights, to see if they tingled on her tongue as much as they sparkled in her eyes.

"It's electric," the boy said. He knew more of human ways, and was pretty sure that electric was the name of those lights' colour.

"It's a wish. It looks just like one," the littlest argued.

They all held their breath. Their faces were softer, more similar, in its impossible light. As they stared at the tree they had made together, the warmth of the delicate future chased away the forest's chill.

TWO LOYAL DOGS
(AND A HORNHEAD IN AN APPLE TREE!)

Rhonda Parrish

THE BOYS WERE happily frolicking through the snow, snorting and snuffling, digging their noses into the powder and tossing it around as they roughhoused with each other, tails wagging hard. It wasn't late, only about eight, but it was dark and the park was deserted except for the three of us. It was exactly the right amount of cold—brisk but not painful—so I looked on, my hands shoved into my pockets, breath clouding the air, but not the least bit impatient to get back home.

Back home I had work to do, responsibilities to deal with, losses to mourn, but here . . . here I could just enjoy the snowflakes twisting and twirling through the pools of light cast by the streetlamps, the sound of the dogs happy frolicking, and the way the trees swayed ever so slightly in a breeze that reached the tops of their boughs but didn't quite make it down to the ground.

I scanned the tree branches, looking for the pair of ravens that had been shadowing me of late, but if they were there, I couldn't see them.

Looking at the trees around me reminded me of the artificial tree I'd unpacked but not set up back home. I'd thought that putting it up would help me find the Christmas spirit—whatever that was—or at least a little light to brighten my days, but it had only made me more depressed. As soon as I'd pulled the pieces out, I'd been struck by all the memories of last year. All the ways it was different from this one.

Last year Omma had still been living in her home.

Last year Lyle had been with me.

Last year the world had made sense.

Ulf's growl, almost immediately joined by Bjorn's, dragged my attention from the treetops and back to the ground.

We were no longer alone.

The woman was backlit by one of the Narnia-like streetlamps that were scattered throughout the park. Its light surrounded her like a warm halo, but cast all her details in shadow. What I could make out for certain, though, because it stood out stark as a lightning bolt against the night sky, was the giant rack of antlers which spread over her head like the crown of a tree.

"You," she slowly moved her arm without bending it to point at me. It felt over-dramatic and weird. Like a little kid pretending to be an imperious queen. "Will bring me an apple."

"That," I said, lowering my voice and matching her level of melodrama with my tone. "Seems really fucking unlikely."

She took a step toward me, which moved her away from the light just enough that I was able to make out a few more of her features. She had long curly hair and a beautiful face. Her sharp eyes and hawk-like nose somehow added to her cold beauty rather than took away from it, and the antlers I'd thought looked like the crown of a tree actually were a crown. Like a crown-crown. It looked like it would be heavy and uncomfortable, but she walked as though the antlers were as much a part of her as they might be to the animals they'd originally belonged to. And she did that walking, through the snow, on high heels. Very high heels. She almost looked like she was walking en pointe, which was appropriate given that she was also wearing a brown ballet-style bodysuit that might have been made out of leaves.

I dropped my hands to the top of the boys' heads. They were wolfhounds, and big even for their breed, so I was able to touch them without bending over, and the feeling of their coarse fur beneath my fingers gave me the strength I needed to stand my ground rather than take a step back.

"I said," she paused and again reminded me of a little kid trying to act grown up. "You will bring me an apple."

"Safeway is that way," I said, pointing to the southwest. "Get your own damn apple."

It had only been a few weeks since I'd been introduced to the realities of our world—of magic and monsters and all the crap that came with it. There was an awful lot I didn't know but I wasn't an idiot. I knew this woman, whoever or whatever she was, didn't mean the sort of apple you could pick up at Safeway. I didn't have a clue what kind of apple she did mean, but I didn't actually care either. I'd had a lot taken from me since learning magic was real, and I was still very much grieving those losses so I didn't have the spoons to deal with some arrogant, antler-headed woman who thought I was her gopher.

"Bring me an apple of immortality," she said, her face impassive.

"First, I have no idea who you are. Second, I have no idea what you're talking about, and third, I am not your servant."

"I will not explain myself to an ignorant mortal, feathered or otherwise," she said. "Do as I command. The way will open tomorrow at midnight. Come to me then."

"Look," I said, faking much more patience than I actually had. In fact, it was probably a good thing I'd left Omma's magical sword at home or I'd have been tempted to draw it. "I'm not about to follow your commands. And as for my being an ignorant mortal, it seems to me that if you weren't also mortal, you wouldn't need something called the apple of immortality. So how about you fuck off and leave my dogs and I to enjoy the park, and we'll just forget this ever happened."

That brought the first change of expression I'd seen on her face, only the slightest furrowing of her brow, but it was something. She pointed at us again, but this time her arm transformed. From elbow to finger it was no longer human flesh, or even magical flesh, it was an antler. Or, more specifically, a horn. One single bone-coloured horn which tapered to a brutal-looking point.

Seeing her hand and forearm morph into a weapon made the boys go wild. Snapping and snarling, they lunged toward her and then backed up against me once more. Over and over again. "Bring me an apple," she said one last time. Her voice a warning, her horn-hand-sword-thing pointing menacingly at me, and then at the dogs. "Or else."

She stepped backward, and the boys must have interpreted that as a retreat, a moment of weakness they could capitalize on, because they burst toward her. And then it was like reality was a curtain and she parted it, just a bit. There was a ripple, a shimmer, and suddenly she and Ulf were gone. Bjorn, half a step behind his brother, ploughed through empty space and then spun around and looked to me for an explanation. But I was just as confused as he was.

I DROPPED BJORN off at Omma's house. I suppose I should just call it my house because I'd officially given up the downtown condo I'd shared with Lyle and moved back in, but it still felt a bit more like Omma's house than my own. Which was ridiculous. It was the house I'd grown up in, and these days only the boys and I lived there, but this was one of those things where logic didn't matter. I still thought of it as Omma's.

I wished, not for the first time, that I didn't live alone so there would be someone here to keep an eye on Bjorn in my absence, but though I was hoping to move Omma out of the care home, I hadn't yet lined up in-home care for her, so it wasn't safe yet. In my defence, I was dealing with a lot these days, and everything seemed to take more energy than it should, more effort. I went through most of my days feeling as though I was wrapped in batting. Not the soft cottony kind you want to rub your face against, but the squeaky polyester kind. Everything was a bit muffled, a bit harder, and a bit frustrating. And I was doing it all alone because Lyle was gone. Murdered right in front of me.

And now I was facing Christmas without him.

"Nope," I said to Bjorn, patting his shoulder as he leaned up against my legs. "We're not going to think about that right now, are we? No we're not."

I knelt down so we were at eye level with one another and rubbed behind his ears. His big brown eyes looked into mine. "I'm going to find out how to get Ulf back, okay boy? I just need you to stay here. Be a good boy. I'll be back as soon as I can."

He blinked at me, long and slow like a cat, his tongue lolling from his mouth, his sides heaving with his panting.

Bjorn was a charcoal colour, and Ulf, who Lyle and I had always called his brother but I had no reason to think was actually a litter mate, was a tawny colour. They were never apart and I'd taken to joking about Bjorn being Ulf's shadow. Now with Ulf missing . . . what was a shadow without its object?

"I'll be back as soon as I can," I said.

He'd be safe in the house despite the lack of supervision—after everything that had happened around Halloween, the safeguards on the house had been refreshed. Whoever the bitch was who took Ulf would not be getting Bjorn as well.

I FLEW TO Ash and Elm—the bar where I worked part-time. I'd worked there for years but only recently learned my boss was Odin. Like, the god Odin. He called himself Erik but it was a whole thing. And I'd only made that discovery shortly after sprouting wings. Great, white feathery wings like a freaking angel or something. Only I wasn't an angel, I was a Valkyrie. Ish.

Anyway, normal people couldn't see my wings but magical beings like gods and giants could. And the wings were physical, but also kind of not?

It was complicated.

The upshot was that they didn't get in my way as I tried to live my life, wear clothes, and all that stuff, but I could use them to fly. Not super effectively—flying as a skill took a fair amount of practice and I didn't trust myself to go very high just yet—but I didn't have a driver's license or a car so at night, when I was less likely to be spotted than during the day, they made a much faster form of transportation than a bus. And I hated taking cabs.

Folding my wings behind me, I opened the door to the bar so hard that it bounced off the wall, leaving a dent in the drywall. Only one table, way in the back, was occupied, and those patrons jumped and turned to look at me but something on my face inspired them to quickly mind their own business. "She has my fucking dog," I said.

"Who—what?" Daniel stammered. He was standing behind the bar—where he had no business being—with an empty pint glass in his hand and a stunned look on his face. The latter was par for the course, the former was not my problem right now.

"Some deer-faced bitch has my dog. Look. Where is your father?"

"Deer-faced—?"

"Where. Is. Your. Father?" I bit off each word, trying and failing to remind myself that it wasn't Daniel I was pissed at. Erik came out from the bathrooms, tucking in his shirt. I still marvelled that at one time I'd thought him just an ordinary bar owner. These days I could see through his magical glamour to the god he was. A diminished god, it was true, but a god nonetheless.

"What's going on?" he asked, using the sort of tone I imagined he must have mastered when Daniel was a kid.

"Some woman, with an antler crown and an arm that can turn into a horn-sword-thing came to the park and threatened me tonight. And when she vanished through her magic portal or what-the-fuck-ever it was, she took Ulf with her."

I'd never been one to shy away from profanity, but apparently this woman really inspired it in me. I hadn't sworn this much while I was sober in months.

"An antler crown . . ." Erik let the sentence trail off but he didn't say it like a question, more like something to fill the silence. I narrowed my eyes.

"Yes. Who is she and how do I get my dog back?" I asked. One thing I had learned over the past several weeks was that the direct route was the best route. Especially now that the magical armband my Omma had given me would let me know if people lied to me.

"Take a seat," Erik said, gesturing to the barstool beside the one with the plaque which read RESERVED FOR ERIK screwed onto the back of it. I'd had the plaque attached to his stool as a joke.

I crossed my arms over my chest and didn't move from the middle of the bar. Daniel raised an eyebrow at me—Erik was very much unused to not being obeyed which Daniel would know better than anyone. "I don't want to take a seat," I said, recognizing that I sounded like a petulant teenager but not giving a shit. "I want my dog back."

Erik gestured toward the seat once more and then slid into his and waited, drumming his fingers on the countertop until Daniel passed him his favourite IPA. I stomped over to the bar and leaned against it. I thought of it as a compromise. I was willing to come over to where Erik wanted me but not sit where he wanted me. Childish, sure, but I was absolutely knotted up about Ulf being gone. I didn't know where he was or what was happening to him, and I was not okay with it.

The dogs were the main thing that were helping me deal with Lyle's death. Well, them and learning how to wield a sword. The swordplay lessons helped me fall asleep at night—it's easy to do when your muscles ached from use and you'd driven your body to its limits—and the boys helped me get up in the morning. I felt like I was slowly fumbling my way through my grief but losing one of the dogs would . . . well, it would destroy me.

And Erik should damn well know it.

He accepted my compromise with a nod, took a drink, and then said, "I can't know for sure without seeing her, of course, but it sounds like a nature spirit. What did she threaten you about?"

Daniel filled a pint glass for himself and scooted around the bar to come join his father and me just as the actual bartender, Stephanie, came in the back door where she'd obviously been taking a smoke break.

"She said she wanted an apple," I said.

Daniel was standing just behind me, about to slide into the seat on my left sandwiching me in between him and Erik, but at my words, he froze. I swear he even stopped breathing. Erik's reaction was smaller but no less profound. His eye got wide—eye singular. The other was covered by a patch—and he made a soft coughing sound.

"An apple," he said. "Did she say what kind of an apple?"

"An apple of immortality," I said.

Daniel still hadn't moved and Erik's posture was weirdly erect. "What?" I snapped. "What's going on? I just . . . I can't deal with this right now, Erik."

"She's definitely not just a nature spirit," he said, "if she knows about the apples."

"What about the apples?" I wouldn't say I yelled, exactly, but I raised my voice enough that Stephanie turned to look at me from halfway across the bar and Daniel jumped in surprise—the first movement he'd made since I mentioned the apples—and slopped his beer all over the bartop.

Erik cocked his head in a way which reminded me of his

ravens, and took a deep breath before letting it out slowly. Trying to control his temper? Part of me thought, "Good, welcome to my world," but another voice said, "Dial it back, Autumn." I needed him on my side, not angry with me. The leeway he'd give me on account of Lyle's recent death was limited, and I suspected I'd just about reached the end of that particular tether.

When Erik replied he spoke slowly and carefully, his voice low and sizzling with tension.

"The apples are a closely guarded secret. Very closely. Only a very few know they exist, fewer still are allowed access to them, and I can count on one hand the number who know where they are."

"I don't want one," I said, not trying to hide the exasperation from my voice, but keeping my tone respectful. "I'm not exactly a 'give in to blackmail' kind of girl. But I do need to know what they are, why she wants them, and how to find her and teach her a lesson about pestering me and my dogs. I just can't have nature spirits or 'definitely not a nature spirits' popping up in my life whenever they feel like it and messing with me."

Erik nodded, and I felt Daniel's exhalation of relief against the back of my neck. "We can take care of it for you," Erik said.

The temptation was real. I was in so far over my head. I'd been making progress, learning to tread in these new waters enough to keep my head above water, but this was like a giant wave that had come and slapped me in the face. But the thing about waves, if I was going to milk every drop out of this metaphor, was that one always follows another. If I didn't learn how to deal with this sort of thing on my own, I would be forever running to Erik and Daniel for help and I'd never learn to swim.

I wanted to learn to swim.

I wasn't against accepting a helping hand when the situation required it but I didn't want to turn dependence into a lifestyle choice.

I shook my head. "I just need to know what you know."

Erik smiled, and I saw an expression of something akin to pride flash over his face before he wiped it off and gestured to the barstool beside him once more. This time I sat.

"Short version," Erik said, "is that the apples are what make us immortal. Once, there was a whole orchard of them but Loki—"

That's what he called my dead boyfriend. I knew him as Lyle

but to the All Father he was Loki. The trickster. The sly one. The pain in the ass.

"—did what Loki did best and now there's only one tree. One tree whose fruit needs to be shared among many. It's why only a select few of us remain, why we've diminished. If this woman, whoever she is, knows about the fruit she's more likely to be a demi-god than a nature spirit. And if she gets her hands on an apple it would increase her powers and extend her lifespan. At the expense of someone else."

Lyle/Loki had also been demi-god—the son of a god and a giant—though I hadn't known that until after he'd died. I'd assumed that if he hadn't been murdered, he'd have lived forever, though. After all, didn't that just come along with the whole "god" gig?

"So all you gods aren't immortal?"

Erik shook his head. Daniel snorted and said, "I wish."

"And the giants?"

"No," said Erik. "The apples are what allow us to live so long but, as you should know by now, Autumn, we can all die."

"Why don't you just plant more trees?" I asked, momentarily distracted from my immediate problem by the obvious solution to theirs.

"The apples don't have seeds," Daniel said, at the same time Erik said, "It doesn't work that way."

Of course it didn't. Magic never worked in a nice straightforward way that made sense. If it did, it wouldn't be magic.

"So, if I can't give her what she wanted even if I wanted to— which I don't," I hastened to clarify. "How do I get my dog back and make sure she leaves me alone from here on out?"

"Kri—" Erik began and then stopped, correcting himself. "Ms. DeBall has a book that makes all oaths sworn on it unbreakable. Maybe you could make a deal with her to borrow it."

"Except that I can't imagine a world where she'd let me borrow her stuff. Especially her magical stuff." Ms. DeBall ran the old folks' home where my Omma lived. She and I had a bit of a complicated relationship. We were allies, of a sort, but neither one of us liked the other. "Besides, how would I make the antler woman swear an oath to leave me alone?"

"You'd have to force her into it," Daniel said, and when I

looked at him for the first time since sitting down, I saw excitement lighting his face. There was very little in the world Daniel liked more than a good fight. He used to occasionally join Lyle and me when we watched *Monday Night Raw*. Lyle's favourite wrestlers were always the ones who were really good on the mic, witty and sharp. Daniel preferred the big, bulky type of wrestler who won their matches based on sheer size and brute strength.

"Her arm turned into a sword, Daniel," I said. "My sword skills are nowhere near good enough to take on someone whose sword is literally a part of their body. How am I supposed to force her?"

"I could come—"

I mean, maybe. Bringing some brawn with me to a confrontation didn't feel quite the same as just asking Daniel and Erik to take care of the problem for me, but it wasn't too far removed either.

"Nah," I shook my head. "I guess I'm going to see Ms. DeBall."

MS. DEBALL LOOKED human—middle-aged with pale skin and white hair she wore in a super adorable mini-beehive-type thing. Despite how she looked, however, she was neither adorable nor human. As far as I could tell she was some sort of giant. Of the frost variety, if the temperature she kept her office at was any indication.

I was sitting across her desk from her and she was, quite literally, looking down her nose at me.

"You want to borrow my book?" she sniffed.

"Erik said you might lend it to me. So I can make the deer-woman demi-god whatever leave me alone." I looked her hard in the eye, holding her gaze steadily and trying to impress upon her with my eyes the sincerity of my next words. "I really just want to be left alone. But she has my dog."

That's the other thing Erik had told me last night. Ms. DeBall might be a complete hard-ass, but she was also a sucker for dogs. I was surprised to hear that, but I was absolutely going to milk it for all it was worth.

Her eyes narrowed. She obviously knew I was trying to take advantage of her soft spot, and I almost felt bad for Erik because she was most definitely going to know where I'd gotten my information from. But Erik could take care of himself and I didn't know if Ulf could.

"Please," I added.

She sighed audibly, and I knew I'd won but forced myself not to smile because that was a sure way to make her change her mind. And though this plan wasn't actually much of a plan, it was the only one I had. "Fine," she said. "But I'm going to need something for collateral. And you'll owe me one."

The surge of happiness I felt was immediately squashed down. The last thing in the world I wanted was to owe Ms. DeBall a favour. Or, I corrected myself, the second last thing in the world I wanted was to owe her a favour. The last thing I wanted was for the deer bitch to have my dog.

"Fine," I said. "Will the arm ring do as collateral?"

"That'll do fine," she said.

"And I'll get it back when I return your book to you?"

"You will," she said.

The arm ring in question was magical, and if she was lying to me, it would have pinched me. Painful but helpful. Anyway, it hadn't pinched me so she wasn't lying.

I reached under my sweater and tugged it off while she unlocked a drawer in her desk and opened it. As I handed the ring over to her, still warm from being worn, she passed me a beat-up, dog-eared copy of a paperback book.

"Seriously?" I said, as we made the trade.

"What?"

"*Twilight?*"

She rolled her eyes, dropped my arm ring in her drawer, and slammed it shut with a resounding bang. "It doesn't matter what it looks like on the outside, it just matters what it does. Any oath sworn on that book is unbreakable upon penalty of death."

I put my winter coat on and jammed the book into one of the oversized pockets. "Right. Got it. Thanks," I said.

"And don't forget," she said as I was leaving her office. "You owe me one."

"Goody," I mumbled.

"What?"

"Nothing," I said. "Thanks."

MIDNIGHT FOUND ME back in the park waiting for antler-face to show up again. Bjorn was with me, pressed tight against my leg. I had the book in my coat pocket and my sword in my hand. Honestly, if someone mundane were to come across us just then it would have been pretty difficult to explain myself.

Thankfully, I suppose, no such person just happened to stumble across us. I did, however, notice one of Erik's ravens looking down at us from a nearby treetop. It was better disguised than usual, which told me that Erik was trying to hide the fact he was spying on me, but he was still definitely spying on me. It was endearing in a way, that he cared enough to want to keep an eye on me. But also felt sort of like pressure. Like he was checking up on me as well.

I tightened my grip on the hilt of my sword and then relaxed it again. In part because I was super nervous, but also to keep my hands from totally freezing up. Using a sword while wearing winter mittens was not something we'd covered in my sword-fighting classes yet.

I'd actually thought about leaving the sword at home—I have a lot of practice with hand-to-hand combat and self-defence and only the barest of broad strokes with swordplay—but honestly, I thought it made me look a bit badass. And if I was going to try and force this woman to swear to leave me and the dogs alone, I was going to need every bit of badassery I could summon up. So the sword came.

But it was fucking cold.

Then, in the space between one heartbeat and the next, something changed. Bjorn, the raven, and I were alone in the park waiting for Hornhead to show up, and then the raven was gone and Bjorn and I were in a totally different park.

When I'd watched the woman vanish before it had been like parting a curtain in reality and slipping through it. In this case, however, it was as if Bjorn and I had fallen through that same opening.

I hadn't noticed the low-key sounds of the city around us until they were gone, but one moment they were there and the next they weren't. The trees looked exactly the same but the streetlamps were gone, leaving the moon and stars as the only sources of illumination. I heard an owl hoot somewhere in the distance and much closer, the scream of a fox.

Bjorn began to growl.

"Did you bring me an apple?"

The voice came from behind us and Bjorn and I turned at the same time. The woman with the antler crown was sprawled out across a throne which looked like it was made of bones and antlers, a white fur blanket-type thing tossed across its seat. She definitely had an aesthetic, I'd give her that.

She was still wearing her crown and the brown bodysuit-type thing. And the way she was lounging crossways over the seat of her throne let me see that the ridiculously high heels she'd been rocking before were still on her feet and also made of antlers.

"Do you really like deer or really hate them?" I asked.

She blinked, slow and controlled, and I was surprised to realize that her eyes were just a little bit too big. A little bit too dark and luminous. How had I missed that under the light of the streetlamps back in reality? How was I able to see it now with only the moon to light the scene?

"What?" She sounded sincerely taken aback.

"Do you really like deer, and that's why you're copying their aesthetic everywhere and covering yourself in their bones and shit . . . or do you really hate them so you sit on their corpses and wear them as a warning to others?"

She rolled her eyes hard—really, this woman could teach Ms. DeBall a thing or two about eyerolling—and then slowly unfolded herself from the throne. She was quite beautiful. The way she moved, silently, elegantly, despite the huge crown of antlers from her head and the stilettos on her feet. And she had the longest legs of any woman I'd ever seen ever. Even without the heels. Her legs definitely make up a disproportionate amount of her body. It was eerie but lovely.

"Did you bring my apple?" she asked.

"Where is my dog?"

If we were just going to sit and ask each other questions I was at least going to change them up now and then.

She quirked one eyebrow and then raised her arm and pointed at Bjorn. Again without bending her elbow.

"My other dog," I said, dryly.

"Ran off as soon as we got here," she said.

"An answer. Fantastic. Now we're getting somewhere," I said. I think I sounded nonchalant but I didn't feel it. Ulf wasn't here. How was I supposed to find him now?

She took a step toward me, and I watched her right forearm elongate and transform from a flesh hand to a single, lethal-looking horn.

"My apple?" she said.

"Why do you need an apple?"

"Because I don't want to die."

"We all die."

"Have you seen death?" she asked, snarkily. "Have you? Because I've seen it. I've seen its ugliness. Its finality. I don't want to experience it."

I thought of Lyle. Thought of the horrible way he'd died right in front of me. And I nodded. "Yes." I didn't trust my voice to say more.

"I need the apple," she said simply. As though that explained everything.

And in a way, I guess it did.

But I couldn't help her and I said so.

"I don't want to die!" she screamed. And in that moment, she was terrifying and terrified. I could hear it in her voice, the raw, brutal fear.

She attacked.

She was really good with that horn. I was significantly less good with the sword.

Bjorn helped though, lunging forward again and again, trying to bite her, to knock her off balance. It was working, too. She couldn't keep her sword/horn thing pointed at both of us at the same time, but the cold was making my movements sluggish, and the sword was really heavy. Plus, she had home court advantage.

I've heard people describe fights as a dance but dances are coordinated and choreographed and beautiful, and this was the opposite of that. It was primitive and ugly and dirty.

And it ended most anticlimactically when she drove me backward until I tripped over something buried in the snow and spilled to the ground. A star burst before my eyes as the back of my head bounced off the ground and my sword slipped from my numb fingers, landing somewhere in the blanketing white with a soft *fwump* sound.

Then her horn sword was pressed against my throat, and Bjorn was crouched just behind me, his stinky dog breath warm against my face.

"Stay," she snapped, pointing a finger at Bjorn. Then she pressed the bone sword against me just hard enough to break the skin and repeated for emphasis, "Stay."

I suspected he was going to listen. I hoped he was. He was fast but not fast enough to reach her before she ran me through.

The way she was towering over me on her tippy-toes in those fucking shoes just added the perfect little cherry of humiliation on my defeat. As if laying on my back in the snow with her sword against my throat wasn't enough, she'd beaten me on high heels. In a bodysuit.

And now I was going to die with a copy of *Twilight* in my pocket and whoever investigated my death was going to think it was mine.

At least she had the good grace to look a little bit winded. I could see her chest moving as she panted at about the same rhythm as me.

"I need an apple," she said between big, gasping breaths. The beauty I'd seen in her face before was erased by her desperation. "You need to bring me an apple."

"I don't have a fucking apple," I said.

"You can get one."

"I can't. I really, really can't."

"I will kill you if you don't," she shouted. And I believed her. But there was nothing I could do about it.

"I can't," I said. And for a moment I wondered if it might not be better if she killed me. If everything just ended. But then Bjorn growled and I remembered that I had things to live for. I had dogs to live for. And friends. And family, small and broken as it may be. I shook my head, hoping to distract her while my hand felt around for the sword I'd dropped. "I just can't. But maybe I can help some other—"

She lifted the sword, drew it back, and I knew she meant to run me through. Her patience was done, and it was time for me to die.

But then a flurry of tawny fur burst out of the darkness, tackling her and knocking her to the side.

Ulf!

I didn't waste any time with relief or glee but scrambled to my knees and dug around in the snow for the sword. I couldn't tell where it had fallen and was forced to flounder blindly for it.

Meanwhile Ulf and Bjorn were fighting with the deer woman. I could hear their snaps, snarls, and growls mixed in with the heavy sounds of her breathing, the meaty sounds of their struggle. When one of the boys yipped, I gave up on recovering the sword and threw myself into the fight unarmed. No one hurt my dogs and got away with it.

Bjorn, Ulf, and I fought together like a well-practiced team. We weren't, but we gave a good impersonation of it. They kept her pinned against the trunk of a tree, dodging her sword hand and creating just enough chaos to keep her off-balance, while I punched and kicked her like any opponent I'd ever faced in the ring.

Soon she was bleeding and her attempts to defend herself were slowed and half-hearted.

What two of us hadn't been able to manage, three of us did handily.

The dogs darting in and out at her had uncovered something shiny and silver half-buried in the snow. I thought about picking it up, about using the sword to end her life, to eliminate the threat she'd posed to the dogs and me, but then I remembered the pathetic way she'd sobbed and screamed, "I don't want to die." And I stayed my hand.

Aside from that one moment of weakness when I lay on my back and thought all was lost and so I may as well be too, I also wanted to live. The last few weeks had been hard and depressing. I'd been sad and struggling, but I wanted to live. I wanted to live with a ferocity I didn't even know I'd possessed until I'd been faced with Lyle's loss.

I didn't want to be the one to kill this woman. Goddess. Deer. Whatever.

I reached in my pocket and pulled out the copy of *Twilight*.

Despite her wounds and her weariness, the woman looked from the book to me and, with disdain dripping her from voice, said, "Really? *Twilight*?"

I half-laughed. In other circumstances I think I might actually have liked this girl.

"You're going to swear an oath," I said.

BACK HOME WITH the boys, I couldn't bring myself to do Christmas carols. I just wasn't ready. But I cleared a space in the book-filled living room, streamed *Monday Night Raw* on my phone, and set up the Christmas tree.

As the wrestlers on Lyle's favourite television show pretended to beat each other up, I took my time decorating the tree, and the dogs supervised.

When I was finished, the tree was a bit more sparse than any of the trees Lyle and I had shared—his style was much more grandiose than my own—but it was sparkly and colourful.

When I turned off all the other lights in the house and switched on the tree's, it shone like something in a movie, filling my heart with warmth and bringing a smile to my lips. And, when I reached down to where Ulf and Bjorn stood at my side and scratched their ears, for a moment, just a moment, it almost felt like Lyle was there with us. Looking over us.

But probably that was just the rum in my eggnog talking.

Probably.

ℙLAYING THE 𝕆DDS

JB Riley

"DO YOU KNOW the chances of pulling an inside straight?"

I shrugged. "Somewhere less than eight percent, depending on the number of—"

Jamie looked at me with a growl. "That was rhetorical." He picked up his glass of whiskey, tossed it back, and signalled for and accepted another. It was early on the twenty-ninth, and I had planned a full day of inventory and cleaning to prep for New Year's. I needed to clear out the storeroom, scrub the bathrooms, get my order in to the beer distributor by 5:00 p.m., and my liquor guy had already left a message reminding me if I wanted those cases of champagne for the Midnight toast, I'd need to let him know ASAP.

But instead of counting bottles and washing chalkboards, I was watching my little brother get drunk. Not the first time by any means, but not my plan for the day.

Maybe I could move him along. I put a pot of coffee on, then leaned my forearms on the bartop. "So you lost a bet? To who? Did Death forget to collect you?"

Jamie always looked a little seedy, but right now "seedy" was aspirational. With clothes torn and dirty, eyes sunken and red-rimmed, hair a birds' nest of tangles and several days' worth of beard, I'd almost chased him off my front step as a vagrant before catching his scent. He tossed back his whiskey and held his glass out for another. "Look, it wasn't my fault. I should have won, but the witch drew the nine of clubs. Couldn't believe it."

Eyes distant, he didn't notice me grab a bottle of cheap whiskey from the well and pour. After three shots in about five minutes, he wasn't going to taste the difference, and I knew from experience just how big a dent he could put in my stock of Bushmill's. He took it and tossed it without comment, held his glass out again.

"When do you have to pay it?"

He accepted the (cheap stuff) refill but placed it in front of him, rolling his shoulders and neck until I could hear pops. "It's paid, but things got a little complicated."

Things always got complicated around Jamie. I waited in silence, watching him fidget until he finally opened his mouth again.

"See, I sort of bet the pack."

Jamie saw the look on my face. "I had three jacks, Brenda!" He picked up his glass and studied its amber liquid. "The witch had five curses, three protection charms, and a love potion in the pot. Vlad was out, Khzaran was out, everyone else folded after the ante. The pot was huge, and it was down to just the two of us." He slammed his glass down. "I had three jacks!"

"I don't care if you had a royal flush with an ace back." It was my turn to growl. "What happened?"

He couldn't quite meet my eyes. "I put the pack up—one task, no more than one day, no killing. It should have been safe."

I leaned forward across the bar, pulling his gaze. When he met my eyes, I growled harder. "What. Happened. Jamie?"

Jamie sighed. "She sold us to Santa Claus."

I GOT HIM to switch to coffee, though I had to Irish it up before he'd continue the story. Apparently, one of the elves had left the wrong gate open and the reindeer got into the apple orchard. Reindeer love apples of all sorts, but these had been fermenting at the base of the trees since the beginning of October, growing a nice fuzzy layer of mould and fungi that had somehow attracted a strain of wild yeast. The resulting hallucinogenic mash created a crisis just in time for Santa's annual giddy-up.

"So the sleigh isn't getting airborne while Dasher and the gang are tripping balls. They'd fly right into a wind turbine over Topeka and that would end things. The operation needed a plan B and we were it." Jamie shrugged. "The witch made bank all around.

"Mrs. Claus got us oriented," he gestured with his mug. "Did you know 'Santa' is actually a hive mind? There's thousands of them. Every single Santa you see at the mall, the corner, parades . . . they're just drones, all linked together. Mrs. Claus is the queen and she's . . ." he shuddered. "Let's just say she's terrifying. She runs the whole show and it's one tight ship. Amber moons, what an Alpha she'd make."

Jamie scratched the stubble of his jaw. "Anyway, the witch sold us as a replacement team. The sled itself is what creates flight—I guess there's an Efreet caged under the seat who's working off a few millennia of debt. He provides the lift, the reindeer are only there to give forward propulsion. Mrs. Claus had the elves adapt the reindeer harnesses to dogsled hitches for us."

He drank some coffee. "So remember there's thousands of Santas? Well, in addition to the Efreet there's other major mystic hoodoo in there somewhere. As soon as we're hitched up to the sleigh one of the Santas jumps in and yells 'go!' and—" He stopped.

I didn't have time for this shit. "And?" I prompted.

Jamie peered into his coffee mug. "And this is tough to tell, you know? Traumatic. Makes a wolf thirsty, is all I'm sayin'."

"I swear to Lunos, Jamie, if you don't keep talking they will never find your body."

"Um," he coughed and took a hurried swig from his mug. "So the Santa yells 'go!' and we lunge forward and . . ." he paused again, then held up a hand. "I'm not being a jackal, I'm trying to explain. We lunged forward and ran but stood still at the same time. It was—it was really weird. I knew I was running, pulling the sleigh with the pack around me, but at the same time I was standing there, in the traces, waiting, with the sleigh behind. Then another Santa jumps onto the sleigh where we were standing and yells 'go!' and off we go again except we're *still* not moving."

He shrugged. "It happened I don't know how many times. Every couple seconds, a Santa would jump in and off we'd run. I was so many of me running so many places at once that I'm grateful I was running on air, you know? If I was running on four paws, I'd have tripped myself in half a step, but you can't trip on air. My feet got tangled together sometimes when another me started to run, but it didn't matter, we still moved forward."

"Are you sure you didn't get into the reindeer acid?" Screw the inventory, I needed a drink. I grabbed a glass and pulled out the Bushmill's. Jamie perked right up and held his mug out so I poured for both of us.

While Jamie busied himself with his mug, I tossed the whiskey back and thought for a moment. Pack magic helps us run as one during a hunt. We know where each member is, what surrounds them, if they get hurt or lost. It *is* like being in multiple places at once.

"Okay. So you sort of felt like when we hunt?"

Jamie thought for a moment, nodded. "Yeah, only dialled way up. This went on until each Santa had a sleigh. It felt like there were thousands of me, running through the sky in all directions."

I nodded. "I got drunk one night with a Buffalo shifter, an old bull from back in the day. He talked about how his herd ran like that, when they filled the Plains. Reindeer are designed to run in herds of thousands. Maybe their magic works the same way ours does. Maybe Claus needed pack magic or the Santas couldn't fly."

"Maybe. So anyway, we ran." He leaned backward on his stool, upending his coffee cup to catch the last drops on his tongue. "We pulled that sleigh and here's another thing. Do you know how many time zones there are?"

"Twenty-four."

"That was rhetorical. There's a shit ton. Christmas arrives in Tonga almost twenty-four hours before it hits American Samoa, which means the whole 'no more than one day' had us going for forty-eight hours straight." He rubbed his face with his hands. "Amber moons, I'm tired. Anyway, we ran for forty-eight hours. If one sleigh stopped, another was in flight. All those Santas jumping off with presents, diving down chimneys, popping back up with cookies, jumping back on again. I don't know how it works, I just know my job was to run so I did.

"Finally, we got back to the North Pole and the sleighs landed one at a time, the Santas jumped off, and another piece of me came back together. The last sleigh landed, the Santas went back to their hive, and then it was cleanup. We had to help the elves corral a bunch of seriously baked reindeer, and that was hard because by that time I was starving. My Santa didn't share even one of those damn cookies, and I could have eaten Prancer *and* Vixen.

"Finally, Mrs. Claus released us from our debt, and poof I was home."

I thought for a moment. "So that was the big complication?"

Jamie slid his eyes to the side.

"Jamie?"

"Lee . . . said he felt tricked. Said he wouldn't get harnessed like a husky just because I'd screwed up. He said it wasn't fair, but turns out the witch placed a curse to make us pay up on the debt."

I could feel my pulse quicken. "What happened, Jamie?"

Jamie wouldn't meet my eyes. "He fought, Brenda. He fought long and hard but the curse was too strong. He's—" He wiped his eyes. "He's not Lee anymore."

I reached for the cooler behind me, leaned against it as my knees buckled. Lee was Jamie's twin. Tall, strong, and merry. Fierce, brave, and kind. Stubborn, oh so stubborn. "Tell me."

There was a *meow*, and I snapped my head toward the front door, stared at the mackerel tabby cat sitting at the entry. It lifted a leg and groomed briefly, then sauntered in and jumped onto the bartop to bonk his head against my shoulder.

It took some time to find my voice. "Jamie?"

He shrank back. "I'm sure the curse will wear off." The cat laid back his ears and hissed. Jamie shrank back further. "Um, eventually?"

I stared at the cat for a long moment, then looked at Jamie. With a yelp, he was off the barstool and sprinting for the exit. I caught him by the shirt collar two strides from the door.

"There's a white witch in Seattle who I trust. She should be able to do something. In the meantime?" I dragged Jamie toward the back room, scooping the cat up and settling him on my shoulder as I went. "Lee, you're going to clear all the mice and spiders out of the storeroom. Jamie, you're going to scrub the bathrooms. You both can help me inventory after you're done."

They groaned in mutual protest.

"Stuff it before I make you work off your bar tabs, too. Lifting a curse is expensive, and you are going to settle *this* debt up front or I swear to Lunos I'll sell you both to the Easter Bunny." I pointed Jamie toward the closet where I kept the cleaning supplies and shrugged Lee off my shoulder. "Now get to work. We have New Year's to prep for."

"I don't have to listen to you," Jamie sulked. "You're not my boss."

Some things never change, most especially little brothers. I moved until I was staring straight into his eyes, lifting my lip into a snarl. "Want to lose another bet?"

They got to work.

The Curse of Christmas Present

Louis B. Rosenberg

IT WAS THE only gift still sitting under the tree. That's because there wasn't a note saying who it was for and none of our guests would admit to putting it there. Personally, I suspected weird Uncle Marcus, the jokester of the family, but his denials seemed genuine.

Everyone's did.

Eventually my wife got fed up and moved it to the dining room table, as it was already late Christmas morning and most of us were just sitting around relaxing over coffee and doughnuts, plus those amazing meringue cookies that Grandma only makes once a year. "Come on, folks," my wife pressed the group, "which one of you fools brought this thing here?"

Everyone just shrugged.

I probably should mention that it was an unwrapped wooden box about twelve inches on each side, weathered and worn with a tattered red ribbon around it. I'm no expert, but I've watched enough episodes of *Antique Roadshow* to know it was definitely Victorian, with dovetail joints that were obviously handcrafted and a darkened lacquer that had to be at least a hundred years old.

That's when Aunt Jenna noticed a faint inscription carved into the lid. We all leaned forward and looked, baffled by the strange

47

words. I was pretty sure it was Latin, so I typed it into my phone and this translation came back:

"Make a wish and guess what's inside—the winner claims both."

Smiles erupted around the table, everyone eager to play along.

Even our dog Mugsy jumped up on a chair and barked. He was a fat little shih tzu, his pug face so cute he could get away with just about anything, and right now that meant slobbering on the tablecloth next to my annoying cousin Howard and his prissy new girlfriend Cynthia.

"Who did this?" my wife asked again, delivering suspicious looks at every member of the family, expecting someone to crack.

Nobody did.

"Fine, we'll play it that way," she laughed and laid down the ground rules, suggesting we go clockwise around the table, everyone casting a silent wish and then guessing the contents of the box out loud. "Whoever comes closest to what's inside, wins."

Everyone agreed.

Grandma went first, making a silent wish and guessing fruitcake.

My dad went next, guessing a bowling ball.

Uncle Marcus guessed raw monkey brains just to freak us all out.

The twins, little Jimmy and Jenny, made their guesses from under the dining room table, as they were far more focused on their new Lego Star Wars kits than some boring antique box with a ratty old ribbon around it.

We continued around the room like this, Mugsy sniffing and growling the whole time. He even tried to get up on the table, which was a little odd, but I assumed it was because he wanted a doughnut. My wife had already scolded Cousin Howard for sneaking him half a cookie.

Finally, I went last, making my silent wish and then closing my eyes so I could visualize what might be hidden inside the box. I'm not sure why, but I was pretty sure I was going to win by guessing a vintage Japanese tea set—the kind that's handmade with unglazed clay.

My brother gave me a look, as if to say—*Seriously, dude?*

I stood by my guess, for I'd recently seen an episode of *Auction Kings* on the History Channel where someone brought in an old

Japanese tea set in a rickety wooden box. He found it at a garage sale for forty-five dollars and his wife was sure he was totally ripped off. To everyone's surprise, they appraised the damn thing at fifty grand. The curator made a big deal about the unglazed clay, saying that a glazed finish would have been the easiest way to spot a modern knock-off.

"Ok, folks—let's see whose wish is coming true!" my wife declared.

Everyone sat forward, excited.

Even Mugsy put his paws up on the table and howled.

My wife pulled the ribbon off the box, carefully setting it aside. A deep breath and she slowly lifted the lid, inch-by-inch for dramatic effect.

Everyone eased closer.

And finally, we saw it.

I'd like to say we all gasped with delight, but it was more of a collective groan. That's because the box was totally empty except for a single large bone, cracked and bleached with age. It was obviously too big to be human. My annoying Cousin Howard said it was horse bone, most likely an ulna or humerus. He was an orthopaedic surgeon and somehow managed to remind everyone of that fact any chance he could.

Regardless of the biology, we all just stared at the dusty old bone, weathered and faded, nobody knowing what to do or say. After all, it was a creepy thing to find under your tree, especially when nobody would admit to putting it there. So creepy in fact, my wife didn't want to reach in and touch it, so I tilted the box and let it slide out onto the table.

It was just an ordinary bone.

No strange markings.

No embedded jewels.

No hidden inscriptions.

To be honest, it looked like the kind of thing you'd stumble over in the tall grass behind an abandoned farmhouse and continue walking without giving it a second thought.

That's when Mugsy jumped up onto the table. He delivered two quick barks, grabbed the bone in his mouth, and ran off to his little bed in the corner.

"It looks like we have a winner," I laughed.

Everyone did.

But it wasn't a laughing matter.

That's because my brother-in-law suddenly got down on all fours and started sniffing at my wife's behind. I thought she would turn around and smack him, but instead she bent down and started sniffing at Aunt Jenna. And Uncle Marcus started sniffing our neighbour Vanessa, which was a particularly offensive sight, as he was more than twice her age and she was wearing an absurdly short tube skirt.

And before we knew it, all of us were on our hands and knees, sniffing and growling and barking and howling. Even Grandma barked a few times, which made her dentures fall out on the floor, and yet nobody seemed to notice or care.

And there was Mugsy, the bone in his mouth as he watched us from the corner of the room, his tail wagging wildly as he relished his wish come true.

REX INVICTIS

Robert W. Easton

"ADAM, I DON'T like the look of this place."

Ugh. Humans are so blind. That was a goat skull nailed to the sign! I'm a dog and know this isn't goat ranching country.

"Come on, Janet, give it a chance. It's the last one."

She crossed her arms. "The only one."

He reached over and touched her chin. Her tense shoulders softened at his touch. Revolting.

"Okay, Adam. Let's look."

I lay down in the back seat of the SUV and sighed my best harumph. It's not easy being an immortal wizard cursed to be endlessly reincarnated as humans' pets.

The crunch of gravel stopped and they opened the door for me. I hopped out and shook my wiry grey coat. Being a dog is the worst of all the forms I've taken. But shaking out my coat? That's the good stuff.

Nobody notices when a cat does something clever. "Oh my god, the cat managed to open the garage door! And filed our taxes! They're so sneaky!" But they spend so much time monitoring the behaviour of their dogs, nothing gets by them. If I'm discovered, I die. Curses suck.

"Rex, heel," Adam commanded, staring at me. Twit. I moved up and sat by his right leg, then circled around and sat by his left

51

leg and looked up at him. He nodded and ruffled my ears. "Good boy, come." Puppy training was going well, just not *too* well.

Together we walked up to the gate. It was a sandstone fence maybe three feet high, with a wrought iron gate topped by a stylized sun. The gravel path was that sort of fake red rock people like, and prickled my paws. The place reminded me of a Victorian pastiche of hermetic occult orders. I sat and scratched my left ear with my rear paw.

Janet pushed the gate open and went inside. She was nice enough. She liked to pretend to be put out all the time, but I could smell how much she really cared about Adam. He needed her and she wouldn't let him down. She wasn't fond of dogs, but that's just good taste.

A bearded man greeted them in, believe it or not, a Roman toga. He held his hands together forming a circle between the fingers. I shook my head disapprovingly. Too much, dude, too much. A little goes a long way.

Adam stepped forward, his right leg buckling slightly, and caught his balance. I whined, the smell of his bone disease always present, like a rancid layer of oil in my nose.

He held out his hand. "Adam Cabot. This is Janet Singh. We called ahead about the chapel?"

"Flamen Aurelius. We spoke on the phone. Please come in." The man held his arm to the side and walked beside Adam where I was supposed to heel. I held back, following behind, tail drooping.

Janet jumped in. "We want to look around first. I'm not sure that this is the right place, but we're here to look."

Adam smiled at her. She was trying.

The Flamen—I knew that was a title—would be the head priest here, dedicated to the order of worship of a single god. By the stylized sun on the gate, I surmised that god was Sol. People have been worshipping the sun since they were living in caves. How about something new? So boring.

"The Sun Garden, I'll show you that first. The building is styled as a Roman villa, a square with an open middle. Tomorrow is our holiest day, Dies Natalis Solis Invicti, or the Day of Birth of the Unconquerable Sun. I have to say, we're really excited about a wedding here, especially tomorrow of all days. I hope we can convince you."

They stepped into the building, and Adam asked, "Is he okay, my dog, Rex?"

"Rex? A king is indeed welcome."

Buttering me up? Suspicious.

Janet was fidgeting. "Um, Mr. Aurelius, what is the significance of the goat skull out front?"

"Yes, well, first, just call me Aurelius, or Aurie. As to the skull, well, our order did sacrifice animals in the ancient days, almost two thousand years ago. We obtained that skull from a local butcher and placed it there as our first and only one. A nod to tradition, I assure you, nothing more."

The man smelled weaselly. He was lying. They did indeed sacrifice animals still, I was sure of it. If I could get away from Adam and his cancerous leg, I could probably track down what. If I really cared, that is.

I lay down on the grass beside the front door and yawned my biggest dog yawn.

Adam looked over at me and smiled. "Stay," he commanded.

I gave him my saddest droopy eye look and lay my head on my paws. It's my best move and worked like a charm on the sap. He smiled and the three humans went inside. As soon as they moved out of view, I concentrated on enjoying the warmth of the sun on my fur.

Of course, I could still hear them, so it wasn't the best snooze. If only they could just be still for a couple hours, that would be great.

My mind drifted back, through long hazy years. Through endless births and youths, before the repeated and inevitable deaths, to a lazy day in Madrid. It was hot, and I was desperate. I remember the hunger, consuming me. Countless had died, in a warm snap after a brutally cold winter. Fend for yourself, or die of starvation, a terrible passing of the harshest agony and torment. I stretched out with my will and levitated the last loaf of mouldy bread off the shelf, right over someone reaching to get it. He called foul. "But my babies!" he shouted, yet I threw my coin at the merchant and fled. His voice called after me, and I spun as I heard the magic resonate around me like ripples in a still pond. The loaf slipped from my hands, fell to the dirt street. I curled into a foetal position, burning in the sun, then crawled to an alley. My bones snapped one by one, my skin tore, my flesh burned.

When I was done, I was not dead but an ass, a donkey. The first form.

Here in the present, voices drifted in and out of my awareness. Okay, that's not true, I heard everything. Stupid dog body. I was attuned to them both, Adam most of all. He had raised me from a pup, and despite my efforts to the contrary, my canine anatomy was entirely dialled into him. The depravity of the curse was boundless. If I ever discovered who hexed me back in Renaissance Madrid, I'd find a way to travel back in time and bite them, and I'd growl and shake my head back and forth. Ugh, being a dog sucks. I sighed wetly.

"The light in the Sun Garden is wonderful. The altar is designed to reflect the sun best tomorrow, specifically at noon. The altar lights up and fills the courtyard with golden light. It's hard on the eyes, and if you have any witnesses, they wouldn't see much for a quarter hour or so."

"No, no guests. Just us." Adam's voice was even, but I could hear the regret. My ears drooped, curse them, responding involuntarily to my master's drama.

"Oh, well, that's a lot to ask then. As much as we'd like to share the special day with you, rearranging our ceremony hinders other people's plans. Maybe a justice of the peace?"

Adam was quiet, his thoughts to himself. It was a good question. Even I didn't know why he was so set on being married tomorrow of all days.

Janet nudged him. "Tell him, Adam. It's important enough."

My left ear raised. What's this now?

I could hear his jaw creak from the tension, but then he relaxed. "I have stage 4 leukaemia. I don't have long to live. The drug therapy hasn't worked. I won't see next Christmas, unless a bone marrow transplant can happen. Even then . . . well, it's not a sure thing. My family just lost my mother. There is no way they'd fly out here for a wedding, I couldn't ask that of them. I know it's not important, it's selfish even, but I always dreamed that I would be married on Christmas."

I could hear his voice crack. A low whine rose in my gut.

"I had nearly lost hope that I'd meet someone like Janet. And there she was. Perfect in every way a man could want. I wish we had more time together, my love. I'm sorry it's turning out to be this way. I want to marry you, here, in the sun. A brief shining moment to celebrate our eternal bond. Let's banish the shadows, for a little while, shall we?"

I could hear Janet weeping, and then the sound of their embrace. Even the Roman priest was struggling, his breathing shallow with shared grief. Me? I was a hard-nosed hound. I wasn't affected by this. I . . . damn it. I think a bug flew in my eye.

"Look, I'm sympathetic, by the God, who wouldn't be. If you had fifty guests, even twenty, I'd make the call, add you to the ceremony. I can give you twenty minutes, at eleven a.m. After that, we'll need to rush you out to organize Dies Natalis. I'm sorry, but that's all I can do."

Adam squeezed his fists, tendons straining, and Janet murmured some obscure human noise like she just swallowed a sad cookie; you'd know the sound if you heard it.

"Thank you, we accept. You've saved us, really," he said, offering his hand.

Aurelius shook the hand, their palms meeting gently. "Let's go talk about the ceremony you want to have. My office is just through there."

I stood up, my ears drooping nearly to the ground. Even my wiry coat felt flat, as if I was being pulled into the ground. I was a grey melting mess of sad dog. They had so little time, and while I knew he was sick, he had never told me anything about it. Stage 4, that sounded bad. How many stages are there? Ten? No, only four. I felt that in my own bones as if they too were writhing from the corruption.

I had to help. I loped off, looking for a phone. And some thumbs.

I jogged around the corner and tripped and fell. Stupid big puppy feet. No, that wasn't it. I cocked my head to the side, one ear up, one down. Oh, it was my belly. Agh, the sudden pain rippled through me again. What is that?

I heard it then, the chanting. Okay, creepy monk seminary to a forgotten Roman god, no problem. Chanting? Come on, what is this, the Dark Ages? Forgetting the stomach pain, I loped to investigate. As I got closer, the cramps ran through me again, but I was ready for it, so I only tensed up. I felt waves of energy, like heat mirages rising from hot sand, but not hot, more like . . . waves is a good word, let's stick with that.

Around the corner, at the back behind the "Roman villa",

sneer sneer, was a path. The magic was coming from there. Oh, yes, it was magic. I'm a wizard, not a clumsy mutt puppy. Time to think like a wizard. Ah, so the magic feels like, well, like turmeric tastes. So, transformational magic! My heart froze. My fur shivered. Those black hearts were transforming something. Another wizard sent to hell on the wrong end of their curse, no doubt! I ran.

At the clearing were six vile cultists, performing their profane magics to send another innocent and well-meaning soul into a wasteland of—

Alarmed by movement, my head twisted to the side, ears up. Damn it, just a chipmunk. Whoa, big one. Bet that would be tasty—Focus!

I crept back to the clearing, belly on the ground in the brush, my nose poking out through a willow bush. At the centre of the clearing, between the sextet of sorcerers, was a bassinet. They were sacrificing a baby? And where was the high priest, back at the temple trying to cajole Adam into opting for the extended shiny ceremony only for an extra two hundred bucks? So they were entirely routine about the human sacrifice, got it, no big deal here.

I charged in and tripped over a twig, rolled to my feet, and darted forward. Two of the Roman wannabes grabbed for me, but I got through one's legs, grabbed the bassinet in my teeth, and dashed into the woods.

The dirt path unwound before me. I focused on my feet. Can't trip now, don't want to harm the—fruit? I skidded to a stop and looked inside. Grapes. I rescued grapes.

Huffing my best huff, I turned around and carried the basket back to the drunk romans.

They halted where they were and then let me pass. I placed it back in their sad little circle and then used a paw to align it the way it was. I moved away and sat, watching.

"That's not a dog."

"It's ugly, sure but—"

The others laughed, but the first one continued, "No, look closely, look at its aura."

They all peered, and one by one, an expression of wonder overtook their wine-summoning faces.

This was it. The moment I die. Again. They found out I was a person in an animal body. It had happened six times before, mostly in the early days, before I began to protect myself.

"It's a person, trapped in a dog's body."

Any second now.

"Well, we can fix that. Can't we?"

I looked at the leader, the first one that noticed me. He stepped closer and squatted before me. He was in his forties. Had a pointed beard, greying a little. His eyes seemed kind, wise.

"My name is Flamen Merro, or Doug Cartwright, if you want. We're an order of monks, dedicated to Sol Invictis, the sun god. But we do have some magic. If you want us to help you, please write 'yes' in the dirt."

My wizardly grey dog eyebrows rose on their own, echoing my feeling of hope. The unfamiliar sensation buzzed inside me, like a cold drink of water, for the first time in hundreds of years and scores of lives. Feeling not unlike a trained horse, I scratched "etiam" in the dirt, Latin for "yes".

He nodded and rose. "You're in luck. You're cursed somehow. Curses are our speciality, or rather, breaking them. A fair bit of preparation, meditation, and your magical aura will crack like an egg tomorrow at noon during our ceremony. There is a problem, though. Your aura is very unstable. The magic of our grounds appears to be keeping you together, but as soon as you leave, the curse will likely trigger. I don't know what that will do, but curses are called curses for a reason. Stay with us tonight, meditate, drink some sacred wine, and when your aura is weakened enough, tomorrow at noon, you should be fine."

I nodded. *Vale*, puppy feet! That's Latin for farewell.

They led me to their rectory, seminary, monk cell place, and closeted me in a room. It was stone, with a door and a bamboo mat, but little else.

Doug gave me some water in a bowl. "Meditate, clear your mind of your desires. Concentrate only upon the sounds and feelings of your body. If you begin thinking, try to cleanse the thoughts by feeling your breath in and out of your, er, snout."

I get it, he wanted me to attune to the magic of the place.

"Once your mind is clear of all thoughts," he continued.

I'll attune, got it.

"You'll search about for the aura, the essence of this place. The magic of the structure."

I gave him my best doggy death glare.

Unhindered, he continued, "When you've become in synchronicity with the place, you'll—"

If you say it, I'll bite you. I swear to Sol Invictis.

"—attune to the energies of our magic."

I lay down and whined, a paw over my nose.

"Good, get to it. This will be hard work, don't leave this room for anything. If you aren't perfectly in tune, the magic could backfire. You could trigger the curse, or possibly make this state permanent. Yes, that's more likely. The curse would end and you'd be this, a dog, for the rest of your dog life. But at least you're a puppy, so that's . . . longer, I guess. Sorry."

It had been a very long time since I'd attuned to anything, but I settled down to do the work. It's hard not to think.

AT LEAST AN hour went by, maybe two. My mind flashed unbidden thoughts, and I banished them, thinking of air going in and out of my snout. A chipmunk burbled up from the recesses. I ignored it. The feeling of shaking my coat arose, but I repressed the irrepressible urge and focused. Adam's leg. I blinked. No, ignore that. I'll be human tomorrow. I can help him better as a wizard. Breathing, in and out. One with the monastery. What do Romans call monasteries? No, push that away. The air enters me, that is everything.

"Rex," came the sound, a memory of running in the park, chasing a cloth frisbee. My heart pounded, but I pushed it aside. Dog stuff, gone tomorrow.

"Rex!" The sound was real, not a thought. Somewhere far away. Didn't he know . . . no, he wouldn't know. His nine-months-old puppy was missing, that's all he knew. It was fine. I didn't care. I'd lived with dozens of families and they all went away eventually. I didn't care, that was dead in me.

"Rex!" I could hear the timbre, his worry, his love for me. How? It had only been eight months since he picked me from the litter. My ears sagged, my thoughts betraying me.

Concentrate. It doesn't matter. He'll live. Oh my god! I . . .

I whined. But he wouldn't, would he. Not for long. His last months in life would be spent wondering where I went, missing me. Even if I became human and told him, and somehow he believed me, it wouldn't be the same.

This was my chance! Sol Invictis only comes once a year. If I leave the grounds, the curse could trigger, and although they didn't know, I knew that I would die, to be reincarnated again. Somewhere, likely nowhere near here. How would I get back here, as a gerbil, or a parakeet in Australia? And if I die, Adam would still be heartbroken.

It's my life. I can't sacrifice my future. It's been too long. I can't bear—

"Rex! Please come!"

My heart nearly exploded. Anxiety coursed through my body. He loved me. How could I turn my back on him? If it meant my life, so be it, I couldn't stand feeling his pain a moment longer. Damn it.

I pawed open the door and ran. I ran for Adam.

The hallway opened before me, blurring past. At the stairs, I tripped and banged my jaws together, paws scrambling to keep running. Gaining purchase, I darted up the stairs, careened off the wall, and ran toward the voice.

"Rex?"

I banged off another wall, cornering too wide, and then ran up to him. I spun in a circle and licked his face as he ruffled my ears and tried to hug me. I was too squirmy, and moved in and out of his arms. He laughed and finally I deigned to allow him to squeeze me tight.

"Where did you go, boy? Were you in the kitchen?"

My ears perked up. Kitchen?

Adam laughed once more and scratched the thick hair on my neck. "Come on, let's go to the hotel."

I happily followed him out to the car, where Janet was looking at the woods through her bird-watching binoculars, then skidded to a stop. The attunement! They said if I left, the curse could trigger. I whined.

Flamen Aurelius (what was his real name, I wondered, Melvin?) jogged out. "Wait!"

Janet came running over and gave me her own hug (which I allowed, and even licked her cheek); she tasted like sunscreen.

"Melvin" came over and huffed once. "The guys have been talking. Did you want to stay here tonight? Our dormitory is only half full. You could each have a room, or share one, your preference."

Janet giggled. "Spending the night before apart is a tradition."

Adam beamed and took her hand. "Do you really want to? I'd be okay with that. We'd have to get some supper and then come back."

The head priest shook his head. "Oh no, you can stay. We'll have a small dinner tonight and a feast tomorrow at sunset. Really, the others had fun playing with Rex today. They'd love to have such a noble friend around as long as you can share him."

Janet and Adam looked into each other's eyes with growing grins. She nodded and Adam said, "Okay! Thank you, you're making this a great event. I really appreciate it, so much. I just wish that . . ." He looked at her. "No, I wish for nothing else. This will be wonderful."

He didn't smell that way. Regret and love battled within him. I sensed that he would do anything to marry this girl, and a Christmas Day wedding was special to him. But not sharing it with family was a bitter note. He had to choose, and he chose her over them.

Why did he choose again? Oh right, his mother had died, and his family was mourning. As was he, I knew. He wished for more, but took what he could get.

Wish. Oh, I wished I was a wizard. My magic could have made short work of some of these problems. Still, an idea formed in my head. Maybe I wasn't a wizard these days, and maybe I wasn't as sneaky as a cat, but I surely could do something.

I just needed time, and time was a dwindling bowl of kibble.

DURING DINNER, I snuck out of the dining room. It was the south side of the four-sided complex with one side looking at the trees to the south and the north side overlooking the square in the centre. I gobbled down my plate of lightly fried hamburger meat and, when no one was looking, crept out.

I dashed for Doug's office. I could smell which was whose and found his computer. I'd watched people use these devices over the last few lifetimes, and sort of knew what to do. The time before last I was a cat in a place called Frankfurter—my mouth just waters at that name—and my owner thought that my affectation for sitting on her desk beside the computer was because I wanted to be near her. No, dummy. I was memorizing your passwords and learning the ins and outs of search engines. You didn't really get drunk and order me treats from Amazon all those times.

Adam's social media of choice was Facebook, so I started there. My paw stretched out, and I worked the mouse gently, gingerly pointing and clicking by rolling my paw forward painfully. With a great deal of care, I typed, one letter slowly after another.

THE NEXT MORNING, we had breakfast. Adam and Janet exchanged colourfully wrapped gifts, trinkets of some sentimentality lost on me. I'm not heartless, I was just too busy chewing on my giant rawhide bone I had to unwrap savagely. I didn't even see them kiss, but I sure heard it. We then went for a long walk through the countryside. It was a beautiful day, crisp and cold but sunny and serene. I heeled nicely by Adam as he held Janet's hand.

When they returned, the cars were pulling in. The extended cult members, but also a bunch of folks who had never been here before. They gawked and leered and climbed out of their rental vans. They were dressed up and I recognized them from the funeral.

Adam burst into happy tears, running and hugging his father, his sisters, two nephews and a niece, and four aunt/uncle pairs, with their assorted children.

"How did you get here? How did you . . . ?" He looked at Janet, but she was crying in surprise, too.

His father—I knew him as KarlCabot#4511—held him roughly by the sides of the face. "I got a Facebook message from someone named Doug, saying you were getting married here, and couldn't ask me to come because of the funeral. I love you, boy. Of course we came. God bless you for being so considerate. Oh, sorry, can I say that here? This will be the best Christmas gift a father could have. The new beginning we all need just now."

They hugged again and laughed. I spun in circle after circle and played keep-away with the children, stealing the bowtie they wanted me to wear, and leading them around the villa. The kids were wearing elf and Santa hats, and after their energy was depleted (mine was boundless, never mind the lolling tongue) they all exchanged presents.

Since I'd left a note for Doug on his machine, he knew what I'd done last night. He claimed that he had done it as he wanted the day to be extra special for Adam and Janet.

The ceremony was wonderful. I knew I'd only have a dog's life to remember it by, so I soaked it in. My gift to Adam. Aurelius led a strange procession around the Sun Garden, six acolytes dressed as horses, while he walked backwards, directing them. It was a metaphor about driving the sun around the earth each day. Did you know that the word Sunday came from Emperor Constantine, who named the day of rest Dies Solis, or day of the sun, after Sol Invictis? That day, I learned that too.

The Romans gracefully included a benediction to Sandra, Adam's late mother, and the ceremony was all about new beginnings and rebirth. It was lovely, entirely beautiful, and I looked smashing in my bowtie—I got a good look at it when drinking out of the toilet.

After the wedding, the ceremony had the couple blessed by the order, and at noon, the Sun Garden glowed with the day's brightest light, filling us with a remarkable glow. We bathed in the radiance of their Sol Invictis, the unconquerable sun.

I felt something break inside me then, and understood. Long ago, I had been cursed for using magic selfishly. By sacrificing my best shot at a cure, I'd earned the end to the curse. When I died this time, I'd finally be reincarnated as a human. I'd passed on the last loaf of bread for another more needing.

I was content to wait, to live this life with Adam and after he passed, with Janet and hopefully their children. It wasn't so bad being his dog. Not so bad at all.

O HOWLY NIGHT

Jennifer Lee Rossman

BELLA STRUGGLED TO keep still. Odin had told the hellhound puppies to sit and stay; failure to do so might cost them the status of very good dogs, and only the best got to go O-U-T into the human world.

So sit and stay they would, though excitement trembled through their bodies and threatened to make their tails wag uncontrollably. Only Bella escaped the ordeal of controlling her tail, as she had lost it in a scrap with that three-headed dog a few afterlives down the way. A blessing, really, as she had never quite gotten the hang of being a very good dog and had never gone O-U-T.

She and her littermates watched as Odin went through his routine. Feeding the ravens, getting Sleipnir's reins from the hook by the door, putting on his going-out eyepatch. Then he turned to them.

"Oh, hello puppies," he said, smiling beneath his beard and pretending he hadn't seen them. "Hmm. I wonder . . . would any of you like to . . ."

Thirteen little black heads tilted sideways.

Odin smiled and raised his voice to a falsetto, addressing all of them, even Bella. "Go for a ride?"

Thus released from the mighty power of the sit and stay

63

command, the puppies cried havoc, bounding at Odin's feet and baying loud enough to wake the dead. Assuming any of the dead had been able to fall asleep that night, anyway.

Odin opened the door, letting slip the puppies of hell to join the others already assembled. The Wild Hunt had begun.

As THEY BURST through the barrier between worlds, the deathly hunting party took on a spectral quality, becoming one with the winter wind that swept through the woods and countryside. All who heard the cries and the hoofbeats and the howling dogs ran for cover, for the legend was well known and nobody dared get caught and be doomed to run with the Wild Hunt for the rest of eternity.

Especially not on Christmas Eve.

The holiday meant little to Bella, this being her first time going O-U-T and her hailing from another realm, but the mortal world just seemed to exude a sense of hope and joy and love. Most likely a result of the indoor trees she saw through the windows as they gambolled through a quaint little town. If she had an indoor tree to piddle under instead of having to whine at the door and wait for Frigga to let her out, she figured she would feel pretty joyful as well.

The others did not share her wonder, but she expected as much. Her fascination for the human world, for mortal creatures and the general concept of being alive, was one of the main reasons she was pretty sure nobody liked her.

The hunting party, tens of thousands of spirits strong, charged through the streets and fields at the whims of the leader. They would take off after a deer, running the creature nearly to exhaustion, then the scent of a far-off bear would catch their attention and they would all veer in that direction.

Bella ran faster and further than she ever had before, feeling as if the endlessness of the world was matched only by that of her energy. She wound around the legs of the ghosts and their horses, baying and howling along with the trumpeting of countless bugles. Ancestral hunting instincts surged through her body. But still the others pushed her back; her siblings, the older hounds, even some of the human spirits.

A sobering wave rippled through the hunt, turning even the most raucous hellhounds and demons serious. When the smell reached Bella, she understood. The wild beasts were but diversions; the real quarry were mortal humans, and they had just spotted one.

HE TASTED LIKE fear. Fear and cinnamon. Bella wasn't quite sure how she knew, as the Wild Hunt didn't actually kill and eat him so much as *absorb* him, but a phantom flavour filled her mouth just the same. Fear and cinnamon.

He walked in the back, forced to join yet somehow still unwelcome, and Bella took it upon herself to befriend the new kindred spirit. She barked, lowered her front half in a play bow, and raced to keep up with him as he and the rest of the hunting party continued sweeping through the countryside.

He paid her no mind, just followed the others as if he had any choice in the matter, despair turning his eyes empty and lifeless. Even when she broke off from the pack briefly to find the most perfect fetching stick in all the world, or at least the county, he just looked at her blankly.

The poor man. He had no idea how to play fetch.

WHEN THE WILD Hunt stopped for a brief rest—they may have been spirits and deities and denizens of the underworld, but they still had to tinkle—Bella tried a more powerful approach, something no one could possibly resist.

A puppy belly.

She plopped on the ground, the infernal heat from her body melting the snow almost instantly, and rolled over in front of the man, her belly on full display. He gave her a cursory glance before returning to his despondent sighing.

Was she not doing it right? She had never actually experienced a belly rub, but she thought this was how the other dogs did it.

Bella let out a soft whine, attracting the attention of Sleipnir, Odin's favourite horse and second favourite grandson. The dappled grey stallion, just one of many glorious beings to come from the underworld's loose understanding of physics, pawed at the snow with two of his front hooves and snorted at Bella.

"What's the matter with you, pup?" he asked, not so much out of concern but because he considered it his duty to ensure every animal member of the hunting party found the night fulfilling.

"The human ghost is sad even though I'm cute and bring him sticks," Bella grumbled, rolling onto her stomach and resting her head on her paws.

The man squinted at the animals, as if suspecting they were talking about him, then went back to staring at the photograph in his hand. His own smiling face stared back, along with three children.

"It takes them a while to love being dead sometimes," Sleipnir said. "Doesn't help that it's Christmas. Important holiday to a lot of humans, especially ones with families." The horse swished his tail thoughtfully. "He was carrying a bag when we got him, wasn't he? Probably presents for the kids."

Bella tilted her head to the side, regarding the man curiously. Unfinished business didn't make for a good spirit. A fun spirit, yes, one that threw pots and pans and made the walls bleed, but not a *good* spirit, not a happy one.

She rose and walked over to the man, giving his hand a gentle lick with her sulfuric tongue. There was nothing she could do to give his children their father back, but she could at least give them Christmas.

IT WASN'T HARD to sneak away; besides Sleipnir, no one paid much attention to Bella.

Once she left the ghostly aura of the Wild Hunt, a most peculiar sensation came over her body. She felt . . . well, alive, she supposed. She began to pant, exhaustion from the miles-long run catching up to her, and one of her paws throbbed as if she had stepped wrong somewhere along the line.

Bella looked back, but the hunt was nearly invisible to her, just a vague patch of existence that her eyes kept sliding off and an uneasy sensation deep in her gut. She decided she didn't want to look at it anymore and set off to find the bag.

THE FIRES OF Hel burned within the pup, but she was tiny and winter was persistent. More than once, she thought about abandoning the bag and running back to the Wild Hunt for a nice, warm cuddle puddle with the other hounds. Not that they would comply.

She pushed on through the blowing snow, following the scent of humans to a little town decked in evergreen swags and shiny baubles and bells. Fear of the Wild Hunt left the streets empty and the doors locked up tight, but warmth spilled from cracks between curtains and the smell of Christmas Eve dinners permeated the air.

She was the only being around, but already Bella felt less lonely than ever before.

The scent on the bag led the hellhound to a house locked up tighter than the rest, with so many decorations and lights that it resembled the halls of Valhalla in terms of sheer shininess. Bella scratched at the door, barking softly.

Of course, what Bella thought of as barking softly, most people would call "unearthly howling," and the children wisely did not answer. But she continued late into the night, and the longer she was in this human world and away from the influences of the other spirits, the more her voice quieted until it was an almost pitiful whine.

The door opened, just a crack, and three little human faces peeked out. The older ones regarded the hellhound with fear and suspicion, for their father taught them well, but the smallest one, the runt of the litter, her eyes lit up. "Puppy!" she cried, throwing open the door and wrapping her arms around Bella.

"IT IS DEMONIC," the eldest whispered. "Part of the Wild Hunt, no doubt."

His younger brother nodded reluctantly, his eyes never leaving the little beast curled up on his sister's lap. "It brought his bag to torment us. They got him, didn't they?"

There was a long moment of silence, then, "We don't know that. But we do know there's a hellhound in our house, so what do we do about that?"

"Maybe there's something about fighting them in Dad's folklore books. I'll go check. Just . . . just watch it, all right? Don't let it get her too."

Bella heard this conversation, but distantly and through the impenetrable fog of peacefulness the likes of which she had never experienced until now, until the little girl child introduced her to the joy of belly rubs. Oh, if she had a tail to wag . . .

". . . and I'll take you for walks, and brush you, and you can sleep in my bed," the little girl was whispering, and it all sounded so lovely that Bella briefly forgot about the Wild Hunt and her siblings and the underworld altogether.

That is, until she heard the horns and the howling. Her ears perked up. Did they come back for her?

The boy humans went to the door, the taller one peering through the peephole. "Dad!"

A low growl rumbled in Bella's throat as the girl squealed and stood up, holding the pup as she ran to join her brothers. No, they did not come back for her. They came for the children.

Bella struggled to free herself from the girl's arms as the middle child opened the door. She placed herself between them and the ghostly apparition of their father, raising the hair on the back of her neck and making her eyes glow like hot coals. These children would not go O-U-T. Not if she could help it. They would sit and stay.

She was hardly formidable in the underworld, though, and even less so here among the mortals. At best, she looked a little more puffy and like her eyes might benefit from some moisturizing eyedrops.

"Demon dog," one of the boys growled. "Get out of the way."

"No, puppy," the girl—and already Bella had started thinking of her as *her* girl—pleaded. "That's our daddy. It's all right, he's good."

"No," her brother whispered. "Something isn't right."

Bella couldn't say exactly what the children saw. The utter lack of light in his eyes, maybe, or the vague patch of existence behind him that made people uneasy to look at. But they saw *something*, and though it broke their hearts, it saved their lives as well because they did not go running into his arms to be captured by the Wild Hunt.

From somewhere behind the veil, Odin whistled. Bella sat perfectly still, as if under the command of sit and stay. He called her name, and she pinned her ears back and growled in defiance.

After a moment, a great grey stallion emerged from the fog, stamping all four of his front hooves. "If you live with the mortals, you will be one," Sleipnir warned. "You will grow old, you will experience pain and hunger and fatigue, and one day you will die."

"One day," Bella repeated, in a very quiet and shaky voice. "But not today. Not like the children will if I let you get them."

She glanced at the father, at the kids. They would be together, yes, but running with the Wild Hunt meant never reaching Valhalla or Helgafjell or any real afterlife. They would never find peace, and so being together would be meaningless as they slowly became the bad kind of spirits.

"I'm staying. For a little while, anyway. They need protection, I need a family that will love me."

"You will regret it."

"Maybe. But you'll be back. Every Christmas, you'll be back."

With that, Bella turned and escorted the children inside. After all, they still hadn't opened their Christmas presents.

WHERE THE HEARTH IS

Lisa Timpf

AI-ENHANCED BORDER collie Pepper twitched her nose, keeping her eyes tightly closed as she processed her thoughts. That dream she'd just had, of their mission on Altimus—it had seemed so vivid. Right down to the scent of the pine trees that dotted the forest they'd trudged through, enroute to the Syndicate headquarters, the rasp of sedgegrass against her muzzle as they skulked through the meadow.

Wait. That didn't feel like sedgegrass. And it's still there . . .

Though she'd been retired from the Galactic Space Services for three months, years of rigorous training enabled Pepper to transition instantly into a state of full wakefulness. She scrambled to her feet and shuffled backwards, noticing, as she did so, a black form twitching erratically in the air just above where she'd been sleeping.

On closer examination, the form proved to have eight legs that spanned an area as broad as her dinner bowl.

Spider! Pepper bared her teeth in a snarl. She cocked her head and lowered her lips back over her teeth as logic kicked in. *Spiders aren't native to Arcadia*, she thought. Of course, one could have come in via the spaceport . . .

. . . But there were so many checks and balances to prevent that! No, a simpler explanation lurked somewhere near. She felt

71

certain of it.

Pepper ducked her head. Her irrational fear of arachnids had been a source of embarrassment throughout her career as a canine operative in the GSS, though most of her ship-mates had been kind enough not to tease her about it. Most, but not all. And one of those who had derived immense pleasure from leveraging her fear for his own entertainment happened to live with Pepper and her handler Minna, now that they'd moved planet-side.

"Quicksilver!" Pepper yelped.

A handsome silver-grey feline poked his head through the branches of the pine tree that Minna and her partner Allie had erected in the home's living room. The cat yanked the string on which the fake spider was suspended one more time for effect, and grinned.

"Very funny," Pepper remarked, making sure her tone conveyed, clearly, her complete lack of amusement. "You'd better not let Minna catch you in there."

"She won't." The cat's voice oozed with self-confidence.

"How can you be so sure?"

Quicksilver clambered down, then picked his way carefully around the brightly-wrapped packages arranged at the base of the tree. "Because. I heard her leave in the car. And I'll hear it come back."

Pepper turned away. *She* hadn't heard the vehicle depart. She'd been too deep in sleep. Was she going soft, now that they'd moved dirtside?

"Look, I'm sorry."

Pepper whirled back to face the cat. *It's not like him to apologize.*

"You've seemed down in the mouth lately. I was just trying to cheer you up."

Pepper chuffed softly to herself.

"Is there a problem?" The cat took a step closer.

Nothing I'd tell you, Pepper thought. She believed her reticence to be justifiable, having been the butt of Quicksilver's practical jokes all too often in the three-plus years since she'd first made his acquaintance. Still, with Minna out and Allie having left this morning for Mailletville, two hours' travel each way, the cat presented the only confidante available to her at the moment.

Pepper shuffled her forepaws, uncertain what to do. She shifted position so she could see out the window. See the yellow sky. She still hadn't gotten used to that. Oh, sure, they'd gone on-planet on assignments, back when she, Quicksilver, and Minna had been active GSS operatives. But always, in between, they'd returned to the *Meech Lake*, their vessel. To Minna's comfortable bunk room. To the exercise area. To the mini-caf, where one of the crew members could often be prevailed upon to dial up a dog cookie from the synth-server . . .

"Do you know what they're doing on the *Meech Lake* right now?" Pepper asked, her voice thick with emotion.

"Barrelling off on some mission to risk life and limb?" Quicksilver sat facing Pepper and curled his tail around his front toes.

Pepper shot the cat a disdainful look. "Getting ready for Christmas."

Though Nibo Salvar, their commanding officer, had been Harsovian, she'd made a point of honouring the winter festivals celebrated by various planetary cultures, including Earth's Christmas. Pepper closed her eyes, remembering the fun of accompanying Minna on her Secret Santa expeditions through the hallways. The smell of special meals programmed into the auto-servers—meals which Minna had often shared with her. The fun of opening gifts, the day of, in Minna's cabin.

"The smell of pine, pumped through the air vents," Pepper said dreamily.

"Are you daft? That was synth-smell. You've got the real thing right in front of you." Quicksilver jerked his head toward the tree.

Pepper ignored the comment. "The carols."

"You can't carry a tune in a bucket." Quicksilver smirked. "I, on the other hand—"

"You call that caterwauling singing?"

"Insults will get you nowhere." Despite the remark, the cat fired Pepper an approving glance. Quicksilver had always encouraged his canine counterpart to show more spunk. Trading verbal barbs was something the cat would happily do 24-7. Or, in Arcadia's case, 25-8.

But not Pepper. She yearned for action. "What're you planning for today?"

Quicksilver stretched and yawned. "Well, if there was a blaze going in the fireplace, I'd curl up on the hearth. But instead I think I'll just head over to the master bedroom for a nap."

"Don't you ever get tired of sleeping?"

Quicksilver shot the dog a green-eyed glare. "I have *years* of sleep to catch up on from the *Meech Lake*. And I'd best get started."

Tail in the air, the cat headed for the back bedroom. Pepper snorted in disgust.

Maybe when Minna got home, she could be prevailed on to go for a walk or engage in a rousing game of fetch. Something to look forward to.

Pepper's spirits rose, then just as quickly plummeted.

Who knew when Minna would be home? And lately, she'd seemed too busy to pay much attention to Pepper. Why would today be any different?

A spark of defiance deep within the dog's black and white head flared into a small flame.

Yes, it had been Pepper's own decision to retire. But that didn't make it any easier to accept that life was different now. Harder, in a way, knowing it was her choice. That she feared, deep down, she might have made the *wrong* choice. Perhaps it would have been better to go out in a blaze of glory instead of sitting around the house all day . . .

Suddenly restless, Pepper slipped through the dog door before she could change her mind.

ONCE OUTSIDE, PEPPER hesitated. Did a nap sound like such a bad idea? Not necessarily . . .

She shot a longing glance back at the house and snarled under her breath. If she returned, Quicksilver would never let her hear the end of it.

The breeze ruffled Pepper's fur and tickled her snout. The dog lifted her head, cataloguing the scents. Nothing threatening, nothing surprising. But that, there—

The tang of fish-smell and kelpweed. Which reminded her. Living planet-side might not be as exciting or purposeful as her service on the *Meech Lake*, but they *had* made some friends in the three months they'd lived on Arcadia. And the smell of the large ocean upon whose shores New Caraquet had been built jogged the dog's memory.

Rimbaut Salvage, a business owned by some of those new friends, was a brisk ten-minute trot from her home. Well, eleven minutes, the last time she'd made the trip. *I've let myself get out of shape.* The thought failed to dampen Pepper's spirits, now that she had a goal to shoot for.

Her emotions ratcheted up another notch when she slipped through the salvage operation's open gate-way and spotted Anna Rimbaut. The woman, who worked with her three brothers and her father Lazare at the firm, had started keeping dog cookies and cat treats in her desk since befriending Pepper and Quicksilver.

Licking her lips in anticipation, Pepper trotted up to Anna, who stood, tablet in hand, studying one of the vessels the crew had brought in.

Anna lowered the tablet and smiled when she spotted the dog. "I was just about to have my tea break," Anna said. "C'mon in."

Obedient to a fault, particularly when it suited her, Pepper trailed the woman through the door of her office, then plopped her behind on the floor and watched, gaze riveted on Anna's right hand as the woman slowly opened the top drawer of the desk.

"Is Minna with you?" Anna asked, tilting her head so she could see back through the corridor.

Pepper woofed twice and shook her head.

Anna laughed. "You do understand a lot, don't you?"

Pepper rose to her feet, wagged her tail, and extended her snout to accept the cookie that Anna held out. She munched on the treat as Anna busied herself with heating the kettle she kept on top of her filing cabinet.

"You know," Anna said. "Dad's just getting the boat ready to go check out a potential salvage site. You'd be welcome to come along. I could check with Minna—"

Pepper raised her head and gazed intently at Anna. A ship— she felt a surge of enthusiasm that quickly ebbed away. The notion of activity appealed, but the realization that the *Northumberland* wasn't the type of ship she yearned to feel under her paws weighed down upon her.

Pepper nodded toward the cookie drawer and woofed softly, a gesture she hoped Anna would interpret as a thank you. Then she squared herself in the direction of the door, looking back over her shoulder at Anna.

"I get it," Anna said, laughing. "You have business of your own to attend to. Another time, perhaps."

Another time. Pepper dipped her muzzle in acknowledgement, then jogged through the door, her pace quickening as she proceeded. Anna's suggestion of taking a trip had brought to mind a different destination. One she knew that Quicksilver would mock her for, if he knew of it.

He won't know of it, Pepper thought. She gritted her teeth.

THE SPACEPORT SAT on the far edge of town, beyond a low hill that provided ample separation from the residential and business areas. As she approached, Pepper could detect the sweetish smell of the plant-based fuels that powered the servicing trucks and luggage trains.

There. Pepper, having crested the hill, looked down at the spaceport and sighed. She hadn't realized how sore her eyes had been for such a sight. She squinted as sunlight bounced off a shuttle from a passenger liner. A swirl of colour surrounded the vessel as brightly-clad tourists disembarked. Noting the day-packs and the binoculars many sported, Pepper surmised they'd be headed to the Arcadia outback, hoping for a glimpse of the local fauna—the chienchats or the cerfelan or perhaps some of the brilliantly-feathered birds that abounded in Arcadia's woodlands.

Beyond the shuttle, spaceport staff collected a delivery smartpod that'd been dropped from a transport freighter to parachute down, making auto-corrections with tiny nav-jets to position itself for landing. Two other smartpods squatted on the spaceport tarmac, waiting for their turn to be processed.

Pepper knew the pods emptied on the previous visit had already been reloaded with Arcadian exports, then shot into space to re-join their parent vessel before it departed for its next stop. She cocked her head and studied the pods, wondering whether they held any goods that Minna might have ordered. Or, for that matter, the special shipment she'd requested . . .

I should have done this sooner. The bustle of the spaceport, the mere affirmation that their quiet planet was linked in some way to the busy commerce of the galaxy, had already lifted her spirits. Pepper glanced at the remaining ships. Two J-class cruisers, the kind favoured by many for sabbatical space-jumps with extended family, sat fins-down further out on the spaceport's surface, and three other vessels rested further toward the periphery.

Pepper's eyes narrowed as she studied the most distant of those, seeing the charred nose-cone, the distinctive outline. *It couldn't be. Surely Port Authority would have recognized it . . .*

But how would they? They weren't the ones who'd run across a vessel very much like this one back on Altimus. Pepper narrowed her eyes, studying the distant shape. If she was right, the vessel was a derelict salvaged from a long-abandoned Greenoan spaceport and rendered space-worthy once again. Only someone desperate would stoop to such measures.

Someone who operated on the fringes of the law, for example.

They'd run across Syndicate operatives in three vessels almost identical to this one, fast-moving smugglers. And captured two of them. But the third had escaped, much to Commander Salvar's chagrin.

And now, it looked as though the fugitive vessel had made landfall here.

The ship sat apart from its fellows, its nose pointed skyward, its sharply angled fins suggesting a readiness for flight. Pepper tilted her head and tried to remember the landing schedule. It was impossible, where they lived, not to hear the growl of incoming jets. She'd thought she detected a rumbling in the night, just after moon-high. Against regulations, but then again, what did Syndicate members care for such niceties?

The nighttime landing argued for a short visit, a quick turnaround. Here to do their business and then gone before anyone could raise alarm.

If only she could contact Minna!

Not wanting to be tracked, Pepper hadn't brought her com. She raised her lips in a grimace. *I didn't think I'd need it. I'll know better next time.*

Should she contact Xavier Thibodeau of the Arcadian Defence Team? That'd be her next stop. But it was one thing to share a half-baked theory with Minna. Quite another to alert the Defence Team commander about a peril that might or might not be real . . .

Pepper trotted back down the hill, moving at an angle. Her motions infused with purpose, now, she loped around the berm that circled the spaceport, skirting the scrubland. Noting a tall buroak she'd marked from her original position, she nodded to herself. *Should be able to get a good sightline from here.*

She trotted up the berm, moving with purpose, hanging her tongue out to the side. To a casual observer, she hoped to convey the image of a family dog on the lam.

Her eyes intent, she crept to the crest of the berm, then looked down, feeling a flush of satisfaction. She'd been right, this location provided an excellent vantage point. And there was no mistaking the vessel. The scarring along the sides, the barely-legible markings that had once been Greenoan lettering—it was the same ship they'd encountered on Altimus.

And she was certain it was up to no good.

Now to alert Xavier, before these ones took off.

PEPPER HAD MEANT to leave immediately. But her yearning for what she had lost, what she had left behind, froze her in her tracks when she heard the rumble of a departing jet.

On the opposite end of the field, flames shot down from below the fins of one of the family cruisers. Ah, to be off for adventures in the skies! She wondered where they might be headed. From here? Maybe Tosorontia, out in the next system. Or Space Station Three, which boasted the galaxy-renowned shopping and clearance centre offering the goods from Karspan Sector. Minna had bought her a blanket there, made of the softest naava spider silk. She still remembered how soft it had felt . . .

Pepper watched the skybound vessel until it disappeared into the sky. Then she shook herself. She had places to go.

She was about to turn and lope toward town when she heard the scuff of space-boots behind her.

"Well, lookie here."

She didn't recognize the voice, but there was no mistaking the undertone of menace. The fur along Pepper's back bristled.

She turned, slowly, muscles tensing as she readied herself for flight.

Most Arcadians knew her, and she knew them. But the scent

of this one was different. He'd been in the outback, she could detect that much. Underlying that was the smell of the space traveller—recirculated air, body smell. Water was at a premium on most ships, but some accommodation was made for periodic bathing. Still, for many spacers, a trip planet-side meant a chance to visit the showers for a real clean-up. This one had not taken that opportunity. Which argued for being on business. In, and out.

Grey form-fitting slacks and tunic, with no insignia. And the weapons slung at his belt—he couldn't have gone to town, not carrying the disruption blaster that hung at his right side. Banned in all sectors. Favoured by outlaws.

A poorly-healed scar from an old wound had lain a lash across his cheek. Pepper whimpered low in her throat. She'd seen such, only once, aboard the *Meech Lake*. Knew how long it had taken the bearer of that scar to recover.

Feeling a surge of empathy, she met his gaze. And shivered, seized by a sudden chill. She'd never seen eyes so cold.

Pepper drew to mind the skit nights aboard the *Meech Lake*, entertainments to while away the long hours. Minna had worked patiently with Pepper and Quicksilver, laughingly coaching them in the finer points of play-acting. Time to apply those teachings now.

She nodded politely and turned to go down the hill. *Just a dog out for a walk*, she told herself. *Pretend to be that with all your might.*

She took one step, then another.

"Not so fast."

Pepper turned back to look at the man, her gaze dropping to the blaster he now held in his right hand. Despite her determination to play the role of a carefree family pet, at the sight of the weapon her tail slipped between her legs.

This evoked a sly grin from the spacer. "Hmmm. Now how would an ordinary mutt on Arcadia know what a disruption blaster looks like?"

Pepper offered a slow wag, then cocked her head and studied the man with the most vacant look she could muster. She saw doubt flit across his face, and allowed herself to nurse a small spark of hope.

The man glanced at his wrist chrono, then back at the dog.

"Gotta make tracks," he said. "Liftoff's in two hours, and it wouldn't do to be left behind." The sincerity with which those words were spoken resonated with Pepper. He meant every word. "And whether you're smart or not, you're coming with me. There's a market for your sort, out there."

Pepper bared her teeth. Fight, or flight? Despite the threat implicit in the weapon, would he destroy a potential source of income?

She knew the answer to that. If it came down to dealing with a potential threat to the ship, he'd do far worse. Besides, the less lethal paralyzer slung on the other hip would provide a way to deal with her without killing her.

Pepper paddled her forepaws on the ground, expressing a genuine distress.

"Ahead of me. Nice and easy. And don't try any funny stuff." The man bared his own teeth in a grin.

What was it Commander Salvar always said? As she stumbled along ahead of the Syndicate man, Pepper clung to the memory of her former boss as an island of sanity in what had become an upside-down world. Stay in the game, that's what she'd said. Stay in the game, and look for your chances.

Pepper darted a glance at the vessels drawing ever nearer. Was it just this morning that she'd longed to go back into space?

Be careful what you wish for. That was another saying Commander Salvar had been particularly fond of.

She wished she'd paid greater heed.

Pepper slowed her pace as the Syndicate vessel drew closer, scuffing her feet.

Should she run for it, in spite of everything? She glanced ahead.

Nothing even faintly resembling cover, to hide behind. He'd have a clear shot, and unless he had an abysmally poor aim—

Pepper cut the thought off right there. Syndicate operatives with lousy aims didn't typically survive for long. And this one's facial scarring and arrogant air argued he'd been around for a while. No, she'd have to come up with a different plan.

Where there's life, there's hope. That thought had sustained her through difficult situations before.

But as the ship's entry-ramp loomed closer, Pepper's thoughts turned to Minna, and to the possibility that once the ship blasted, she might never see her handler again. Despite all of her training, despite all of the difficult situations she'd been through, she couldn't help it.

She raised her head and gave tongue to her despair in a long and wavering howl.

PEPPER AWOKE WITH a stun-inspired headache. *Not the first time,* she told herself, raising her head and regretting that too-quick movement immediately.

She had the sense that some sound had woken her. If so, it had since faded from earshot.

Pepper raised her head. Despite a wave of dizziness, she forced herself to focus. Time was short, and she couldn't afford to waste it. Giving voice to the howl of despair must have triggered her captor to hit her with the paralyzer. Which meant she'd been out for thirty minutes to an hour, depending on the duration of the raying.

Pepper closed her eyes and focussed on what her nose could tell her. The distinctive smell of ship-air, cut with disinfectant. Whoever had done the cleaning hadn't been super-thorough. Bio-smell of body oils and skin flakes could still be detected, albeit faintly.

There. The scent of haava smoke. Pepper coughed. Marcat spice, too, tickled her nose, telling her the vessel had among its crew a Galvan. Then again, if one of the eye-stalked natives of Galva paced the corridors on a ship like this, she couldn't count on their normal reputation for empathy for all living things. That would have been distorted, somehow, for him to serve on a ship such as this one.

The dog opened her eyes and began a visual examination of her accommodation. Metal surrounded her, too close on all sides. She had barely enough room to turn around. The thick criss-crossed wire of the enclosure's door offered the only large opening, though a fine meshwork in the back of the pen offered a flow of air. At least there was an auto-fill water bowl, with the usual taste of recirc water replaced by the clean spring-fed Arcadian liquid. So, they'd taken time while portside to refresh their supplies. Which could be a bad thing, Pepper thought. It could signal their intent to make a long jump back into space.

One thing at a time.

Voices, just outside the door to room in which she'd been penned, alerted her to danger. Striving to present an image that might look, for all the world, as though she still slept, Pepper curled into a ball, covering her nose with her tail. If she was lucky, her captor would believe the stun-shot still held its effect.

The door slid open with a hiss.

"You were freelancing." Words spoken in an accusatory tone, by a voice she didn't recognize.

Pepper inhaled deeply, detecting the scent-signatures of two individuals—her captor, and another.

"Providence sent her," Pepper's captor grunted. "She'll fetch a good price at Beta Station."

Pepper's spirits sank. *Beta Station.* Reputed to be the Syndicate stronghold, though no-one was certain of its location. If she'd worn her homing device, she might lead the GSS to its location . . .

But she wasn't GSS anymore, was she? And who would come to look for her? She hadn't told Minna where she was going, Quicksilver either. For all they knew, she might be out on the waves with the Rimbauts, or exploring the outback looking to make contact with the elusive chienchats.

"Well cared for, by someone," the newcomer said. "Greater odds somebody will come looking."

"We lift in an hour," Pepper's captor replied. "No time. They wouldn't have even noticed she was missing. And the fact that she's in good shape will mean she'll draw a better price."

"If Harfor finds out what you've done . . ."

"When does he ever come down to the cargo area?" A pause, then the Syndicate man answered his own question. "Never. We're safe here."

"I'll keep my silence. But there'll be a price."

"Isn't there always?"

The voices moved away, and Pepper rose to her feet, stretching to relieve a kink in her right haunch. *An hour,* she thought. *That's not much time.*

In that case, she'd better get busy.

EVERY INSTINCT URGED Pepper to batter herself against the door of her cage. To dig at her housing, hoping to find a weak point, until her paws bled.

But she forced herself to slow down. To use the superior intelligence the AI implant afforded her.

Best start with the door-latch.

The door wouldn't have been designed to open from the inside. But then again, it was meant to keep ordinary animals penned. And she was not an ordinary animal . . .

Pepper studied the door's opening mechanism with care. When her examination was concluded, she breathed a sigh of relief. Such had been made to keep in non-sentient beasts, and would, she was certain, do an admirable job of that. But for an AI-enhanced entity such as her, mastering the lock would be possible. Move her unusually-agile front toes so, and so; support the catch mechanism with her muzzle, thus—the door popped open.

Pepper stood framed in the opening, triangular ears pricked at their highest to catch any scintilla of sound. Then she pushed the door open and hopped out onto the floor.

Now, to find the entry-door to this cramped tin can. Driven by urgency, she padded down the narrow corridor, all senses on high alert.

Look for high traffic. And follow the trail back . . .

There, she'd done it. The entryway stood before her. And with it, her hope of reunion with Minna . . .

She was in luck. No Syndicate operatives in sight, though surely they'd have set an alarm to alert them to the presence of anyone breaching the perimeter defence without the access code.

So, she'd set off the alarm when she went through that. But if she was lucky, if she ran quickly enough, there'd be a chance . . .

About to leap through the opening, Pepper heard a commotion above her, toward the passenger decks.

Nothing to do with me, she thought.

Then she heard Minna's voice.

MASTERING SHIP-STAIRS had been one of the toughest tasks in Pepper's GSS training. The border collie appreciated the skill now, clambering, despite the lack of mag-boots, with an agility born of long practice and heat-of-the-moment urgency.

As she scaled the steps, her mind churned. What was Minna doing here? Had her foolishness drawn her master into peril?

Pepper whimpered to herself as she ascended the final rung and popped out onto the next floor.

To her relief, she spotted Minna's tall, slim form in the corridor that led to the right.

"All clear," a helmet-and-armour clad Port Authority officer told Minna. He paused. "But no sign of . . ." His eyes widened as he spotted Pepper.

Minna, curious as to what had caused his sudden silence, turned to look. She dropped on one knee and seized Pepper's head between her hands. "There you are. I was so worried."

"Worried?" The Port Authority agent raised his eyebrows. "You mean, you didn't send her here on surveillance?"

"No." The response was short, sharp, and emphatic. Minna rose to her feet, her expression grim. "In fact, I just happened to be at the customs office picking up a parcel when I heard her bark. If it hadn't been for that . . ."

"Excuse me a moment." The officer turned away, right hand pressed to his ear, then turned back. "Well, either way, her presence proved fortuitous. Gave us grounds for a search. And we found a large quantity of snort and other contraband. So this ship won't be lifting any time soon."

"Good," Minna said.

The officer put his hand to his ear again, then said, "Something I need to check on. You're okay to see yourself out?"

"Yes, and thank you."

The officer departed, and Minna turned her full attention to Pepper. "We," she said, her voice low, "are going to talk. At home. Unless you'd rather stay shipboard?" She shot the dog a keen look.

Pepper shook her head. Home it was.

The dog turned toward the stairs, then shot a yearning look

back at her master. That backward glance proved fortuitous.

Because just behind Minna, she saw the wall moving, where the wall shouldn't be able to move.

A hidden compartment, Pepper told herself. Of course. Such a ship would be full of those . . .

She jerked her head toward the threat, then leaped.

And realized how out of practice she was.

Her shoulder slammed against the now-visible door in the wall, and she fell to the ground with a grunt of pain. She should have waited, timed her jump differently . . .

The door flew open. Minna stood, gun drawn, face grim. Pepper staggered to her feet. *I'll be too late,* she thought, bracing herself for a leap.

And she might have been, had the young man hiding behind the panel been carrying a weapon.

But he was not.

This was no hardened criminal. A nav-man, or perhaps a tube-jockey, working an apprenticeship down in the ship's power plant. He'd simply sought refuge the first place he could think of. And elected to show himself too soon.

Lucky for us, Pepper thought.

She exchanged a look with Minna, tail tucked.

THOUGH THE START was less than auspicious, the promised talk when Minna and Pepper got home wasn't as bad as it could have been.

They'd waited till Quicksilver was out of the room. Then Minna had sat on the couch, Pepper seated in front of her on the floor.

"Look, you shouldn't have taken off like that."

I know. I know. Pepper lowered her head. *I'm not sure what got into me. Well, I am. But it shouldn't have. I wish it hadn't.*

As though sensing her troubled thoughts, Minna had reached down to rub Pepper's ears, just the way the border collie liked.

"You know, don't you, that it was the right time to retire?" Minna asked.

Pepper whimpered softly.

"I miss them, too. But we can't jump back into the past,"

Minna said. "We need to live in the present. Find a purpose here. It's an adjustment for all of us."

Pepper tilted her head. She hadn't considered that others might share the same feeling.

"Look, it's been crazy busy since we got here. There's been a lot for us to do, to get organized. I don't expect you to understand."

Pepper looked up at Minna, seeing the doubt in her eyes. The yearning to be understood.

I'll try. Pepper rested her head on Minna's knee.

"There is—something. But I don't want to get your hopes up." Minna bit her lower lip, then shook her head. "Not yet." She paused. "Want to go for a walk?"

Is the sky blue? Er, I mean yellow? Can we? Can we?

"I'll take that as a yes."

Sensing that she'd been forgiven, Pepper wagged her tail.

TWO WEEKS LATER, Pepper felt only contentment as she sprawled on the rug at Minna's feet. She raised her head, looked around the living room, and opened her jaws in a grin. Anyone entering the house without understanding the context might have thought the place had been invaded by plimrats, the gopher-like creatures in Arcadia's outback that loved to steal and hoard anything they could get their dextrous paws on.

What do you expect, on Christmas Day, Pepper thought. Quicksilver, lying on his side, batted lazily at the box of hardplas spiders she'd bought him. When he'd opened the gift, he'd shot her a quizzical glance. She'd shrugged and told him the current lot were getting tatty. If he wanted her fright to be real, he'd best up his game.

So you like it, being scared, he'd asked her.

She'd just given him an inscrutable border collie look. Let him think what he wanted.

"So, Pepper, d'you like it?" Minna held up the locally-fabbed flak jacket she and Allie had given the border collie as a gift.

Pepper tapped her tail against the floor twice to signal her approval. Then a thought hit her. *When will I get to use it?*

Did it really matter? She'd realized, back on the Syndicate

ship, that retirement was a reality she had to face, not a situation she needed to run from. She'd just have to learn to cope, that's all.

Allie cleared her throat. "That leaves one last—gift, I think." She raised her eyebrows and looked at Pepper and Quicksilver in turn. "Not the kind you wrap."

Quicksilver laid back his ears. "If you couldn't wrap it, then it's not something you can eat, play with, or sleep on," he whispered to Pepper.

Pepper shifted position, unwilling to confront the cat but disagreeing nonetheless. Her new-found acceptance of her lot in life seemed like a gift, in and of itself. If only she could convince Minna that she was okay, now . . .

Allie cleared her throat. "This's what we've been working toward for the past few months." She exchanged a goofy grin with Minna. "We just had to deal with the red tape, first."

"Tape?" Quicksilver rolled smoothly to his feet. "They should have called on me. I know how to take care of tape, for Pete's sake." He stood on his hind legs and swatted the air to demonstrate.

"Not that kind of tape," Pepper hissed.

"We've got our detective licence. We're cleared to operate on Arcadia, now. Take on cases."

Afterward, Pepper would tell anyone who was willing to listen that she'd tried, really tried, to contain herself. But she couldn't help it. She was on her feet, chasing her tail, before she could stop to think, and did three complete rotations before succumbing to dizziness.

She flopped to the floor, waiting for the mocking comment that was sure to come from Quicksilver. But the cat, it appeared, had launched himself on a quick circuit of the room, leaping on and off each piece of furniture he encountered, then clambering up the tree for his finale. Right up to the tippy-top.

Said tree was, at the moment, swaying perilously, leaving the cat clinging with all his might, his expression morphing into something resembling seasickness.

Allie walked over to rescue him, and he flowed gracefully onto her shoulders, looking imperiously down at the dog as the tall woman returned to her chair.

"Sorry we didn't tell you earlier," Minna said, after allowing a couple of minutes for everyone to settle down. "We didn't want to get your hopes up if it wasn't going to come to fruition."

So that's what she was talking about. Pepper rose, shook herself, then walked over to Minna and gazed up adoringly. It was the best way she knew how to say, *Everything's going to be okay for sure, now.*

They stayed that way for a long moment, communing silently.

The last of the discontent that had nagged at Pepper two weeks ago ebbed away. Everything she needed was right here. Minna was happy because she was with Allie. Pepper was happy because she was with Minna.

And, of course, there was Quicksilver, too. She'd gotten used to the grey cat, she realized. What if he'd gone off, instead of her? She'd have missed him, that's what.

"Look," she said, looking up at the cat. "I'm sorry I ran off without saying anything. I—wasn't myself."

The cat stared down at her, his expression inscrutable. For a moment, Pepper thought he was going to play the usual card of unconcern. But instead, he twitched his whiskers and said, "So. You'll be helping us on cases again. That's good news, I suppose."

"Me? Helping you?" Pepper sputtered. "Why, I'll have you know—"

Sensing one of their interminable arguments about to erupt, Minna intervened. "What about a few carols, huh? Like old times."

Pepper, knowing which "old times" that remark referred to, shot her master a look. Another affirmation that Minna, too, harboured some nostalgia for the old days.

"Wreck the Halls," Quicksilver suggested.

"Bark the Herald Angels Sing!" Pepper yapped.

The cat shot a meaningful look at the box of fake spiders, then at Pepper. "Have a Crawly, Jolly Christmas."

Allie rolled her eyes. "Silent Night it is."

AFTER A SPIRITED round of carol-singing, Pepper curled up on the floor, making sure to lie on Minna's foot so that she'd be aware if the woman were to move.

"D'you really think everything's going to be okay with them?"

Minna asked Allie. "You know, after—"

Pepper eased an ear backward, the better to take in the conversation.

"It'll be fine. You'll see. It's all still new. But in time, they'll accept this place as home. We all will."

Home, Pepper thought. She yawned. Some days, her memories were vivid. But on other occasions, the adventures they'd had aboard the *Meech Lake* seemed like they'd happened to someone else, the stuff of space-vids.

The dog raised her head, looking around the comfortable room. The handmade rug that provided just the right amount of padding from the floor. The fireplace which, thanks to Allie's efforts earlier that morning, set out an agreeable warmth.

She thought about the close quarters on board the Syndicate ship, and shuddered. She hadn't realized how claustrophobic a vessel could be, once you'd become accustomed to open air. Of course, if Minna chose, she'd follow her right back onto the *Meech Lake* or any other space-faring vessel. But if she had her druthers, she realized she'd be just fine with staying on Arcadia for the rest of her days.

Pepper blinked lazily at Quicksilver, who padded over to touch noses with her.

"Well? Are you home to stay?" The cat studied her with yellow-green eyes. "Not that I care. Although I would hate to waste those excellent spiders. I suppose I could scare Allie with them."

"Scare Allie? That'll be the day."

Quicksilver turned to shoot an appraising look at the woman. "Everyone is afraid of something," he said. "We just haven't found out what."

"Let's hope we don't."

"Well? You haven't answered my question. Do I need to keep an eye on you in case you wander off again?" The cat's whiskers twitched.

"No," Pepper said. She opened her mouth in a grin. "I'm home, now."

"Home," the cat said. He stalked across the room and settled himself comfortably on the tiled flooring in front of the fireplace. "Home is where the hearth is."

Pepper shot him a glare. "*Heart.* It's where the *heart* is."

"Hearth." His voice raised, ever so slightly.

Pepper replied in kind. "Heart."

"Hearth."

"See?" Allie's voice contained a hint of laughter. "Things are pretty much back to normal."

"Not yet," Minna said. She glanced at Pepper, then Quicksilver, mock-frowning. "Knock it off, you two," she said.

That's what she used to do on the Meech Lake. *When we got too rowdy.* Instead of experiencing a pang for her former residence, Pepper felt a sense of rightness. Of a cycle, come complete.

Home, Pepper thought, suddenly feeling drowsy. *Home is where Minna is.*

She turned to tell the cat. *Already snoring.*

Would a nap be such a bad idea? She thought not. And the hearth was plenty big enough for both of them . . .

ALL BARK

Rachel Sharp

"BABE! YOUR BOOTIES!"

Kendra stopped spinning circles at the door, thwapping her tail repeatedly against the scuffed banister post. She couldn't help it. A few days into her lunar shift, the essential *dog*-ness always started to take over, and it was easier to just let it happen. Her mother hated that she called herself a dog, even in her own head, but she was what she was; she lived indoors, she enjoyed a good rope toy, and she hid in the bathtub when there were thunderstorms. Her mother was more regal. And less splotchy of coat. Kendra, on the other hand, had a hiccup in her howl that knocked any impression of wild majesty right out of people's heads.

Snow, though.

She loved snow.

Annalise knelt beside her, offering a thick sock printed with a high-top sneaker design, which Kendra obligingly dipped her paw into. It stretched to its limits. Though Kendra disliked the W-word for herself, she *was* a little big for most dog-sized things. The booties were "extra large." The picture on the packaging had shown a mastiff. Her padded foot barely fit. It was okay to stick out a little here, though—she and Annalise had found a place to rent in a neighbourhood that was mostly shifters. Down the street, the bookshop even had a "pets welcome" sign with a winking cartoon cat on it. Like queer folks, shifter folks tended to blob together socially.

Kendra felt Annalise pat her flank and lifted that paw for dressing.

The socks felt unnatural, but even her canid brain had learned to connect booties and snow. She couldn't see it outside yet, but she could smell wisps of clean crystal coming in around the aging back door.

One more foot. She resisted the urge to bounce and spin, switching hind legs instead.

"Do you want your jacket?"

Kendra *mmrph*ed. She had a fur coat like Marilyn Monroe. Jackets were for chihuahuas.

"Okay. Have fun." Annalise opened the door.

The doorknob turned, and Kendra lost it. She wedged her head through the crack, widening it with her chest, and cold flakes immediately clung to her eyelashes as she exploded into the backyard. The snow wasn't deep yet. She dropped the front half of her body at a full run, slid her face through it, and did a barrel roll.

She could hear Annalise laughing through the closing door.

Shovelling snow into her mouth, Kendra chomped and mumbled contentedly while it melted on her tongue. Something in her bones loved this.

One ear pinned itself back when a twig in their poplar tree creaked, but she didn't process it. She rolled left, then right to even herself out. Her massive body was displacing all the snow they had. Kendra started tugging on one bootie with her teeth so she could feel it under her paws before it went away.

She was peripherally aware of the elderly lady hawk watching her from the third-floor window next door, probably grinning. That was fine. Let her enjoy the show. Kendra rolled again, wiggling, clowning it up, but then stopped.

This time, both her ears swivelled. Something was scratching against the side of the house.

She rolled to her feet, growling before her last foot landed on the exposed yellow grass.

There was a squirrel climbing the shutters. It stopped, looking at her.

Kendra didn't think. She charged the house, briefly condensing herself down onto all four massive paws before shoving gravity away in a vertical leap that shocked the squirrel into motion. His tail whipped just out of her teeth as he propelled himself back into the poplar tree and disappeared over the rickety fence.

She could have cleared the fence, but she couldn't climb a tree or a telephone pole. He was out of her reach.

She howled. One of the neighbours howled, too.

Annalise threw the back door open.

"Babe?"

Kendra ran to her and pushed up against the side of her leg, gently forcing her back into the house.

"Babe, what's wrong?"

Kendra stared at her girlfriend and whined. She couldn't use her words. She could barely *think* in words. It wasn't just a full moon, it was also the eve of the Solstice. The W-word, normally a fraction of a fraction of herself, was running the show tonight. She had no way to tell Annalise what had happened.

She laid her heavy head against Annalise's thigh.

"Okay. I don't know why, but outside bad. Got it. Let me lock the door, and I'll put your blanket on the couch so we can watch a movie, okay? How about the Christmas one with the otters."

Kendra felt the tip of her tail swing minutely against her will. She knew that locking the door was good and that a whole movie meant getting rubbed behind the ears for a near eternity. Everything that wasn't happening right now was slipping away. Her senses, still alert, detected nothing to fight.

Annalise locked the door.

Feeling like a bag of copper bones in a lightning storm, but unable to think hard enough to do anything about it, Kendra padded through the house to the couch and sat waiting for her blanket. Her tail thumped, but she couldn't stop whuffing in breaths through her squared-off black and white nose, vibing the hunt, until Annalise had rearranged the couch, sat down, and patted a cushion beside her. Kendra stepped up, taking most of the space. Annalise rubbed behind her ears. Soon, the movie overwhelmed her with sensory nonsense. The human in her was already a thin presence. The dog in her fell asleep.

The wolf, though, pressed her chin a little harder than necessary on Annalise's thigh, and waited.

IN THE LONGEST night of the year, Kendra started awake with no idea of the time. A noise. There had definitely been a noise. Her body was off the couch and stalking to the little kitchen before any other aspect of her had bothered to wake up. Annalise made a semiconscious noise from the couch behind her. Kendra froze between the hunt and her girlfriend with one paw still in the air. She had to protect Annalise. She had to find the source of the noise. She struggled to think.

Finally, she side-tracked to the wall and reared, bodily shouldering the light switch on before thudding back down on all fours and heading for the kitchen again. If Annalise could see, she could protect herself.

A glass smashed in the kitchen. Someone cursed.

Kendra slid around the corner, scrabbling on the wood laminate floor, and came face to face with someone in the dark. Looked like a man. Smelled like a squirrel. She barked her loudest bark, which was not inconsiderable, and he fell back, stepping on broken glass and cursing again.

He could change shape at any time. Some shifters were lucky like that. Canids were tied to the moon. Owls were tied to the dark. But squirrels were so pedestrian that they were always in their element. Not wanting to let him get away again, Kendra squared her back feet and prepared to lunge for his neck. Any shape he took, he would still have a neck, and it would stay between her teeth.

Annalise stepped into the kitchen, flicked on the light, and put two fingers in Kendra's collar. "Babe, let me handle this."

Kendra, wavering between the dog and the other thing, *mrrph*ed and slowly put her furry ass on the floor. Annalise, realizing now what Kendra had failed to communicate earlier, pulled her fingers from the collar, grabbed a meat tenderizer out of the knife block, and waved it at the intruder.

"*Darren, what the hell do you think you're doing here*?!" Annalise bellowed. She looked at the counter and down at the broken glass. "Are you drinking my booze? Did you *seriously* break into our kitchen to drink my good booze?"

"I . . . uh . . . is your new boyfriend a werewolf?"

On being so insultingly misread, Kendra tensed up to lunge at him again, but Annalise put a slim hand right in front of her long face, stopping her short.

"My new *girl*friend," Annalise said, "is going to chew on your neck if I don't stop her. How dare you. I mean, I *knew* you sucked, but how dare you. You break into our home and do the pettiest shit I have ever seen. I should have put down traps."

Darren looked increasingly panicked. "I didn't . . . I just . . . I thought it would be a funny story, y'know, like 'haha, my ex broke up with me so I snuck in and drank her expensive froufrou vodka and ate her generic holiday cookies,' I wasn't hurting anybody."

"Darren, I swear, if you touched those cookies—"

"It was just a joke! I didn't mean anything by it! C'mon, admit that it's a little funny—"

As Darren's excuses dragged on, Kendra found herself increasingly tempted to push past Annalise's hand and show him her teeth. His words were fuzzy to her, but his tone—self-indulgent, unserious—brought the tension of a growl to her throat. The sound was in the air before she could reconsider. Annalise grabbed her gently by the scruff.

"Kendra, stop it. Darren, I'm calling the cops. I'm sure they'll be thrilled to see you again." Annalise marched out of the room to get her phone, leaving Kendra alone with the intruder.

"Annie, don't—aw, man." He looked at Kendra. She didn't even have a chance to show off her smile before he started to change, leaping over the kitchen table as he shrunk to try and get away from her. She careened into a chair, demolishing it. His tail was already disappearing over the edge of the counter. He was *quick.*

Kendra tried to bring all her brain cells together even as the rest of her chased after him on instinct. How did this little rodent get in? How was he going to get out?

The squirrel leaped off the counter and scurried out of the kitchen. Bunching every muscle to change direction, Kendra tore off after him. When she bounced off the wall, she left a dent.

He turned a corner and bolted up the stairs. Dimly, Kendra realized that he must have gone right by them while they were asleep on the couch. She howled at him as she tried to make the corner, oblivious to the fact that she was probably waking the neighbours.

The scent stopped her at the door of the upstairs bathroom. By the nightlight, she could see that the vent of their washer/dryer combo was loose, and a wispy tail was vanishing into it. He was going to get away again.

She lunged for the foil hose, but it was already empty. Leaving it crumpled behind her, she flew back down the stairs.

Annalise was on the phone. They couldn't trust the police to know about shifters, so she was trying to work the story around the fact that her ex had been inhumanly small when he broke in. She looked up when Kendra hit the back door with her shoulder. Kendra hit it again. Annalise frowned, strode over, and opened it. Kendra once again shot out into the yard, hoping she wasn't too late.

Darren was standing frozen in the middle of the yard, his tail on end and looking more threadbare than ever. He was surrounded. Kendra's howl had indeed brought the neighbours, and the neighbours were not having any of Darren's nonsense. A cat from two blocks over, who Kendra had met once at a game night, was sitting on the fence with one paw raised and claws casually flexing in and out. The owner of the bookstore had his vulpine head stuck through a hole between two fenceposts. In their poplar tree, an owl she didn't even know was stepping side to side and flexing his wings.

Annalise came to the door and switched on the outside light. Everybody blinked. Darren, showing his indecision in little twitches, finally decided he had been better off inside the house and turned, flying over the ground towards Annalise's feet. Kendra moved to intercept, but she never had the chance.

The elderly hawk from next door came out of nowhere. Apparently having seen enough to decide which side she was on, she yanked him out of the thin snow by his tail and shot back up and over the fence, carrying him off into the deep dark.

Kendra sat down in what was left of the snow. Annalise, frozen for a moment with the phone held to her head, suddenly remembered what she had been doing.

"Actually, you know what, he's gone now. Never mind. Everything's fine here. Thanks!" She ended the call, mumbling, "For *nuthin'.*"

Kendra, finally feeling relaxed, padded back inside.

Annalise rubbed behind her ears. "You don't think she'll

actually eat him, do you?"

Kendra wagged. A wag could mean a lot of things. Annalise locked the door again and started to walk away. Kendra followed.

"That bastard. That total bastard. He thought he could just come in here. He thought it was funny. If he does that again, you have my permission to snap his little rat neck."

Kendra wagged a little harder.

"He got in upstairs?"

After staring hesitantly at her, Kendra tried to nod. Not a natural motion in this shape. Still, Annalise got it.

"Okay. I think he's gone for now, but I'll fill whatever hole he got in through with concrete later."

Annalise flopped down on the couch, leaving plenty of room for Kendra to squeeze in. Kendra flopped directly into the empty space, rolling onto her back. Annalise absentmindedly rubbed her behind the ears with her knuckles.

"We can talk about all this in a few days, when you get your words back. And we can make more cookies. For now, let me just say . . . good girl."

Kendra thumped her tail.

CORN DOGS

Sarah L. Johnson and Robert Bose

THE RUSTING PICKUP drifted across the gravel road outside Taber, dust and snow filtering through the open windows. With a curse, Solomon wrenched the wheel and fishtailed back into their lane.

"Ode stomping grouds? Driven this woad a thousand tibes?" Trace sat cross-legged on the cracked vinyl bench seat with a wad of bloody napkins held to hcr nose.

"It is and I have." He glanced at her, caught between a heater stuck on high and the winter wind tornadoing her curls straight into the '80s. A decade he remembered fondly and one she probably didn't remember at all. "Ever owned acid-washed jeans?"

She side-eycd him. "Ever ow'd parachute pants?"

He let out a sigh he'd been holding onto since the restaurant. "What the hell is wrong with you anyway?"

"Cosmetic. Id'll buff oud."

"This is farmville, Trace. People's roots go all the way down, they hold grudges for centuries, and you can't go around making jokes about their sisters."

She pulled the gory napkins away from her nose. "How was I supposed to know that guy was his sister? Or that you've got some antediluvian blood feud with the local Mennonites?"

"All because you wanted a taste of the local cuisine."

99

Trace grunted. "Where else am I going to get a Ukrainian taco? God damn, that tank knocked one of my molars loose." Frigid air cut the volcanic furnace venting through the jagged hole in the dash. "And your mechanic couldn't have lent us something . . . road-worthy while she repairs the Winnebago?"

"This is a classic. Seventh-gen Ford F-series Ranger. Two tone. Chrome trim. Rosewood accents."

"Ever driven anything from the twenty-first century?"

"It's just for the week. By then the Chief'll be purring like a kitten, you'll be on your way to pretty again, and we'll be outta here. If not, my folks probably have something younger than you kicking around the farm."

With a bloody smirk, she reached over to flick his ear. "You mean a car, right?"

Snow clotted the windshield and when Sol flipped on the wipers, they tore away from the glass with a time-glued shriek.

"Your folks won't mind you bringing me home for the holidays?"

Sol pinched a smouldering cigarette from the ashtray and coaxed it to life. "Sure, just don't, you know—"

"—bring up religion. Right." Trace snapped her grimoire shut. "Better stash this then, though the Book of Honorius has lots of invocations for talking to God directly. Like summon-to-the-pub-and-have-a-piss-up direct."

"Never meet your heroes."

"Well, your parents' heroes."

"To tell the truth, I'm not sure what they'll think. Been a while." Sol rolled through a four-way stop and turned into a long driveway leading to a wide-windowed yellow farmhouse. Smoke belched from the double chimney tucked under a brick-clad crown. A triple garage sat to one side, a chicken coop and collection of barns on the other.

"Looks Hallmark."

"Looks neglected." Sol pointed to the field on the other side of the road from the farm, where frost-coated corn stalks jutted from lightly drifted snow. "That's prime land. Should've been harvested and ploughed in the Fall."

"Bet there's a possessed scarecrow lurking out there, a sad sack of sticks that never got invited to the Solstice Party. Takes its revenge on off-key carollers."

A shiver ran down Sol's spine, faded memories tickling the back of his brain, a rhyme his grandfather once told him. About the devil and something waiting in the snow. He looked back at the farmhouse, the lights glowing in the window. Warm and inviting.

"Definitely the place to go if you need your nose cranked back into joint," he said.

Trace plucked the butt from between his lips, finished it off, and stubbed it out in the tray. He shivered again as her lips brushed his neck. "Scared?"

He stared at the house again.

The truck coughed.

"We're not going to make it anyway," said Trace, laughing off Sol's pained face.

He floored it and tore into the yard, slamming on the brake before they collided with a garage door beat to shit from years of slapshots from him and the same crew they'd tangled with in the restaurant. Before things got . . . complicated.

Cold knifed through Sol's Hawaiian shirt as he clambered out of the truck. He thought about slipping on his jacket, but by then the front door of the house was open and a woman stood on the stoop backlit like a saint. Tall boots, jeans, buckskin coat. And a .30-30 Winchester.

Sol raised his hand in a wave. "Hey, Mom."

SOL'S MOTHER PROPPED the rifle in the crook of the kitchen counter and retrieved a clay jug from the cupboard. "Shoulda known the first time you show your face in over twenty years you'd be draggin' a stray."

"That's me," Trace laughed.

"Hold still," his father scolded, still in his scrubs, holding Trace's head between purple nitrile hands.

"Some things never change." His mother clapped four glasses onto the scarred oak table. "Half-dead gophers and feral cats. Surprised none of 'em ever gave Muffin rabies."

Sol grimaced at the memory of his mother's neurotic Pomeranian. Geriatric when he'd left, and surely long dead by now.

His mother poured a measure of moonshine from the jug into the glasses, shoving one at Trace. "Best down that in one, girl. Acquired taste, but it'll help."

Caustic saskatoon berry fumes wafted out of Sol's glass, like a chemical bomb of memories.

"Fuck!" Trace honked a spray of blood into his father's face as he crunched the cartilage of her nose back into alignment.

"Quite a homecoming, son." Newell Black removed his mask and glasses, wiping them clean with a piece of gauze dipped in moonshine. "From the looks of it you've already caught up with your cousins. Nickels? Klassens?"

"Rempels. Rudy and Brad." Sol rubbed his bruised knuckles. "And Donita."

Newell pushed his smudged glasses back up his nose. "Surprised I'm not scraping the both of you into the Taber ER."

"Misunderstanding over tacos," Trace said. "I was talking about her *food*, for Christ—uh, gosh darn it." She gingerly palpated her face. "Damn, that was a slick realignment. How's the perichondrium look?"

Newell shrugged. "Fair amount of blood and edema, but intact from what I can tell."

"How are you at draining septal hematomas?"

"I could ask the same. You have training?"

"Medic."

"In the service?"

"Could say that. Sol never said his dad was a doctor."

"Trauma nurse."

"Figures. You actually know what the hell you're doing."

Newell clinked glasses with Trace and they tossed back their shots. "I'll have a look once the swelling subsides, assuming you're staying a few days."

"Course they are. Tomorrow's Christmas Eve." His mother picked up the clay jug with a work-hardened hand and refilled Trace's glass. "Any gal with the balls to fight a Rempel on her first day is welcome in my house."

Newell raised an eyebrow. "Curious as to what you've been up to, son. Your postcards weren't exactly illuminating, though we did appreciate them."

"I'll catch you up later," Sol interjected. "But is everything okay here? Why's the corn on the stalks and the field unploughed?"

He thanked his mother's White Catholic Jesus for the uncomfortable look exchanged between his parents, if only because it took the spotlight off him, the complicated past he'd walked away from, and the complicated woman sitting at the table where he'd eaten eighteen years of family dinners. What could he say anyway? Grey market relic hunter wasn't exactly a career you could bring home to your parents.

"Tradition," his mother said. "Your Grandfather said a good farmer gives the land back once in a while."

"Grandpa was a dog catcher, not a farmer."

"Last fallow season you'd already left, and the one before that you were too small to remember." She shared a look with Newell and then peered out the window into the winter dark. "Gotta keep an eye is all."

"With your Winchester?" Sol asked.

"Nothing bad happened before. Not until Muffin run off."

"Rosemary . . ." Newell trailed off, as if realizing the pigs were already out of the barn and all he could do was wait for them to come back.

Sol swallowed, the moonshine fire in his belly making him brave. He wasn't a little kid anymore, this wasn't church, and he was allowed to ask questions. "Muffin? The same Muffin? How goddamn old is that dog?"

"Language," Rosemary scolded, crossing herself. "Thirty odd years and spry as a puppy. Who am I to question the Lord's will? Run off a few weeks ago and she weren't the only one. Some dozen missing dogs around these parts."

"Not exactly headline news," Newell said.

"There's demons roaming that field at night, Newell. And you'd hear 'em too if you didn't sleep like a dead horse."

"Sounds like children in your corn," Trace slurred, eyes glassy with moonshine.

"It's late," Newell said. "You two have had an adventurous return. Why don't we catch up over breakfast?"

Trace slumped in her chair, snoring lightly through her broken nose, and as much as Sol wanted to know more, a day on the road and a hometown brawl had him exhausted. The field wasn't going anywhere.

"Girls' rooms are already made up," Rosemary said as Sol

scooped up a limp Trace. "Fresh sheets for your bed in the linen closet."

"Separate rooms? I'm forty-three."

"Old enough to know the rules. Until you put a ring on that child bride of yours, Solomon Black."

"Wouldn't hold my breath," he said, hefting the snoring pugilist in his arms. "She'll never marry an old man like me."

"Heaven forbid you should live in sin your whole lives," Newell said, winking at his wife.

"Don't get smart," she tapped his knee with the Winchester. "Off to bed, the lot of you."

Sol deposited Trace in his sisters' room and got his own bed made up across the hall, grateful for some solitude to sort out his thoughts. Home. On the twin mattress of his childhood, staring up at the ceiling and a tattered *Monty Python and the Holy Grail* movie poster. What had called him here? And why now? Something felt off. Rosemary Black was not a nervous woman, but her hands trembled as she poured that moonshine, stealing glances out the window at the darkened field of winterkill. His Grandfather's so-called tradition he'd somehow never heard of until now? And how the hell did a Pomeranian live to be thirty years old?

He dozed until awakened by his bedroom door squeaking open. "Boo!"

"Jesus." Sol popped up in bed. "You can't be here. My mom will shoot me."

Like a ghost, Trace slid barefoot through the shadows. "Solomon Black's childhood bedroom."

She perused the space, trailing fingers over tattered science fiction paperbacks stuffed into bookshelves, and over the desk, bearing angry teen etchings of stick men and pentagrams. "So, what kind of inbred prairie gothic situation are we dealing with here? Your folks are way too cool not to be psychos."

"Well, they like you. So, there's gotta be screws loose."

Trace stiffened. "You hear that?"

"Only your busted nose whistling up a storm."

"I'm serious. Listen . . ."

Sol cocked his head, and sure enough, a shriek whipped through the darkness outside the window, a window that happened to be facing that fallow field. More mournful howls and chattering that almost sounded like laughter. The kind of laughter that froze your marrow and set your lizard brain on fire.

Trace approached the window. "I don't think that's a Pomeranian."

Charging through a cornfield in his boxers in the dead of winter was a bad idea. But ever since Trace dropped into the passenger seat of his old Winnebago two years ago, bad ideas had taken on a certain shine.

He plunged his feet into his boots—always by the bed because you just never knew—and dashed to the closet, shoving aside the winter coats and Sunday suits hanging stiff and empty for decades. There it was. His old .22. Still loaded, Jesus. How had he not shot himself a hundred times over with how reckless he'd been? He thought of his grandfather, who would have given him an incredulous look and asked what the hell good an unloaded rifle was. Sol never took to guns the way his sisters had, and Grandpa always seemed disappointed.

"A lot's changed, Gramps."

"What?" Trace asked.

"I'm gonna check it out," Sol said, opening the window to a blast of snow-tinged December.

"This is fun!" Trace whispered, bouncing on the balls of her bare feet. "Sneaking out at night on the farm. Can we tip some cows? Steal a tractor?"

"Cow tipping isn't a real thing. And you're staying here."

She frowned. "That's bullshit."

"It's survival," he said. "My mom has ears like a goddamn African elephant, and you sneaking down the hall to get your shoes would rather defeat the purpose of me sneaking out the window, so stay put. I won't be long."

He clambered out, somewhat less gracefully than he had as a wiry teenager, landing with a crunch on the frost-sharpened grass. Trace leaned on the windowsill, wearing a dangerously neutral expression. She could be planning anything.

"Stay," he warned again, like it would make any difference.

He jogged across the road and stood at the edge of the field. The chittering and yowling were definitely coming from nearby, but he couldn't tell which direction. Gripping the rifle, he stepped into the forest of eight-foot corn stalks. Frosty leaves brushed against his skin like dead hands and he desperately wished he'd brought a flashlight. A rustling had him spinning around. Then a loud bark, and he turned back just in time to see a shadow darting deeper into the corn.

"Muffin?" he whispered. "Oof—"

Something huge slammed into his back, knocking him to the ground. Viselike pressure clamped onto his spine and ribs, and a hot sheet of pain ripped through his shoulder. Carrion breath blasted across an ear. Then, with a tinkle of bells and a sharp bark, the weight lifted. A swish of leaves, and the strike of paws vibrated through the frozen dirt. Heavy paws. No way it could be Muffin, but that bell was familiar.

He spit the crumbling earth out of his mouth, tasting a full cycle of hometown seasons, of long green summers gone cold and brown. When he attempted to push himself up, his right arm buckled in agony. Dammit. "Trace?"

In terms of hard facts, he knew almost nothing about Trace, her past being an enigma, but of one thing he was certain: Trace did what she damn well pleased and the day she took orders from Solomon Black would be the day after never. He'd told her to stay, ergo, she had to be nearby.

"Trace," he whispered, wincing at the responding yips and cackles. "Trace!" he shouted, and the corn rustled, but it wasn't Trace. The one time she actually listened to him would be the time he got eaten alive by whatever those things were.

Rifle in hand, he managed to crawl out of the corn and back onto the road. The front door of the house flew open, and he'd never been so happy to see that rectangle of yellow light.

"Nice going." Trace stomped across the yard in a wifebeater, panties, and his dad's boots, like some hillbilly nightmare. "Could have used some backup after all, huh? This arm is a situation."

"Could you maybe gloat later, and get me inside now?" Sol bit down on a scream as cracked ribs grated when she hauled him up and into the house.

"So," Newell said, sewing stiches into Sol's blessedly re-moonshined shoulder. "This is a thing with you two?"

"Dad, there's a wild animal, several wild animals, in that field. I know you don't believe . . ."

"A wise man apportions his belief to the evidence. Clearly, something took a large bite out of you."

Once again, his father was turning something literal into a metaphor deeper than Sol could ever hope to dive. But Sol wasn't too shallow to know it was about more than just corn dogs. It was everything, the surprise homecoming, the brawl, the estrangement that had no malice at its root, only inertia. One year becoming two, becoming ten, and so on. It was the fact that he'd left home to serve a higher power, only to abandon that calling for a life on the wrong side of every law he'd been raised with. And there'd been girls, women, probably too many. But this one, this wiccan wilding, was the first he'd ever brought home.

"Dad . . ." he said, unsure of what to apologize for first.

His father placed a gloved hand on the side of Sol's neck. "Life is funny, son. But it's all right."

Sol looked up to see Rosemary hovering in the doorway.

"Solomon." She tightened the belt on her housecoat. "There's more to this family business than the farm. You left before we could explain it proper, but now the Lord's brought you home."

"Family business?"

"Superstitious clap trap, I'd always thought. But now . . . you're gonna need to see your grandfather."

"I'M NEVER EATING again," belched Trace. Before Newell vanished for an early shift at the hospital, he'd served up a leaning tower of pancakes, peameal bacon, sausages, biscuits, and scrambled eggs.

"Prepare to loosen that belt, babe," said Sol, starting up the truck and wincing when both his shoulder and the serpentine belt squealed. "Tonight's the traditional Black Christmas Eve feast. Tomorrow is Christmas Brunch and after, the main event, the Big Christmas Dinner."

"I'm going to explode."

"Then Boxing Day leftovers."

"I'd have a smoke, but with all that grease I think I'm flammable."

"Just gotta pace yourself."

"Says you." Trace reached over, slid a hand under his bomber jacket, and rubbed the belly straining against his shirt buttons. "When I was a kid, you learned quick to never pass up a meal."

Sol didn't know squat about her childhood, but with all his background on full-frontal display, he decided to take the risk. "Was it rough?"

She stared out the window as if she hadn't heard him, then snuggled up, head on his shoulder as they headed towards town. "Want me to drive? You can't steer and shift with that arm."

"I'm good."

"Like hell."

"Good'sh." He missed the shift, the resulting gear grind shivering every tooth in a hundred-yard radius.

Trace fiddled with the thermostat and settled for tugging off her sweater and stuffing it into the blower hole. "Isn't your grandfather dead?"

"As a doorknob."

"So, we're going . . ."

"Yes."

"You know, black dogs are common in European mythology. Where'd you say Grandpa was from?"

"Pretty sure these are just strays." He sounded unconvinced, even to himself.

"And your mom's Pomeranian is thirty years old and weird shit happens in the fields every fifteen years." Trace tapped her swollen nose. "Stinks."

"To high Heaven." Sol froggered the highway, bustling with jacked up trucks heading into town for last-minute Christmas shopping. Finally, they turned off into a quiet industrial area sprawling around a potato chip plant until the lane brought them to a cemetery wrapped by walls of spruce trees.

He parked inside the gates, slid out of the truck, and rolled his shoulder. "Should have asked dad for some Oxy."

"Why didn't you?"

"Know how bad I had to be hurt just to get a band-aid as a kid? Maybe if I'd lost the arm."

"Breakfast endorphins'll have to do then." Trace followed him down a row of frost-furred headstones. "What's his name?"

"Ezekiel Braun."

"I see Goertzens and Thiessens. Oh, there's a Rempel. Ivan. Probably the progenitor of those taco thugs. Got a hammer?"

"Be nice. He's a cousin."

She gave the stone a boot. "How many damn branches does your family tree have?"

"One for every Mennonite and half the Catholics here." Sol stopped in front of a tall black slab of marble. "Ezekiel Braun. Born 1910, died 1994. Father of Rosemary. Wolfjäger."

"Wolf hunter," said Trace, brushing a crust of snow from the inscription. A Knight of Columbus shield in the top left corner, and on the right, a dog's face in profile, short triangular ear laid back, narrow eye squinting. Elaborate collar. "You said he was a dog catcher?"

"For fifty years." Sol circled the slab, pressed his hand to the stone. "Well now what? Mom wasn't exactly instructive."

Dropping into a squat, Trace pulled the cap off the bronze flower holder and tugged on the securing chain. "Nobody brings him flowers I see, soul hole's full of mulch."

"Pink job, I'll have to ask my sisters."

Trace glared up at him. "Before we leave town, you're going to buy some sturdy fake flowers, come back here, and pretty this place up. Pink job, my ass." She scooped out a handful of grass and leaves. "Wolfjäger. That's some Old Country mojo Ezekiel brought across the pond with him. Not the kind of arcane knowledge you go and do something stupid with, like dying before you can pass it on."

"Are these etchings some kind of clue then?"

"Obviously." Trace whacked his shins with the bronze vase, invoking a yelp. "That pooch engraved here? See that charm on the collar?"

Sol crouched and squinted. "Looks like a cross on a flame."

"Mark of the Bearer of Death. A Hellhound."

"Those are real? How do you know all this?"

"How do you not know it?" She shook her head, muttering in a Slavic language he'd never heard her speak. Old Country.

Sol wondered at that. No hint of an accent, or cultural affinity. He'd just assumed she was . . . what? From small town southern Alberta? Now that Trace knew so much about where he came from, not knowing anything about her felt vulnerable in a way he didn't much like.

Trace pulled the Book of Honorius out of her oversized purse, opened it to a dog-eared page. "Your mom sent us here for a reason. We're more alike than you thought."

"You don't know my mom."

"Neither do you, it seems. Toss me your knife."

Sol surrendered his bone handled blade, a Confirmation gift from his grandfather. She locked it open and cut a circle around the flower holder and herself, murmuring under her breath. Then she nicked her finger and let a drop of blood fall into the hole. Could his mother have known? Rosemary Black was many things, most of all Catholic. She'd crucify herself before knowingly inviting a witch across her threshold.

"Got him," Trace exclaimed. "As I suspected, he was waiting for us. Well, you."

"What? Who?"

"Check this out." Trace reversed her circle, stood up, and shoved her cupped hand into Sol's face.

"Ugh, god I hate earwigs." He cringed at the oblong insect's twitching black antennae. Memories of husking corn for family cookouts and having those ugly black crawlers erupt from the silk. "No . . . that's not my grandfather."

"Is so, and he says he can prove it." Trace let the bug hop on her shoulder, bent an ear, then squinted at Sol. "What's a tallywhacker? Like a toy from the olden days? He says it was your favourite."

Sol flushed. "Jesus, never mind."

"Zeke says we need to go to St. Augustine's Church. Everything we need is there."

Townsfolk in heavy coats milled in front of the Gothic mini-cathedral, awaiting the next Christmas Eve mass. Solomon circled the block and parked around a corner.

"So," asked Sol, suppressing a gag at the revolting earwig perched on Trace's shoulder, "there's a secret vault under the church? A tomb of some kind?"

"Dan Brown shit in small town Alberta," she said. "Zeke also says not to feel bad. Y'know, about being gone so long. Says the Braun men always leave."

"I'm only half Braun," Sol said, wondering what else his grandfather might be telling her.

They left the truck and pushed through a snow squall until they got to a stone shrine adorned with a crucified Jesus and weeping disciples.

"Tomb of the Unborn," Sol read on the plaque. "Knights of Columbus."

Trace nodded to the bug. "This is the access point."

They were checking it out when a figure in a Canada Goose parka broke from a group chatting near the church stairs.

"Solomon Black." A furry hood flipped back to reveal a round face and aggressively highlighted hair. "Course, it's you. Nobody else has that profile."

"Hey . . ." Sol shook his head, fusing memories of the past with the present. "Josephine."

Stood to reason someone was going to recognize him. In a heavy coat. In a winter storm. Two bloody decades later. And it would have to be his high school girlfriend.

Smelling thickly of hand cream and chardonnay, Josephine gave him a rib-grinding hug. "Didn't think you'd ever come back, and looks like you've been busy." She glanced at Trace. "Showing your daughter around your old stomping grounds?"

"Whoa, no—"

"Have three of my own too. I mean, don't we all?" She stripped off a glove to flash a platinum ring with an enormous diamond. "I married Peter Walsh. You remember him, he's a chiropractor now."

"Sounds like you landed in a sweet pair of heels," Trace said.

"Oh, you're a sweet thing, and smart, getting a nose job over the holidays. It'll be healed up beautifully by the time you head back to school. You going to the mass? We should catch up after." And with a wine-soaked laugh, she flitted off to join the gaggle of ladies heading into the church.

"Wow, Dad," Trace drawled. "How'd you let that dump truck get away?"

Sol squinted into the snow. "Shut it."

"Zeke says you dodged a torpedo there."

"He never did like her."

"Is she why you skipped town?"

"One of many reasons," he said. "And she's better off anyway."

Trace nodded. "Chiropractor though, that's more criminal than we are."

Sol turned to the Tomb. "How do we get in?"

Trace listened as the earwig twitched its antennae. "Should be a hidden button in the stone amphora."

With the crowd filing inside the church, Sol found the concealed button and the outline of a narrow entrance at knee level. It slid aside to reveal a compartment full of white sticks.

"Baby bones," said Trace. "You Catholics are creepy."

They both wiggled in and closed the door behind them. He flicked his lighter and handed it to Trace while he worked his fingers around a ring set flush with the floor and pulled up a trapdoor with the scrape of stone on stone.

"So far so good." He looked up at Trace, busily loading her bag with tiny femurs. "Really?"

"You know how hard it is to source these? Zeke says it's fine, and he's in charge here."

Damn woman. Damn grandfather. Damn town. He pried the lighter from her fingers and climbed down the ladder into a hole smelling of damp wood, leather, and gun oil. "Forget those bones. You need to see this."

Trace climbed down as Sol lit a half dozen wall sconce candles and took in the entire room. Ezekiel hadn't been kidding when he said it was a vault. Racks of old swords, cudgels, and armour, next to a cabinet full of relatively modern rifles and pistols. Steamer trunks. Chests. A wardrobe, with various military and municipal uniforms. A wall full of books, which Trace darted to. Another wall displayed a map of Western Canada, with coloured pins and a faded canvas banner with a painted poem.

Puppy dog, puppy dog, where do you revel?

I've gone to Hell to visit the Devil.

Puppy dog, puppy dog, what have you done?

I frightened a Priest and devoured a Nun.

Puppy dog, puppy dog, where will you go?

Into the fields, to lurk in the snow.

Beneath the map and banner was a workbench with a collection of tools. And leather collars. Dog collars.

"Red collar with the brass charm," Trace said. "Zeke says if we get that on the alpha, it should exorcise the lot of them."

"Should, eh? What about this?" He picked up a Vietnam War M72 LAW portable rocket launcher. "Seems more effective."

"If you want to piss it off. Zeke says the only reason you

survived first contact was that Muffin must remember you fondly. She let you off with a warning. Doubt you'll be getting another."

"Damn." He snagged the collar and the shotgun. "But I'm taking the Mossberg."

"Your grandfather says he wants us to leave him here, and he's proud you're following in his footsteps. Anything you want to ask him before we head out?"

"Well, for starters, how exactly does one go about collaring a Hellhound?"

LOW WINTER SUN screamed across the dash of the Ranger as they turned onto the road running past the field of dead corn. Sol kept his peripheral vision trained on any sign of movement while Trace had her nose buried in one of the vault books, determined to suck up every last bit the light would allow.

"Didn't know you could read Latin," he said.

"This isn't Latin." She frowned, finger tracing the line of text. "It's Vedic Sanskrit, which means we're dealing with something a hell of a lot older than the Church."

"Didn't Grampa explain it?"

She slammed the book shut in the dimming sunset. "The dead don't always explain things in a way that makes sense to the living. He said the land has a call, or a song, I guess is how he put it. Sometimes it hits a certain note, like one of those dog whistles people can't hear. Something about the frequency . . . changes them. The collar creates interference. It's basic metaphysical science."

"Isn't that an oxymoron?"

"Could you be any more Catholic?" She twisted in her seat, shadows settling into the black bruises under her eyes. "It's all the same elephant, Sol. Science, magic, monsters, and men. All turning on the same giant wheel, all connected to the same hub."

"God?"

She pointed out the windshield. "Is that your dad?"

Sol pulled into the driveway and cut the ignition. His father ran up to the Ranger and what Sol initially took for a dark thermal under his scrub top was in fact a sleeve of blood. "Dad, what the hell happened? Where's Mom?"

"I got home from work and she was gone, her rifle too. Must have run into that damn field. I went looking, but those . . . things. One pounced on me and dragged me out to the road. Nearly took my arm off." He saw the Mossberg laying across the back seat and reached for it. "I'm going back in—"

"No, Dad," Sol said. His level-headed father's hysteria chilled his guts colder than frozen turkey giblets. "We've got a plan, okay? If that's Muffin out there, and she didn't kill me, or you, she's not gonna hurt Mom."

"Don't count on it," Trace jumped out of the truck. "Zeke said each day they're out there, headbanging to that invisible song, the more feral they get." She pulled a bandana out of her bag and proceeded to torniquet Newell's arm, yanking the knot tight enough to make him wince. "Muffin is more Cujo than lap dog by now."

"Shit," Sol said. "Okay, so now what?"

Trace shielded her eyes, staring into the sunset. "Um, what is that?"

Sol followed her gaze to the giant plume of gravel dust and growing roar of what could only be a sixties era McCormick International Harvester.

"Dad, what did you do?"

"Called your cousins, soon as I saw your mother was missing."

"Last thing we need is a herd of Mennonites tearing around a cornfield full of devil dogs."

The peeling red combine lurched to a growling stop as no fewer than eight strapping farmers hopped down from the back and sides.

"We're gonna mow this field down," said Brad.

"Drive 'em out into the open!" said Rudy.

"Yeah?" said Sol. "And then?"

Rudy shrugged. "You tell me, college."

"You were Ezekiel's favourite," Donita said. "Let's see how well you take after him. Telling me you and your mouthy girlfriend can't bag a few rabid mutts? Let's go, guys!"

"Wait!" Trace shouted. "Damn it . . ."

Quick as they'd jumped out, they'd jumped back on the combine, and were off into the corn with a chorus of hooting and hollering like a hillbilly war party. Stalks snapped and crackled, and Trace grabbed the collar from the truck, tossing it to Sol. "The corn is the only thing keeping these things contained. If those idiots chop it all down before we can collar the alpha, this town is in a world of shit."

Sol and Trace ran along the perimeter of the field, Sol's ribs screaming with the effort. "What's the plan?"

"Your cousins' idea isn't totally terrible," Trace shouted. "We get ahead of that tractor thing, let those mongrels come to us."

"How do we know which one is the Alpha?"

She laughed, because of course she'd laugh, and of course all hell would erupt the first time he found himself at home in over twenty years, with Trace racing through the dusk, wild hair flying behind her, as they tried to collar themselves a demonic pound puppy.

"Wait!" Sol skidded to a halt as a lower, meatier growl than the tractor rose out of the corn. "They're in there."

Trace charged into the corn with him, batting the snowy leaves slashing at her face. "I don't hear them."

"Keep going," Sol shouted, careful to keep her in sight lest she be devoured by vegetation. Cornfields earned their horror rep that way. They played tricks with sound, they swallowed secrets. This was a bad plan. He didn't know if the old Mossberg in his hands even worked.

"Do you hear that?" she asked.

He paused. "Shit . . . those fucking hicks."

The rattling roar grew louder, and louder. Trace screamed as the combine broke through the corn to their left heading straight for them. There was no time. Sol tackled her to the ground, covering her with his body, in the feeble hope that only he would get mutilated. He used to laugh at cautionary tales of tractor accidents. Now the entire town would get the last laugh on Solomon Black. Harvested in his own cornfield.

But the churning blades never descended. Instead, a barking, howling, screaming chorus rang out above, and Sol looked up to see massive furry bodies swarming the combine, cousins screaming and bailing left and right, as the entire tractor swerved in a too tight circle until the reciprocating cutter bar snapped off and the entire thing flipped. Seconds later, an explosion banged through the traditionally silent night, and a cauldron of flame ballooned close enough to singe Sol's eyebrows.

"So much for your Mennonite militia," Trace said, wiping frozen muck from her already wrecked face. "Hmm, smells like the movies."

"We better see if there's anyone alive in there."

"Um, yeah . . ." Trace pointed to the smouldering clearing littered with popped kernels of corn and no fewer than twenty deformed dire wolves—ruby-eyed, drooling through their black fangs, and chewing on shattered cutter bar slats. One in particular, with a busted belled collar tangled in the spiky ruff around her neck, took a step forward from the others.

"Muffin?" Sol said.

"Looks like we have our Alpha," Trace said. "You got her new collar?"

"Why exactly do I get stuck doing this?"

"Blue stuff. And family business besides." Trace pulled the book out of her bag. "Go on, avenge your mother."

"She could still be out here."

"Distract them for me," she said, grabbing Sol's grandfather's knife out of her boot and running towards the burning combine.

"Trace!"

Muffin yipped and every lumpen canid head snapped in Trace's direction as she crouched and started cutting a circle into the perimeter of the clearing.

"Hey, dogs!" Sol shouted, but they were already rushing her. It wasn't enough. If the Alpha ordered an attack, they would attack. "Muffin! *Muffin!* Remember that time I swung you around by your tail?"

The spiky ruff dog cocked her head, bell jingling, her mouth dropped open in a hellish snarl, and Sol swore a dark human laugh rumbled out of her.

"Yeah, I'm talking to you, you little bitch." He raised the Mossberg and curled his finger around the trigger. Too late he saw another mongrel streak through his periphery, crashing into his wounded shoulder and knocking him into the clearing. Then they were all over him. Thank god for his leather jacket, thick reinforced coveralls, gloves, and scarf, but his arms could only cover so much of his head. All the while that evil thing that used to be his mother's Pomeranian chuckled away.

Suddenly they fell back, the laughing stopped, and a jarring silence blanketed the clearing. Sol looked up. Every one of the dogs stood stock still as if the vet had just jammed a finger up their asses. Then they dropped and rolled, bellies exposed, paws lazily paddling in the air.

"Who's a good puppy," Trace murmured, sitting in the middle of the charred corn with the open vault book in her lap, using her fingers to carve what Sol figured must be Vedic Sanskrit into the scorched earth.

"What?"

"Told you, it's a song from the land," she said low and gentle. "I'm just changing the tune a little." She continued to draw and hum and then in a sweet calm lilt said, "You gonna collar that monster, or do I have to do everything around here?"

Sol pulled the strip of red leather from his pocket. "Here, girl . . ."

"SWEET JESUS IN the manger!" Rosemary gasped, standing in the driveway.

"Mom?" Sol cried as he and Trace emerged from the field with an army of scared runaway mutts and seared cousins in tow.

"Rosemary?" Newall stopped short of sweeping her into his arms, though Sol could see it took effort. "We thought you'd been attacked."

"I went to the early Christmas Eve mass. Geralyn gave me a lift." She waved to the elderly lady in a green cutlass who backed out of the drive and drove off as though nothing strange at all were afoot. "What've you done to the field . . . Muffin!"

Sol watched an alien expression of delight take residence on his mother's face as the red-collared Pomeranian jumped out of Trace's arms and scampered across the grass towards her mistress. Rosemary scooped her up and closed her eyes as the dog licked her face.

Tension drained from the gathering and laughter built in its place. Sol counted a more or less regulation number of limbs among his kinfolk and breathed a sigh of relief. He crossed the lawn to his mother. "You take your Winchester to church?"

"I take it everywhere." She cuddled Muffin and a sly smile flickered across her face. "Think I'd have gone if I'd known this would happen?" She gestured to the hacked-up field and smoking remains of the combine.

"What if I hadn't come home?"

"But you did."

"What if I hadn't brought Trace? You obviously know . . . about her."

"I know the Lord provides. Truly a Christmas miracle."

"You can't believe that."

Rosemary frowned. "Since you were knee-high your father and I felt something calling at you. Something you'd have to leave to find." She eyed Trace, bantering exuberantly with his father and cousins, already one of the family. Even Donita had a beefy arm slung around her shoulders. "You're a man of the world now, but that don't break the thread tying you to this place."

"Like a leash?" He bristled as Muffin snarled at him with her nasty little underbite.

"Like a way home, Solomon." His mother kissed the Pomeranian's head. "For when you have to go there."

Sol pulled his mother in for a long overdue hug, even scratching Muffin behind the ears. Then he followed the din of buffoonery back to the ragged cluster of Rempels, Klassens, Nickels, and the lone black sheep, Trace.

The Twelve Days of Dating

Krista D. Ball

WHEN A PERSON makes the decision to move to a space station, they don't usually consider how depressing Christmas alone will be. At least, that was Mandy's situation. She'd spent a few Christmases alone, but there'd always been a routine of familiar things and places to help ease her through the holidays. Walking around looking at lights on Christmas Eve. Or driving on the days that it was too cold. Having a hot chocolate with triple Baileys and way too much whipped cream.

She could do all of those things out here in space, but it just wasn't the same.

She sighed and ate her cheese fries. She was terrible company for Gary, one of her co-workers. He was her standing lunch companion, only today he was also her standing after-work companion because she was homesick and wanted to eat her feelings.

"I hear the first Christmas is always the hardest," Gary said helpfully.

She flicked Gary a smile and a shrug before shovelling another mouthful of cheese fries into her mouth. It was easy for Gary. His parents were amongst the celebrity werepuppies, the accidental product of a car accident in the 70s between a necromancer, a mind witch, and a SPCA van. Everyone was fine, including the dogs. It's just that, somehow, all of the people involved in the accident ended up being merged with the canine personalities in the van. Like most of them, Gary's parents moved to New Sky Station when they retired from the convention circuit and fandom. They all settled down, raised some adorable werepuppies, and had an entire community up here.

"I thought it would've been easier to meet people," Mandy said. "It's been four months and I've barely met anyone."

"What am I? Chopped corgi over here?"

Mandy gave Gary an annoyed look. "The only reason I know you is because we work together. In fact, everyone I know is related to you."

Gary shrugged. "So?"

She wanted to say that it was hard, being an old-school werewolf in a world of shapeshifter border collies, German shepherds, beagles, and a delightful amount of golden retriever and black lab crossbreeds. She wasn't a cuddly were-retriever who made little girls squeak with anticipation of a face lick. Whenever she changed forms, little girls ran screaming to the nearest adult to save them from the ugly, mangy beast.

It wasn't even fair. Werewolves didn't kill little girls. Or anyone. They just wanted to have a nice fish cookout on occasion. And Mandy was a vegetarian anyway, so a grilled tofu steak with a nice salad would be absolutely acceptable.

"Look, I think you should come over for Christmas dinner. Mom's been bugging me to invite you over again anyway, and you know how she gets."

Mandy absolutely knew how Gary's mom got. The woman was a werespaniel, King Charles-cocker cross to be specific. That woman had big, brown eyes as both a human and a dog, and she'd weaponized them. That woman could guilt a fire demon to give up burning things if she put a mind to it.

"Oh, I don't want to impose on her," Mandy said. She really did want to go there for Christmas dinner, just so that she wouldn't be alone, but also she didn't want to go and feel in the way. "I thought you said all of your extended family is coming up to the station this year. I'd be in the way, and it wouldn't be fair to your mom."

Gary snorted. "Are you kidding me? Mom loves company, you know that. Besides, if you came over, my cousins wouldn't change form to prewash the dishes on the kitchen floor."

Mandy laughed. "Oh my god, tell me they don't do that."

"Oh, they absolutely do. They started doing it when they were kids, and everyone let them because it was cute. They're in their forties now, and it's not cute. Now, it's just pathetic and a way to get out of doing the dishes."

"Your cousins should be ashamed of themselves," Mandy said.

"So if you came over, they'd have to help load the dishes and that alone would be worth it," Gary said. He eyed her plate and grabbed one of the cheesy fries. "I'm starving."

"You had two fish burgers!" Mandy said.

"And I hadn't eaten all day," Gary protested. He eyed the tablet on the table. "You wanna stick around while I order fries?"

She rolled her eyes but laughed. They chatted about Gary's spoiled cousins and his family's Christmas traditions. She listened and nodded in all of the right places, but mostly it just made her even more homesick. What happened when they all realized she was a were*wolf*? What if they wanted her to change form? She didn't have anyone she trusted to comb out her mats, and she was too embarrassed to go to the groomers now with the state her fur was in. She was worried she'd need sections shaved, and at that stage, she might as well shave it all.

She could imagine the horror-stricken expressions at a bald werewolf in their midst.

"I think I should date more," Mandy blurted out.

Gary looked up from the food court's order tablet and said, "Yeah?"

"Yeah." She picked up her phone and began clicking icons.

"Wait, are you downloading SkyDates?"

"Yeah, I need to meet people and this is how it's done."

Gary tapped the menu for cheese fries, ordering two plates. He put the tablet back in its spot and said, "Look, this station is small. There's what? Fifty k. Tops. I'm telling you, everyone knows everyone, or *is* related to them. You're not going to find anyone but visitors."

"Oh, just let me try," she said, accepting all of the security options. "I'm just a little lonely and I think I'll feel better if I get out there and meet new people."

Gary snorted. "All you're going to find is fleas."

DECEMBER 22

Mandy stared at her phone in equal amounts disappointment and embarrassment. Her date was forty-five minutes late. She looked about the food court, which had been his choice for a meeting area, but saw no one who looked like his profile photo. She checked the app, in case there had been an emergency or he had to work or some excuse to make her not feel awful.

He'd blocked her.

She managed to hold in the bulk of her tears until she reached her apartment. She texted Gary, who'd asked her to let him know how things went.

Gary: What a jerk. Want me to get my cousins to pee on his door?

Mandy: Best to ask me in the morning when I'm not so mad.

Gary: Okay, but my sisters just said they're on standby for a late-night pee raid.

DECEMBER 23

Mandy was determined not to let yesterday's disaster ruin today.

Now on Christmas holidays for two weeks, she put aside her self-consciousness, handed over her credit card, and had the groomers go through her werewolf coat to comb, clip, detangle, and condition her coat and skin. They even clipped her nails and cleaned out her ears, which were getting a little waxy from all of the fur tangles in her ears. Then, they got her to change back into human form and they trimmed her hair, plucked her eyebrows and wayward chin hairs, and sent her on her way five hundred dollars poorer.

But she smelled like coconuts and oatmeal and felt very fancy indeed.

She glanced up from her table and saw her date walk into the restaurant. He'd not seen her yet and was talking to the waitress at the front. She pointed at Mandy. Mandy smiled. Her date froze. No expression on his face. No smile. Nothing.

Then, he turned and walked out of the restaurant.

And then he blocked her on the app.

Her jaw was trembling when the waitress showed up and said, "Um, so, um, I talked to my manager and, um, a previous table paid for your meal, whatever you wanted to order, so um, you can just go ahead and order whatever you want, on the house, I mean, on the previous customer."

"Thanks," Mandy said. She drew in a ragged breath.

"You should call a friend so that you can share the dinner with someone, since it's free and, yeah."

The waitress was a terrible liar, but Mandy appreciated the kindness of both the waitress and her manager. Mandy texted Gary and asked if he wanted to come over for her free pity dinner. He was there in fifteen minutes.

"Wow! You look fancy!" He leaned in a little. "You smell like coconuts!"

"I went to the groomers today," Mandy said, embarrassed.

"Pawbreakers? My sisters all love that place, even if it's so expensive." He nodded his head and said, "Yeah, I'm guessing he took one look at you, realized you were completely out of his league with that new haircut, and left so that he wouldn't humiliate himself."

Mandy sniffed. "I don't think that's it."

"Well, it's that or he's a colossal twit."

"I'm going with twit," Mandy said.

Gary held up his glass of water. "I'll toast to that."

DECEMBER 24

After the two disasters, Mandy decided it was time to double up. There was no shortage of men wanting to meet up, though her experience thus far was that they didn't want to actually meet her. She had to use the laundromat in her wing, and frankly she couldn't afford to keep washing her good clothes every day.

However, even though it was Christmas Eve and a major gamble to make a match, she hoped there was at least one lonely person on the station willing to form a new pack with her.

Then again, maybe that was just her.

Her first date was a no-show, but he had the decency to message her. He'd completely forgotten it was Christmas Eve and said his mother would absolutely shave him bald if he missed the family dinner. He asked could he make up for it later. She replied she absolutely understood, had no hard feelings, and not to worry about her.

Plus, he didn't block her, so he was already better than the other men thus far.

It was a few hours before her next date, so she ran around doing some errands. She saw Gary and a gaggle of women. Some were certainly his sisters, but the others she didn't recognize. By the way they were acting, though, most likely cousins. They were picking clothes out for Gary and, while she couldn't hear what they were saying, the girls were all clearly berating the poor man. He didn't notice her, and she let him be. He already had enough women on his hands.

However, as she walked away, she looked back over her shoulder twice, just in case he saw her. He didn't. His sisters were dragging him toward a change room with an armload of clothes.

She didn't like the lonely, sad feeling she got walking away from him.

The vertical lift was down, so it took Mandy forty-five minutes to weave her way to the other side of the station to Krunch 'n Kafe, the station's canine-friendly diner. She arrived sweaty, flushed, and feeling very odd about Gary.

Her date was waiting for her. Her date.

Whose name she completely blanked on.

She smiled anyway and apologized for being late.

He gave her a once-over and said, "Sorry, I have to go. My grandmother died while I was waiting for you to show up."

And then he left.

Without another word.

Without even a chance for her to stumble out some sympathies.

She texted Gary, who asked the guy's name. Mandy had to look him up on the app, and thankfully he'd not blocked her yet.

Mandy: Vincent St. Clair.

Gary: Cindy used to date him. His grandmother died years ago, before she'd met him. Cindy wants to know if she and the girls can go pee on him.

Mandy: Tell them not to tempt me.

Gary: Cindy says she can see him in the crowd. She's willing to change form and rush him with a big puddle in the elevator.

Mandy: No, Gary. Tell them no!

Gary: Fine, fine, but I have eight pairs of big, brown dog eyes looking at me now, so I hope you're happy. Are you sure you don't want to come over to the house? Mom's making cheesy potatoes.

Mandy wanted nothing more than to spend Christmas Eve with Gary, but instead she texted back: No, you go have fun.

When she got up the next morning, though, she found a plastic container of cheesy potatoes in a bag on her door handle.

DECEMBER 25

Gary texted Mandy all morning, trying to convince her to come over to spend the day with his family. His entire family wanted to meet her, and she tried not to read too much into that. She made several excuses, including his poor mother already had too many mouths to feed, how she didn't want to intrude, how she was planning to spend the day in her PJs.

But mostly, which she didn't tell Gary, was that she didn't want his family to know she was a werewolf.

She was frustrated with herself for feeling that way, and maybe even a little disappointed. But she couldn't help feeling out of place, as one of the rare werewolves on the station. It's how she felt, no matter how illogical it was.

She got a ping on her phone, saying a match had replied. They chatted for a few minutes before he said, as it happens, he was free for a few hours and offered to meet her at the large food court.

Mandy's expectations were notably already very low for the date, so she only did the most basic of her hygiene routine; she did not want to waste her fancy name-brand makeup on yet another no-show. Her date arrived within a minute of her, and she realized she'd passed him walking in.

They shared the pleasantries of meeting. He preferred to be called Bert, not Robert, and she said she was Mandy, and preferred Mandy. He was already an improvement over her previous dates. She pulled the table tablet and, after tugging on the cord so that she could position it in between them, asked what he wanted to order. There were seventeen restaurants and kiosks in the food court, so there was plenty to be had.

"You go ahead. My mom packed my lunch."

Mandy stared as Bert put his backpack on the table and pulled out seven plastic containers. And a fork. And then a thermos. And then a spoon. And then a water bottle.

"You . . . brought your own dinner?" Mandy asked.

"The prices are way too high here," Bert said through a

mouthful of what looked like potato salad. "So Mom packed me some of Christmas Dinner for me to bring here."

"Oh. So, your mom lives on the station?"

"Yeah, I still live with her. It's cheaper, and since I'm not working again, I can't afford my own place."

Mandy tried not to judge, as plenty of races, werewolves included, lived in extended family units. The pixies might prefer to flee the nest as soon as they turn fourteen, but that was them. She'd even lived with her family after finishing university. It wasn't that strange.

Of course, her mother stopped packing her lunch when she was twenty.

Except maybe on special occasions.

Still, she tried not to judge. Including when he ate over half the fries off her plate, but never offered her any of his food, not even the homemade kibble cookies his mother made which smelled of peanut butter, her absolute favourite.

Then, because he'd eaten her fries and she was still hungry, she ordered nachos.

He ate half of those, too, and then said, "Wow, you can sure pack away the food. That explains your werewolf thighs, I guess."

Mandy suddenly wished the stereotypes about werewolves was true because she really wanted to rip his throat out. Instead, she said she had somewhere to go and left as quickly as possible.

Gary: What's wrong with your thighs?

Mandy: I have no idea.

Gary: I can't believe he brought his own food.

Mandy: I could have dealt with that if he'd shared!

Gary: You can't trust a dog who won't share. Mom wants to know if you want some Christmas dinner. She said you're not allowed to say no.

Mandy: Then, I guess I'll have to say yes.

Gary arrived an hour later with enough leftovers for a week, and they sat and ate, laughing and talking like normal people.

DECEMBER 26

Mandy nearly cancelled the date, but it was only for an afternoon coffee, so she slapped on a bit of coconut oil cream and headed out. She got herself a steamed vanilla milk, and he ordered himself a proper coffee. They exchanged the usual small talk: jobs, station life, apartment location, the usual.

Then, he guzzled his coffee, gave her an appraising look, and asked, "All right. So my place or yours?"

"I'm sorry?" Mandy asked.

"Let's go get furry together."

For starters, Mandy generally didn't do it in werewolf form unless she really knew the person. Also, she couldn't completely remember his name. And she was still drinking her milk.

"Let's wait a bit to make sure, I don't know, we like each other."

He grunted and said, "Well, I better go. I only have an hour before my second shift starts and I don't have time to sit around drinking."

"But . . ."

Mandy: What is WRONG with men on this station? Is there something in the water?

Gary: Seriously, he just left?

Mandy: Yuppers.

Gary: . . .

Mandy: He said he had a split shift, so booked me in between.

Gary: . . .

Mandy: I KNOW

Gary: Mandy, look, I like you, and I'm saying this for your own good. You need to delete that app off your phone. You're meeting all of the weirdos on the station. It should be called Weirdo Dating.

Mandy: There's got to be a normal, single werecanine on this station.

Gary: My cousin, Sam, can stick his tail in his mouth.

Mandy: That's already better than what I've come across so far. God, that's sad.

DECEMBER 27

Mandy was relieved her date was a no-show. Gary's work was just across the way, so he popped over to join her. They shared a plate of fries and vegan chicken gravy.

"I told you the food was good here," Gary said.

Mandy wagged a fry at him. "Yes, you did."

"So, listen. What are you doing for New Year's Eve?"

Mandy made a sound of horror.

"Look, all us kids rent a ball pit. Like, my siblings and my cousins. We get food catered for us, too, so you could totally come. It would be a lot of fun." Gary chomped on a fry and, after a quick gulp of his drink, added, "We all change into dog form and have a blast."

Mandy chewed her fry, suddenly very self-conscious. "Gary . . . so, you know I'm a were*wolf*, right?"

"Yeah," Gary said, clearly confused. "Yeah, you told me that like the first week we met."

"Well, I'll be way too big for the rest of you," Mandy said. She tried to smile, but she felt her shoulders slump without her permission. "Like, I'd probably step on someone and hurt them. I'm just going to order in a pizza and watch movies."

"Okay, but I think you should come."

Mandy changed the subject and felt really sad that she wasn't small like a corgi. She could have a lot of fun as a corgi.

DECEMBER 28

Mandy's date was nice in that he was normal, but weird because he'd decided during their date he was homesick and was going to move back down to Earth. She was happy for him, though wished he'd not told her during the appetizers because she didn't want to appear rude for ordering an entrée.

DECEMBER 29

Thankfully, her date cancelled before she took a shower and she got to spend the evening in wolf form playing with her feet and a marijuana- and catnip-laced cheese ball stuffed inside a plastic ball.

DECEMBER 30

Mandy spotted her date in the food court. He had his back turned to her, giving her one last opportunity to smooth down her dress front and square her shoulders.

He turned just as she approached his table, looked right at her, but then turned back to his drink. For a moment, she hesitated, thinking she'd confused him with someone else. But, no, that had to be him.

Mandy stepped around the square table and looked down at him. He'd already ordered himself food. "Um, hi. Jack?"

"Yes. Oh, are you Mandy?" Jack asked.

"Um, yeah. Hi!" A nervous giggle escaped her and she covered it up with a big smile. "Hi. Nice to meet you finally."

"Have a seat," he said. "I didn't recognize you. You look nothing like your photo."

She wanted to say that he was the absolute douchebag he appeared in his profile photo, but smiled through the moment. She was famished and ordered a vegetarian poutine with extra cheese curds.

"Oh. You're a vegetarian?" Jack asked.

"Yeah," Mandy said. "I have been since my teens. So, how long have you been on New Sky?"

He frowned, but allowed the conversation change. "Two years now, give or take. You?"

"I moved in September. I've met a couple of friends, but it's hard at this age, ya know? Just finding people to talk to and do things with, especially as a werewolf, ya know?"

"Well, I'm not really a part of the werewolf community." He used air quotes when he said community. "I find them all just a bit extra."

"Extra?" Mandy asked. She had no idea what he meant.

"Oh, you know the type. Getting expensive fur treatments, being vegans, and doing CrossFit, as opposed to living the way we were meant to live."

Later, Mandy wished she could say that was the low point of the date. It was not.

When she told Gary over text, he'd called immediately afterward. "I'm sorry, he did what?"

"I'm not exaggerating. He ordered three plates of food and then told the waitress to give me the bill since he was a true feminist."

"But he ordered more food than you!" Gary protested.

"He ate seventy dollars' worth of chicken and ribs!"

"How am I still single?" Gary demanded. "Seriously, my sisters are right. I need to get out there again because clearly the dating pool sucks."

Mandy let out a nervous giggle because she realized all she really wanted was for Gary to ask her out.

DECEMBER 31

Mandy finally admitted to herself that she really liked Gary.

This presented a problem, as she was frozen in awkward terror about him knowing and him not feeling the same way, and then their friendship would be ruined.

She picked up and put down her phone eighteen times before she began berating herself for being the silliest werewolf in all of creation.

Finally, she texted: Have fun tonight at the ball pit.

Gary immediately called her. "Hey! So I was just about to call you. My cousins are coming out with us tonight, and two are bringing dates. So we rented the big dog pit, too. So now you absolutely have to come."

"Oh, I don't want to force myself on to your thing," Mandy said. She absolutely wanted to force herself on to the thing. Then, reality hit her. "Like, I'm really big when I transform."

"Dude, listen. My niece is dating a were-Newfoundland dog. She tops out at one eighty easily."

Mandy cleared her throat. "Um, Gary, I'm at least two hundred."

"Like anyone's going to notice a bit of fur weight. Now, come on. I can't deal with you sitting around all sad all night, and it'll be fun."

"Are you sure?"

"Mandy, come on. You've dated half of the station's weirdos this month. Come hang out with me and my weirdo family instead."

"Like . . . a date?" Mandy blurted.

She slapped herself in the back of the head. It hurt. She deserved it. Friendship ruined. Over. Done. It was never going to be the same now. He was going to blow her off and she was going to be awkward, and it was never going to be the same and—

"Would you like it to be?"

Don't commit, Mandy. Be super cool. Be casual. You can do it, Mandy. Come on, puppy. You got this.

"Um . . ." was all Mandy could say.

"Cause, like, not to pressure you or anything, and we're friends and that's really important because it's really hard to make friends at this age, but," Gary coughed.

In the background, Mandy distinctly heard a scolding female

voice say, "Tell her."

Gary made a shushing noise that he tried to cover up with another cough. "Anyway, um, yeah. I guess I'm asking you out on a date to my family ball pit event. If you want. You can also just come as my friend, because we're friends. Just friends. If that's what you want."

Mandy did not squeal. "I think I'd like that."

"Which part?" Gary asked. Then, a failed whisper of, "Ow. Stop biting me."

Mandy was laughing now. Excited, nervous, gleeful laughs. "I think I'd like for it to be a date."

"Cool," Gary said, really going for the very causal tone.

"Cool," Mandy said, with a nervous chuckle.

"Okay. Cool. It's a date. Go put on some sweatpants and I'll be there in twenty."

An entire room full of dogs began excited howling before Gary could hit the end button. Then, it hit her: she needed sweatpants because she'd need to be able to get out of her clothes quickly to change form. Oh, sweet corgi blessings. Were there big change rooms?

THE YULE WOLF

Rebecca M. Senese

So I WAS lying on my back in the snow, all four paws up in the air, letting the cool breeze tickle the light grey fur on my belly. The sun was high in the sky on this clear day. Just a few fluffy clouds marring the bright blue of the sky.

The air was crisp enough that I could see my breath steaming out of my muzzle. Sometimes I pursed my lips and pretended I was a fire-breathing dragon instead of a great she-wolf. It never failed to crack up the other legendary creatures, although I never did it when the dragons were around.

Dragons weren't known for their sense of humour.

I had chosen a nice, thick snowbank for my lounging, tucked on a ledge between the rising peaks of several mountains in the land of legends. Tilting my head one way, I could see those white-capped tips soaring into the air. Funny how they looked so tiny. I could almost block them from view with a flex of my dew claw.

Looking down toward my tail, I could see the edge of the ledge, hanging over the valley below. Small, jutting rocks lined the wall behind me. The whole ledge was about thirty feet across, lots of room for lounging and rolling in the snow if I so chose.

My tail swished in the snow, brushing the loose surface away. My fur was thick enough that I didn't really feel the cold. If the temperature dropped too much, I could always dig myself a little burrow, or maybe huddle up to one of the dragons.

If they were feeling charitable.

A crunch of a foot on snow caught my attention. A moment later, I smelled the sweet scent of cat.

Rolling onto my right side, I lifted my head.

Jólakötturinn, the Yule Cat, stepped regally across the snow. Black as midnight against the pure white of the snow, her wide paws barely left a mark even though she was almost six feet high at her shoulder. As usual, she walked with her head lifted in the air, her fluffy black tail swishing back and forth. Her fur was thick for winter, puffing out her sides so she looked almost fat. A lot of creatures thought Jóla was a little snobbish but it was only because she either focused on her job or on napping as any good cat did.

I pushed myself up onto my paws and shook, sending snow flying into the air as it cleared off my dark grey fur.

"Hey Jóla," I said. "Getting ready for the big day?"

"Hello Lupa," Jóla said. Her voice sounded a little worn. I noticed her tail wasn't swishing in its usual bouncy way. Her head was dipping a little low. Her black fur, normally thick and glossy, was looking a little flat, like she hadn't cleaned herself properly in days.

"Shouldn't you be better groomed for your job?" I asked. "After all, aren't you supposed to be judging Christmas clothes?"

"I did not tell you how to suckle Remus and Romulus," she snapped, and swiped a paw at my muzzle.

I backed up.

"Sorry, I didn't mean any offense," I said. "I just meant you don't look like your usual well-put-together self. What's the matter?"

Jóla's ears twitched, a sign of irritation, but she sat down, curling her tail around her.

"I am just tired," she said.

"Tired? Is that all?"

She turned her head to survey the area around us. In the distance beyond the edge of the ledge, I spotted a winged Pegasus soaring upward.

"I have no wish to become the fodder for gossip," Jóla said.

"You know me, Jóla," I said. "Anything you tell me is confidential."

The cat let out a sigh. "Very well. I am pregnant."

A yip escaped my muzzle before I could catch myself. I bounded to her side and pressed my head on her cheek.

"Congratulations," I said.

She didn't reply. I stepped back to consider her again.

"Um, are we happy about this?"

Jóla sighed. "I suppose. It is just the timing is bad. I am due soon but I cannot miss work. Not after all my preparation. But I cannot even review the latest edition of Vogue without needing a nap." Her head drooped. "What will the others say if I cannot fulfil my duty?"

"Everyone will understand, of course," I said. "What's one year? You're an expectant mother."

She tilted her head at me, peering with blazing green eyes.

"You think I look for an excuse to forsake my birthright? My mission?" She lifted a paw in a threatening manner.

I sat back on my haunches, lifting my front paws to expose my chest and throat in a show of submission.

"Easy, take it easy," I said. "I never said that you should forsake anything. I know how difficult pregnancy can be. How can I help?"

Jóla lowered her paw, placing it back beside her other one. Her tail twitched.

"Perhaps you can hold the pages of the magazine open."

"Sure," I said. "I can do that."

"Very well." Jóla stood up. Her tail lifted, puffing up. "You may assist me."

She turned and led the way off the ledge. I followed.

Instead of leading me back to her usual tree, she led me to a small, warm cave. At the entrance, she tapped the snow off her paws before entering, then glared back at me until I did the same.

Of course, she wouldn't want any wet to get in here. She had probably picked this cave as a good place to give birth.

And it did look very suitable. The ceiling arched just a few inches over her head. With both of us breathing in here, the cave soon became very toasty.

Jóla headed for the back wall where she curled down in front of a magazine. She placed a paw on it and gave me a pointed look.

Right.

Padding across the hard ground, I sat down across from her. It took a moment for my paws to get the hang of opening the magazine, but I soon realized that I could push the page with my paw then hook a claw under the paper to flip it over.

Jóla settled down, with her chin on her paws. Her eyelids lowered halfway as I started to flip pages. She gave a loud purr to let me know when to turn to the next page.

Humans in strange clothing decorated the pages. I knew even if the magazine wasn't upside down for me, I wouldn't understand the images. But I did not need to. It was not my duty to judge clothing choices on Christmas Eve. That was the mission of Jólakötturinn, the Yule Cat, who appeared on Christmas Eve to ensure everyone celebrated the festive season with new clothes.

Seemed like an oddly specific mission, but who was I to judge? I had been tasked with suckling two infants who begat one of the longest surviving empires in human history.

Being a creature of legend could be a mysterious thing.

Jóla's eyes drooped lower. She was falling asleep. She needed her rest, but I knew she would not be pleased that I let her fall asleep on the job. Still, I watched the thick fur on her sides rise and fall for a few moments.

Wait a minute, her fur was not *that* thick.

Oh dear, she was much further along in her pregnancy than I had realized.

I dipped my head closer to her fur and sniffed. That sweet cat smell filled my nostrils, but now that I knew she was pregnant, I realized what I was smelling.

She was close to giving birth, probably only a day or two away. Maybe not even that long. Maybe only hours.

How was she going to do her job when she was just about to give birth?

I nuzzled her face. She blinked and then yawned, mouth opening wide to let her tongue unfurl. Then she smacked her lips.

"Did I fall asleep?" she asked.

"You did," I said. "Understandable considering how far along you are."

Her eyes snapped open. The fur on her neck bristled.

"What are you saying?"

"Jóla, don't lie to me," I said. "You know you can't do your job this year. Your babies are almost here."

She pushed herself up to a sitting position. Although she tried for speed, I could see how she struggled.

Definitely a matter of hours now.

"I will not forsake my duty," she said.

"What about your duty to your babies?" I asked.

Her ears drooped. She bowed her head.

"I have never missed a year," she said. "I am disgraced."

"Stop being so dramatic," I said. "Honestly, you cats."

She lifted her head and glared at me.

"Don't give me that look," I said. "Or I won't take over for you."

The glare remained for a moment longer, then she blinked in confusion.

"Take over for me?"

I nodded. "My job has been finished for centuries. I'd be happy to cover for you this year. After all, you'll soon be a little too distracted to be judging clothing."

"Lupa, I could not ask . . ." Jóla said.

"You didn't ask," I said. "I volunteered."

Jóla's expression softened. "Thank you." Then she lifted her chin. "If you are to take over, you will need to study. There is no time to lose. You have only two days to review this year's fashions. In the corner by the door is this year's *Vogue, Chatelaine,* and *Fashion Express.* You will need to memorize each issue. I will quiz you before you . . . mrow!"

Another yowl escaped her lips as she rolled onto her side. Her paws shoved the magazine away. It slid across the ground, pages fluttered.

So, not hours then.

Before the day was done, Jóla welcomed five mewling babies into the world. I tried to help, but after a swipe across my muzzle with full claws extended, I retreated to the mouth of the cave where I gave verbal encouragement. When the final kitten came, and I was sure mother and babies were okay, I left. I returned only moments later, bringing along the plain, brown blanket that I had swaddled Romulus and Remus in.

Now that the babies were here, Jóla allowed me to approach. I placed the blanket over her and helped her tuck the kittens under the blanket, keeping them warm.

Jóla gave me a nod of gratitude.

As I retreated to the mouth of the cave, preparing to leave her to rest and care for her young, she called me back.

"Lupa, take the magazines," she said. "You need to study."

"Of course."

I gathered the magazines, bundling them onto my back, before I left to the sound of Jóla purring to her kittens.

NEWS OF JÓLA'S new kittens spread through the land of legend like wildfire. Even the dragons came to pay their respects. Soon my worn, brown blanket wasn't the only offering. Blankets of silk and fur were piled just inside the entrance to Jóla's cave. Bowls filled with fresh spring water and fresh delicacies were brought several times a day.

It wasn't often that new legendary creatures were born. Everyone loved to celebrate.

I joined the celebrations as much as I could, when I wasn't sitting in my den, flipping through magazines. The glossy pages snagged on my claws and I kept ripping the paper.

Of course, it might have had something to do with how fast I was trying to turn the pages.

They all were so boring. Humans wearing clothing. So what? I could not understand the appeal and in fact, I found it rather sad. Imagine living without fur? Without a glossy coat of one's own? I shuddered. Even Romulus and Remus, the two I had suckled and protected until they were grown, had seemed weak and helpless to me. They too had had to swaddle themselves in fabric, draping it over their arms and legs.

These magazines were just the same, only more so.

Of course, I had to admit there was quite a range of colour and shapes to the clothing. The way it sometimes stuck out from the shoulders or flopped across the body. But other than protecting their hairless bodies, I couldn't comprehend the importance of those colours and shapes.

Jóla would not be pleased with my lack of progress.

Fortunately, she was a little distracted.

Soon Christmas Eve came and it was time to put my knowledge to the test. First, I stopped in a final time to visit Jóla for any last-minute instructions.

Five tiny, mewling bundles of fur rolled and tumbled around the cave floor as I stood in the doorway. Jóla swished her tail, gathering the little kittens closer to her as she lay on her side.

"Now remember, Lupa," she said, allowing her attention to waver enough from the kittens to glance over at me. "You are to check that every child has received new, brightly coloured clothes. If they do, you bestow the Yule Cat blessing and move on. If they do not, they are not allowed to feast on the Christmas meal the next day. Instead, you feast on them."

"Feast on them?"

But Jóla's attention turned back to her kittens as they began to nuzzle closer to her teats, looking for their next meal.

I backed out of the cave to give her privacy.

Feast on children who did not receive new clothes?

That was not exactly the kind of Christmas ritual I expected to be undertaking. But I had given my word. Jóla needed to take this year off to look after her new babies.

The duties of the Yule Cat fell to me. Lupa, she-wolf of legend, who had raised twin babies who begat an empire.

What was checking on new clothes compared to that?

SNOW CRUNCHED UNDER my paws as I raced across the land. Soon, the valley of legends fell away as I increased my speed. Faster and faster, I ran. My lungs ached from effort. My muscles worked hard.

Within moments, I passed through the magical barrier into the land of humans.

It had been many centuries since I had been back here. The size of their cities shocked me. Gone were the flaming torches. Now they had harnessed balls of light hanging from tall sticks in the sky. Huge buildings of materials harder than mud soared high into the sky, even taller than the sticks.

Strange, horseless carts rolled down the street. Through windows, I heard music without orchestra and saw shrunken people on square panels, moving and talking.

Humans truly had harnessed the power of the gods.

Strings of different coloured lights hung across houses and were wound around trees, glowing in the night. I remembered Jóla mentioning them. Christmas lights. Part of the festivities.

I liked how the different colours reflected on my fur.

In front of some houses, I saw depictions of Santa Claus and his reindeers. I knew of him but had never really seen him. He spent his time in a different part of the legendary land and didn't visit us creatures very often. I'd heard he was a little snobby. Once in a while, a reindeer would pop in though.

Other homes had snowmen decorated with scarves and hats. I paid particular attention to them. It was clothing after all. But not really presents for the children of the house.

I wondered if those children did not receive clothing, would I have to feast on only part of them since their snowmen had new clothes?

It was a dilemma I hoped not to face.

I spent an hour exploring the planet, familiarizing myself with all the changes that had taken place since the last time I had crossed over from the land of legends.

Then it was time to get down to the business of checking out clothing.

I hoped flipping through the pages of several dozen fashion magazines had prepared me.

I started at a small, two-storey house in Newfoundland. Red brick poked out from underneath mounds of snow and ice. I could sense the family within. A mother and father, and three children. Two girls and a boy. Their minds and bodies all warm and swirling in sleep.

As a legend, I could move where I wished. Within a moment, I stood in a darkened room, in front of a tall pine tree, covered with lights and silver strings and coloured balls. The urge to swat the balls off the tree and chase them stirred, but I pushed it down.

No time for play. I had work to do.

Boxes wrapped in different coloured papers were tucked under the tree. Presents, Jóla had said. In there should be the clothing I sought.

I surveyed the pile of presents. Within them, I could see the various items, toys, games, jewellery. There at the back, I sensed scarfs and mittens, in bright blue and red. Enough for every child.

That was clothing, wasn't it?

It wouldn't make it into fashion magazines, but if I was expected to feast on anyone who didn't receive clothing, I was going to have to make allowances.

No sense stuffing myself. It was going to be a long night.

So yes, I decided scarfs and mittens counted.

Feasting could be deferred for this family.

I moved on.

After the first few homes, I settled into a rhythm. Soon I didn't even have to enter the house to discern the presents and their contents within. The variety and amount of gifts was astonishing. But I ignored the majority of them, looking instead for clothing. Any kind of clothing.

The majority of the clothing I found were socks and mittens and scarfs. Underwear and sweaters were a close second. Pyjamas came third. When the family was just a pair of adults, I found their clothing was usually small scraps of silk.

I tried not to pay too much attention to those.

I did begin to notice that the majority of clothing I found was nothing like the clothing from the pages of the magazines.

I suspected Jóla studied the magazines just because she wanted to, not because it was actually useful to the job. Unless she was feasting on many more children than I thought. I shook my head. No, that wasn't possible. She couldn't possibly maintain her svelte figure if she feasted on everyone who didn't receive designer clothing.

I decided to move east across the planet. I zigzagged through Europe, inspecting houses and apartment homes. Down through Asia where instead of scarfs and mittens, I found bright tunics and great swaths of fabric. Those seemed more like designer clothes than the mittens.

Hours sped by. So far so good. All the homes I had surveyed had had some kind of clothing in their presents.

In every home, I bestowed the Yule Cat blessing and moved on.

I was really getting the hang of this. What an easy job. Jóla was one lucky cat!

I reached the west side of North America and began zigzagging across the continent.

And there ran into my first problem.

It was a small, two-storey, grey brick building in southern British Columbia. It didn't look like a house, more like an office building, but I sensed many people inside. Families, or parts of families. Mothers and children. No fathers.

No Christmas lights decorated the outside. That was enough

to make me frown. Perhaps they did not celebrate Christmas. Jóla had mentioned there were houses like that and told me to pass by them. They were not part of her mandate. I had already skipped huge sections in other parts of the world because of it.

But other places in this city had been decorated, their families bursting with presents. This didn't seem the kind of place to skip.

Uh-oh. Was I going to be feasting here? I wasn't sure how I felt about that.

I passed into the building and found the room where the families were sleeping. It was a large room that took up the entire top floor. Thin fabric walls that did not reach up to the ceiling separated one family from another. Instead of beds, they slept curled on cots. Some even slept inside big, puffy blankets laid right on the floor.

As I wandered along, I noticed fading bruises on some of the mothers' faces or arms. One or two even on the children.

I stopped in the middle of the room and surveyed all.

This was not their home. They had fled their home, to escape pain and fear.

I was reminded of when I found Remus and Romulus, abandoned and crying in the dirt.

And now on a day when these humans should have been feasting, the tenets of the Yule Cat demanded I feast on them.

But I couldn't imagine Jóla doing such a thing. Not to these distressed families, and I certainly couldn't. Not I, Lupa, who had cared for and suckled two discarded infants.

Were these mothers and children also not discarded?

Did they not need to be cared for?

And what better wolf was there for the job?

I puffed out my chest, inhaling deeply.

Then lifted my voice to howl into the night.

Calling to the land of legends.

Requesting the use of their magic.

Soon the air filled with answering calls. The songs of phoenix birds, the rumble of Yetis, the roar of dragons, the whinnies of winged Pegasus. All these and more, sang, gurgled, and thundered their offer of magic to me.

Filling me until the fur on my back stood straight up and my tail quivered straight out behind me.

Magic swirled around me, crackling and sparkling. A few

children stirred in their beds, disturbed by the feel of the magic. They must have been even more sensitive than most children, close to the veil that hid the legends from their world. Most grew out of it when they became adults. Legends became stories, just words on a page.

It kept us safe.

But young ones were close to the veil and sometimes were able to peer through it, to see us.

I would have to be careful not to get caught.

I slunk through the room, keeping low to the floor. My claws clicked on the wood as I moved. I swung my head from one side to another, looking, searching. Every inch of the floor was taken up by these small, sub-divided spaces, filled with sleeping people. There was nowhere for me to gather myself and cast my spell.

Wait a minute.

There in the far corner, an empty space of about two feet across along the wall, narrowing like a triangle.

Perfect.

More than perfect. In fact, it gave me an idea.

I sat on my haunches, lifting my paws. The magic swirled faster. There was so much, it was almost more than I could control. But I would, I had to.

I clawed at the air and howled out my spell.

Pouring magic into the narrow space in front of me.

It sparkled and crackled, at first looking like a column of light flaring up to the ceiling and back down. Up and down, up and down. Then I began to manipulate it.

The column widened at the base and narrowed at the top. Looking like a triangle.

Perfect, that was the right shape.

Next was the colour.

From within the sparkling magic, dark green manifested. At first it was a single blob of colour, then shifted, sprouting branches, changing. The triangle became a Christmas tree.

For a moment, it stayed plain, naked, then the magic flowed again. Red, blue, and yellow balls appeared. Multicoloured strings of light wound through the branches. Those seemed to be standard on all the trees I had seen, then I decided to add some extra flourishes. Candy canes, silver string, a white sprinkle that looked like a frosting of snow.

And for the final touch, I added a rich, fresh fragrance of pine.

I almost lowered my paws to the floor. It was a perfect Christmas tree, lush and beautiful, glowing with colour and light.

No, not quite perfect.

The floor at the base of the tree was too empty.

I was going to have to do something about that.

The magic was starting to wane. I had used a lot of it to create the tree, but I couldn't let it go yet. I was going to have to be fast.

I lifted my paws and howled again.

Magic shimmered around the base of the tree. Soon boxes appeared, wrapped in paper of green, blue, red. Solid colours and multiple stripes. Tiny Santas on some. Reindeers on others. Snowflakes. Jingle bells. Christmas stockings.

As the pile grew, I instructed the presents to select one person on the floor for each of them, to become what that person needed. Some would be clothing, others would be toys, and still others would be something else. Something needed, something loved.

It was as close as I could get to suckling and caring for them all.

As the final presents solidified on the floor, I felt the last of the magic fade. There had been just enough to finish it.

I lowered my paws to the floor and sat looking at the Christmas trees, lights blinking and glowing, reflecting off the shiny paper of the mound of presents.

Not exactly the instructions Jóla had given me for her role as Yule Cat, but I was no cat. I would never be able to do the job exactly as she had done.

I was a she-wolf, and a foster mother. The threat of feasting on children wasn't my style. I preferred to offer the warmth of my fur as I had done for my two infant boys so long ago.

And if there were too many to be comforted by my fur like in this room, I was happy to provide comfort in another way.

It may not be the way of the Yule Cat, but it was my way.

The way of the Yule Wolf.

With a final nod at the Christmas tree, I stood up and padded across the floor toward the windows. The tree glowed behind me like a sentinel against the darkness. I slipped out through the wall and continued on.

There was still more to do as I finished my rounds, but I was no longer going to be so strict in my task. Jóla could take up the mantle for the Yule Cat next year, but I would continue with my own version as the Yule Wolf this year.

Providing my comfort and joy, as only a she-wolf could.

As I raced through the cold, dark night, the clouds parted, revealing the brilliant full moon, shining in the sky. I lifted my head and howled. A Merry Christmas to all.

And to all, a good night.

BARK! THE HAROLD ANGELS SING

Lizz Donnelly

NOBODY WANTS AN old dog for Christmas. It broke Bonnie's heart every year to see the donations go up and the adoptions go down. She'd worked at the Hanging Hills Animal Shelter long enough to know that folks were happy to help monetarily around the holidays, but they wouldn't look twice at any animal that wasn't still roly-poly, cuddly, and most important of the Christmas criteria, new.

It was near closing time, two days before Christmas. Bonnie wandered through the cat room, to make sure everyone had enough food and water for the night. She didn't go into the kennel; it was a rare moment of quiet back there, and it was, of course, best to let sleeping dogs lie. Besides, she didn't need the reminder of a row of cold noses and sad eyes that were going to spend the holiday like they did every day: waiting for their person.

Bonnie was scratching behind the ears of a particularly fat and happy calico named Jello when she was startled by a tap on the glass window. Her co-worker, Lucky, was standing outside waving a newspaper. His name was really Jacob, but if Bonnie hadn't been the one to cut the payroll cheques, she'd never have known it.

"Have you seen this?" he hollered through the glass, holding

147

up the newspaper. "There was a ghost dog sighting!"

"What?" Bonnie asked. She gave the calico one last pat and went to see what Lucky was talking about. He handed her the newspaper and she skimmed it. "Oh, I saw this story this morning in the online version. Little girl was playing on the pond in her backyard and fell through the ice. It's lucky they got her out in time."

"No luck to it," he said. "Did you read the quote from the kid?"

"No, I guess that was behind the pay wall. What did she say?"

"A dog pulled her out of the water."

"Her dog saved her? They should lead with that," Bonnie said. The newspaper had made it out to be a tragic accident narrowly avoided, not a feel-good hero dog story.

"Not her dog," Lucky said. "The family doesn't have one. The girl said it was a little black dog that grabbed her coat and pulled her out. Her mother says there was no sign of a dog. She found her daughter clinging to the edge of the ice and rushed her inside to get warm."

Lucky was grinning at Bonnie like a kid on Christmas morning. She didn't understand the obvious glee.

"What am I missing?" Bonnie asked. "It was a hero stray dog who was scared away by the mother?"

"That's the angle they're going with, but they're wrong. This is Meriden, Connecticut, Bonnie. That was the Black Dog of the Hanging Hills. I'd bet the entire contents of my stocking."

Bonnie was a mid-life transplant to the Hanging Hills area, so she was admittedly not wholly familiar with the story. Lucky was happy to oblige.

"The first recorded sighting was in the mid-1800s and they say it's an omen. The first time, it brings joy. The second time, it's a warning. The third time, well . . ."

Bonnie didn't necessarily want to ask, but she did anyway. "What happens the third time?"

"You die. Not immediately, but shortly after."

"It's a little Dickensian, isn't it?" Bonnie mused. "Three Christmas ghosts, and all."

"I guess it is," Lucky said.

"Why are you so excited? Doesn't this mean the little girl will see it two more times and meet a terrible end?" Bonnie asked. "Is this going to turn into one of those Christmas nightmare stories?"

"Not everyone sees the dog three times," Lucky shrugged. "I've only seen it once. My dad took me camping when I was a kid, and I spotted it from the top of a hill. Although, I've never heard of it rescuing people before."

"Apparently you can teach an old ghost dog new tricks," Bonnie said.

"Well, I'm headed out," Lucky said. "Got to do some last-minute shopping. You in tomorrow?"

"I'll be here," Bonnie said. She came in most holidays. Someone needed to feed the shelter animals and clean, and if she could lend a hand so the others could get back to their families sooner, she would. There was no one at home waiting for her.

Lucky was gone in a swirl of snow. Bonnie set about tidying her desk, making sure none of the office cats were still loose, and all the doors were shut. She was just coming back to her desk when she heard the front door.

"Forget your keys?" she called, thinking it was Lucky.

"I'm sorry, you're probably closed, aren't you?" Bonnie looked up at the woman's voice and found the girl from the newspaper and her mother standing in front of her.

"It's okay," Bonnie said. "We're not closed just yet. I think I read about you in the newspaper earlier today."

"We had quite an adventure yesterday," the girl's mother said tiredly.

"I'm sure that's an understatement," Bonnie said gently. "What can I help you with today?"

"I'm looking for the dog," the girl spoke up.

"Oh," Bonnie said. "We have lots of dogs in the back. I'd be happy to walk you through the kennel to see if there's anybody in there that you might be interested in taking home."

"No, the dog that saved me," the girl said.

"She's looking for a particular dog," her mother explained. "The one she says pulled her out of the ice."

"I'm not making it up," the girl argued. "The dog saved me. It was real, Mom. I didn't make it up."

"Let's go see," Bonnie interrupted, trying to stall an argument. "I'm Bonnie, by the way."

"I'm Belle, and this is my mom," the little girl said.

"Fran," her mother stuck out a hand. Bonnie shook it and then motioned toward the door that led to the kennels.

"Nice to meet you. Shall we?"

Fran and Belle followed Bonnie down the hall and through the door of the kennel. The barking began immediately. The dogs had been fairly settled in for the night, but the sound of the door set them off again. Door meant people, and people meant treats, at least. Bonnie obliged them by grabbing a bag off a shelf nearby.

Bonnie glanced over her shoulder to make sure that Belle was doing okay with all the noise. Sometimes the dogs were a little overwhelming for kids. Belle peered into each kennel stone-faced and unbothered by the ruckus. There was a Cattle Dog mix in the first kennel, followed by three Pit Bull mixes, and a Saint Bernard on the end. He was an elder gentleman whose owner had passed away earlier that month. Belle smiled a little at the big sloppy Saint Bernard, but turned at the end of the row and shook her head.

"These are the only dogs you have?" she asked, disappointed. "He's not here."

"I'm sorry, sweetheart," Fran said. "Do you want to meet any of the others? They all look so nice."

But Belle shook her head. "I wanted that dog."

"If you tell me what he looks like, I can leave a note to call you if any dog matching the description is brought in," Bonnie offered. "In the meantime, would you like to help me hand out treats to these guys? It's Christmastime, I figure an extra one before bed can't hurt them."

Belle smiled and held out a hand for the treats. Bonnie and Fran helped her carefully feed each of the dogs in the kennel. Her gaze lingered a moment on the old Saint Bernard, but not for long. Back at her desk, Bonnie took notes on the dog and wished Belle and Fran a Merry Christmas. When the door closed behind them, the shelter was quiet.

Bonnie hadn't realized how hard it was snowing outside. The wind whipped around her as she brushed off her car, vowing, in her next mid-life crisis, to pack up and move somewhere that didn't have Nor'easters. Once in her car she fumbled with the radio and briefly debated checking her phone to see what the weather was supposed to do, before she decided that it didn't matter. The weather was doing what it wanted and no forecast would change that. The grocery store could wait until tomorrow. She'd just go carefully home.

The drive was fine, until the last big hill. Her wheel hit a patch of ice and her reflexes hit the brakes, even though she knew better than to do that. The car spun twice, completely, like a slow-motion figure skater in the worst free skate program ever, until it slid off the road and collided with a tree. Bonnie's head collided with the steering wheel and her world went dark.

THERE WAS SOMEONE in the kennel. It was Bonnie's first thought when she returned to consciousness with a dog's shrill bark echoing in her ears.

Her next thought was that her head was killing her. Opening her eyes, she saw her snow-covered windshield, her purse on the seat beside her, spilled open and covered in broken glass. She saw the blood on the hand that she'd just held to her head, and her phone on the floor, just out of reach. The barking continued.

Her left arm hung uselessly at her side when she tried to open the car door, and she became aware of the burning pain of dislocation. She knew she needed to call for help and get out of the car if she was able to. Her legs seemed all right. It took her a couple tries to reach her phone but she finally succeeded and dialled 9-1-1. She managed to unlatch the door and kick it open just a little bit.

The phone rang in her hand, and in the snow in front of her was a little black dog, barking furiously. It stopped, at last, just as the operator picked up.

"What's your emergency?"

"I'm at the bottom of Marley Hill. I slid on a patch of ice and hit a tree. I need medical attention."

"Sending an ambulance now. Stay on the phone with me until they get there, all right?"

The little dog turned, as if to walk away.

"Hold on," Bonnie said. "Please, don't go."

"I'll stay on the line with you, ma'am, I'm not going anywhere," the operator said.

"No, the dog. I meant the dog."

"Is there someone else there?" the operator asked.

"No. I mean, yes," Bonnie said. "There's a little black dog. A hound of some sort. I think it saved my life."

She held the phone away from her ear. "Thank you," she said to the dog.

It wagged its tail twice, then turned and trotted off into the darkness. It left no footprints in the snow. "Wait," Bonnie called after it. "There's a little girl looking for you. You saved her too. If you ever decide you want a home, I know the perfect one."

"Ma'am?" the operator's voice came from the phone. "Are you all right? The ambulance will be there in just a few minutes. Hold on, okay?"

"I'm all right," Bonnie told the woman on the other end of the line. "I just wanted him to know that he has options. And friends who are grateful."

BONNIE SHOULDN'T HAVE gone in to work on Christmas Day, but she was determined. There wasn't a lot of cleaning that she could do with her arm in a sling—dislocated, but not broken—but she could bring fresh baked cookies for the staff and fill food bowls, at least. She convinced Lucky to pick her up on his way in.

They were the first of the three scheduled employees to arrive, and when they pulled into the parking lot, Lucky spotted the dog first.

"Holy cats, Bon, it's the dog!"

She'd told him her story on the way; the accident and the dog whose barking had woken her in time to call for help before she froze. She'd been adamant that it was just a stray with good timing, and not the Ghost Dog of the Hanging Hills, but Lucky was unconvinced.

Now, sitting in the car staring at the same little dog waiting patiently for them by the front door of the shelter, Bonnie was starting to question it herself.

"It is," she said in amazement. "It's the same dog." She stumbled out of the car the moment it was in park, nearly losing her tray of cookies in the process, and made her way to the door, Lucky on her heels.

The dog sat quietly, watching them with a preternatural calm.

"It's you," she said softly. "Did you decide you'd like a home, after all?" The dog's tail thumped twice, soundlessly, against the snow.

"Come in, then," Bonnie said. "We'll call your little girl. She'll be so happy to see you."

Lucky unlocked the door and the dog trotted obediently behind them. Their boots left wet puddles on the floor but the dog's paws were remarkably dry. Jello the calico, watching through the window of the communal cat room, yowled in alarm at the sight of it, eyes wide.

"Bonnie," Lucky said in a low voice. "Is this a good idea? This is twice for both of us, seeing the dog. And for the girl, if we call her. What if she wakes up tomorrow and it's the third time? I told you what happens to people who see the ghost dog three times."

"First of all, he's not a ghost dog," Bonnie said, with more conviction than she felt. "Secondly, it's a ghost story, so there's room for interpretation. I think it means if the dog comes into your life three times maybe it's a bad thing, although this one seems pretty set on helping people, so I don't even believe that. But anyway, if she adopts him, he's in her life permanently. No coming and going. No rule of three."

"That's what you're going with?" Lucky asked. "A loophole based on a technicality?"

"I'm going with a little girl who's going to get exactly what she wants for Christmas."

"Procedure . . ." Lucky started.

"Is about securing homes. That's what I'm doing." Her tone left no room for argument.

"Well, I'm going to sit right here until he leaves, because I don't want to risk your technicality if I leave the room and come back."

"Fine," Bonnie rolled her eyes and dialled the number.

A SCANT HALF HOUR later, Belle and Fran burst through the front door. Bonnie had felt bad calling on Christmas morning, but it turned out, her earlier statement had been correct. She was giving Belle exactly what she wanted for Christmas.

"Remember," Fran warned. "It might not be the same . . ."

"It's him!" Belle squealed in excitement. The dog stood up from where it had been relaxing on a dog bed and barked once. They met in the middle of the room, and Bonnie had a fraction of a second to wonder how a little girl could hug a ghost dog, but she dropped to her knees on the floor and the dog climbed into her lap, covering her face with slobbery kisses, as if he'd known her his whole semi-corporeal life.

"I don't believe it," Fran said faintly.

"I'm having a hard time of it myself," Bonnie offered.

Lucky was silent.

"Is there something I need to do to take him home? Sign? Pay?" Fran asked. "Clearly, we'd like to adopt him. I promised her."

Bonnie shook her head. "He's yours. Adoption fees are waived for the holidays. Bring him back next week so our vet can check him over, and I'll have all the official paperwork drawn up then. We'd just like to make sure he's healthy, although he seems to be."

"And not a ghost," Lucky muttered. Bonnie shot him a half-hearted glare.

"We'll do that," Fran said. "And we'd like to sponsor an adoption for someone else, can we do that? Pay it forward a little since you just gave my kid the best gift of her life."

"Absolutely. We can work all that out when you bring him back. You should go home and enjoy the holiday," Bonnie said. "I'll just need to put a name down for his appointment. Any ideas?"

Belle didn't hesitate. "Harold. He says his name is Harold."

"He said?" Bonnie and Fran echoed her.

"Does he say anything else?" Lucky asked. "Like he's maybe been wandering the hills for two hundred years?"

"Lucky," Bonnie admonished her co-worker.

He shrugged. "Just asking."

"He said he wants to go home for some cocoa with a candy cane in it and presents," Belle said.

"With a candy cane, huh?" Fran said. "I guess, because it's Christmas, that would be okay. Come on, you two."

Belle stood up and headed for the door. Harold the hound trotted happily at her heels.

"What do you say?" Fran said to her daughter.

Belle turned to Bonnie, eyes shining. "Thank you for the best Christmas present in the whole entire world."

"You're welcome, although I think most of the credit goes to

Harold. We'll see you next week for that vet appointment."

"Merry Christmas!" Belle said. Harold barked once. Then they were out the door.

Bonnie turned to Lucky. "You survived your ghost dog encounter."

"Second one's a warning," Lucky said. "But you better believe I'm taking the afternoon off next week when he comes back in."

"Deal," Bonnie laughed. "Now let's get our work done. There's a couch and a fireplace calling my name at home, and you know what I think would look great in front of it? A certain Saint Bernard."

"You're going to take Tim?"

"His name is Tim?" Bonnie asked. She'd done the intake paperwork, but never really registered the dog's name.

"Well, the old man called him Timber, but I've been calling him Tim."

"It's perfect," Bonnie said. "Merry Christmas, Lucky."

"Merry Christmas, Bonnie. Let's open the cookies before everyone else arrives."

In Anticipation of Their First Transformation

Adam Israel

DAVE REMOVED THE tray of spareribs from the oven and rested it on the island, already overfull with hot plates, sweetmeats, and side dishes—all the fixings for a holiday celebration.

Through the kitchen window, he could see the oldest pair of kids in the backyard; the winter solstice had brought a blanket of heavy snow and his son and nephew were passing the time by throwing snowballs at each other.

The younger children were in the adjacent living room, arguing over what to watch on the television. His wife and sister-in-law were in a bedroom, wrapping a pile of last-minute gifts. It was a smaller gathering than they were used to, just the two packs. The family spread out further and further with each passing year.

He grabbed an opaque bottle from the fridge and refilled the wine glass in his brother's hand.

"Do you think this will be the year?" Dave said.

Both men knew what thoughts preoccupied the other. The season of change was upon them, and they both had boys who, born weeks apart, were coming of age.

John shrugged. "I hope so, but I'm worried about the

Veränderungen."

Dave shared his brother's concern. The first transformation was crucial in establishing your place as a shifter. Dave and John came from a long line of canids, but both of them had married outside of the family. The boys' first shift could be to a bird, or a serpent, or it might not come at all. Genetics were complicated, especially for their kind.

"Me too," he said. "You know what he told me last week?"

Dave picked up a segment of bone—roasted marrow piping hot. "He tells me that he's a vegetarian. How's that going to work?"

"It might not be so bad," John said. "Your first time, you shifted into the family dog."

Dave grimaced. "Poodles are hunting dogs," he muttered. John never let him live that down.

"Now look at you," John continued, "the most skilful shifter I know. Dad would be proud."

Dave's ego recovered at hearing such high praise. The first shift was always to something familiar, and came naturally to you. Everything else was the result of hard work and study. Even Dave still struggled, at times, to hold the form of a grey wolf, the largest of their kind.

That was one reason both families had stayed in the suburbs; they both invested in a yearly pass to the local zoo. They made regular trips together, trying to see if any of the children took an affinity to any of the animals, but the boys only seemed interested in what they saw on their phones.

The Great Hunt, celebrated at the summer solstice, held great memories as a father-son event. He worried that tradition might become a thing of the past. Attendance had declined over the years as the families spread out further and lives got busier.

Dave realized that the sound of snowy scuffles outside had stopped. He stepped to the window and waved his brother over to join him.

Two nearly identical snowsuits lay on the ground. Inside, something squirmed towards freedom. Both men watched in silent anticipation.

Minutes ticked by.

"Do you think we should help them?" Dave said.

"Nah. Not yet. Give them a few more minutes."

Eventually, a tiny black nose peeked out of the neck of one of the snowsuits. It gave way to an orange and white snout, followed by comically large ears. John clapped his brother's shoulder in celebration.

"A Fennec fox," he said.

A minute later, a pair of grey forepaws emerged. Dexterous hands found the zipper of the snowsuit and unzipped the snowsuit by a few inches. A telltale masked face of white, grey, and black scurried into the snow.

Dave's hand fell to his brother's shoulder and gave it a gentle squeeze.

Fully emerged, the fox and racoon sniffed the air, learning the scent of each other. Once that ritual was complete, the fox leapt into the air and landed on all fours, nose plunging deep into the snow.

The racoon formed a snowball and threw it at their cousin as he raised his head.

Grinning, the brothers raced to strip down, right in the kitchen. Dave was the first to be naked and reach the back door.

The cold and wind whipped at exposed flesh, but he didn't feel it. The hot blood of the transformation gripped him. Animalistic instincts took over. He visualized the form, so natural to him: the family poodle. There was pain—tolerable—as bone shifted, contracted, condensed. Weight displaced in ways that defied logic. His skin tingled as patches of fur broke out like a rash. He dropped to his haunches alongside his brother, the red fox.

There was no need for the hunt, not yet, not with the feast inside. For now, he was content to introduce himself to the newest members of the pack and to frolic in the fresh snow of the longest night.

THE DEAD TREE GIFT

E.C. Bell

THE OWNER DRAGGED a dying tree into the house and covered it with trinkets and a myriad of grey lights, as was her way.

Its dying odour made me sad. Usually, at the Season of the Grey Lights, I could ignore the smell because it seemed to make the Owner and my Chosen happy, but this time it combined with the bereavement scent coming off the Owner. She missed Millie—slave name Patty, unknown birth name—a Being who had been brought to the Owner's house after me, and who had recently died.

I could not understand why the Owner hadn't let Millie outside to die, as was the way. That would have made living in the house tolerable. But now, the smell of death combined with the smell of the dying tree was all too much.

I demand-barked at the back door—even though the Owner hated it, and chastised me every time I did it—and then scrambled down the cursed stairs and out to the backyard.

The sun was setting for the night. The snow stung my feet, and I felt embarrassed at my weakness, until I grew accustomed to the cold again.

I heard a jingle of leash in front of the Owner's house, and knew another Being was "going walkies" with their Owner. I ran to the front fence and huffed a greeting to the female. Heard the

161

Owner say "No," and before the other Being could say anything, she was gone, dragged down the sidewalk and away.

I wanted to follow her. I had no thoughts of mating, because I'd been "fixed", but the female smelled so alive, all I wanted was to be out of the yard.

That was a bad thought. I knew that, but I was desperate to smell life up close, because my Owner had not taken me for "walkies" since Millie died.

"Walkies" weren't perfect, because the Owner walked too slowly for me, but at least I could smell the smells and get the news. At least there was that.

I searched the fence line, slowly. Found a couple of spaces that were almost right, but I'd gained much winter weight and couldn't fit.

I felt a twinge of anger, because the winter weight was the Owner's fault, too. It had come from the complete lack of "walkies" and the abundance of treats just to shut me up.

I found a spot in the fence that I thought was big enough and pushed my way through, flinching as the wire pulled at my skin. I had a moment of fear when my fur wound in the wire, but I kept going. Pain and fear wouldn't stop me this time. I needed to be free.

I scrambled out from under the fence and looked around. I was on the driveway, where the monsters slept. The smell of oil and gasoline momentarily froze me, reminding me of the day I'd become prey for one of those nightmares. But after a moment, I thawed and walked to the front of the house.

I could still smell the scent of the female who'd passed by, but ignored it and headed to the park across the street. I walked to the crosswalk, as was the way when I'd gone "walkies" with the Owner. When the street was clear of monsters, I crossed quickly. Then I marked the ground near the post, as was the way, before I ran into the dark. I wasn't sure where I was going. All I knew was, the world finally smelled alive.

At the far side of the park, a Being approached, and I froze. He was alone, with no sign of his Owner on him. And his smell was not right. Not wrong, exactly, but not right.

"Who are you?" I huffed.

He stared at me for a long, measured moment, and I felt the hair on my back stand as the feeling of being prey flooded me.

"I'm a Coyote," he finally said, and took a small step toward me. "Have you heard of my kind?"

I hadn't, but I lifted a lip and growled. A warning to give me space, and I was happy to see he stopped. But he never stopped staring.

"I can smell humans on you," he finally snorted. "You're a pet. Aren't you?"

"I'm no-one's pet," I said, even though I was. I momentarily wished that I hadn't allowed the Owner to clip my toenails. I might need them to gain purchase if I had to make a quick getaway.

"I think you are," the coyote said, and shook his head. "Are you going to run?"

I snarled again and kept my eyes on him just as he kept his on me. "No," I said. "I run from no Being."

That was not necessarily the truth, because a pit bull had taken offence at my first "learning to be a good dog" lesson, and I'd tried to run from her. I'd half strangled myself pulling against the leash, but she'd been corrected by her Owner and then locked in a room, so I felt that I'd won that event. But after that, I did what I could to stay away from pit bulls.

But this dog who was not a dog didn't need to know that, so I said "No," again, as forcefully as I could muster.

"I see you're missing a leg," the coyote said.

"So?" I tried to sound all cool, calm, and collected because there was no way I was turning into prey within sight of my Owner's door.

"Can you run?" he asked, and he took a slow, measured step toward me.

"I can run faster than you," I replied. "And my teeth are stronger than yours, and you are starting to piss me off with all your questions, so don't test me, pup."

The coyote's neck ruff stood to attention and he lifted a lip at the slur.

Maybe the Owner was right. Maybe I hadn't been as socialized as I could have been. "Sorry," I muttered. "Didn't mean to talk down to you."

"Whatever," the coyote replied, feigning nonchalance. "You're just a pet. Your words mean nothing. I don't understand why you're running around here by yourself, though. Shouldn't you be safely locked in the house of your owner?"

"I needed some time to myself," I said. "I'll probably go back later. Or tomorrow. After I clear my head."

"Huh," the coyote huffed, and sat on his haunches, still watching me.

He did not see me as a threat, but no longer considered me prey. I kept my eyes on him, nonetheless. A situation can change in a moment. I knew that much.

"So, what?" he asked. "Are you looking for a new place to live?" He grinned and scratched, but still with his eyes on me.

"I—I don't know," I said. "If I could figure out a way to stop the smell of sorrow in the house, I'd probably go back, but I'm not sure how to do that."

The coyote's ears perked.

"I can't help with the smell of sorrow or whatever, but I know a place where you can go," he said. "There are pets, like you, living rough. Maybe you want to go there."

I blinked. I hadn't thought of not going back. Not really. I was already missing my spot on the couch, and my treats.

"Why would you tell me about a place like this?" I asked.

"Because my family is tired of your kind wandering around here," the coyote said. "There are more and more of you, every day. Like you don't have a sweet deal. In the warmth, with all the food you could ever want. If you don't want to be a pet anymore, that's up to you." He shrugged again. "You go away and I don't have to run you off. Or worse."

Now, I wasn't convinced that he could do me harm under any circumstances because he was alone and I had strong teeth, but there was something about his suggestion that gave me pause. Finding my own kind, and living with them. Maybe that was what I wanted.

"Show me," I said. "Show me where this place is."

The coyote stared at me a moment more, then gestured with his long snout. "That way," he said. "To the river. You'll be able to find them once you get to the water."

I glanced in the direction he'd pointed, and a small shudder of anticipation made the hair on my back stand upright. I remembered the river, and the valley around it. My Chosen had taken me once, and it had been a wonderful place. Full of smells and noises that had nothing to do with the humans and their monster machines.

"You know where the river is?" he asked.

"I do," I said. More or less.

"Good," he replied. "Go there and you won't see me again." Then he turned his back on me and trotted across the park, disappearing from sight long before his smell left my nostrils.

"The river valley," I muttered, and turned around. "I can do that."

And so I did.

FINDING THE RIVER valley was harder than I thought, because the last time I'd been there, my Chosen had taken me in his monster, and I'd been so disconcerted I couldn't remember the twists and turns he took. Soon I was exhausted, because the humans and their monsters were everywhere.

I remembered when I was hit by one of those monsters. It happened two days after I escaped from my birth home. A nightmare of metal and oil and loud growls worse than any predator. The pain was exquisite as I rolled to the sidewalk and lay there, unable to stand. Unable to walk. I was taken to the Place with the Smell, where they fixed me. Leg and testes, both gone in a flash.

That was where the Owner found me. At the Place with the Smell.

A horn blatted, a monster on the road growling at me, and I panted, my mouth full of fear-water. My Owner called what was happening my own version of PTSD, but knowing what a thing was didn't help get rid of that thing, and I panted like I was hearing the deep sounds from the sky, and I wished I was on my couch with my Chosen.

"It's just thunder," he'd always said as he held me. "It can't hurt you."

Millie had snuggled up to me, too, lending me her strength until I felt strong enough on my own.

I missed my Chosen, and my couch. And I missed Millie.

That thought surprised me. She'd been an aggravation. Until she wasn't. We had been housemates, and I missed her.

I found a small lane behind a line of houses where there were no monsters, and did my best to stick to it as I followed the smell of the river. But it was getting thin, and I was afraid that I'd somehow lost my way.

A Being caged in a backyard let me know I was going in the right direction. His barking alerted his Owners, who yelled at him to shut the hell up.

"Take me with you," the Being whispered when the back door to the house slammed shut, leaving him out in the dark and the cold. "I want to go to the Place That Is Safe. I can't stand it here, with them."

I felt a moment of pity, but it was up to him to figure his way out of his cage.

"Sorry," I said. "I can't help you."

And then I headed to the river to finally find the Place That Is Safe.

ALL RIGHT, SO when I finally found it, it didn't look like much. Mind you, I was cranky because I'd missed four meals and more treats than I cared to think about. And my couch. Oh, how I missed my couch.

In the bush by the river, there were piles of wood so old I could barely smell human on them anymore. Many Beings had marked the area around it, so many it felt like I was walking through an electric fence.

"Hello," I huffed when I got close to the wood. "Anybody here?"

A Being scrambled out from behind one of the piles of wood, like I'd woken him.

"Password," he growled.

"Pass what?" I asked.

"Pass*word*," the Being said again. He had the good ears and snout, but did not look particularly happy to see me. "Now."

"I don't know what that is," I replied, and glanced past him to the other Beings who appeared behind him. "Who's the Alpha?"

The Being snorted derisively. "What makes you think I'm not the Alpha?" he asked. "And how dare you look past me."

He howled angrily, and then a Being, a little smaller but built with good upright ears and long snout, ran up to him and roughly pushed him to the ground.

"Shut up," he said. "You want the cats to hear?"

"Sorry, sir," said the Being, then glanced at me, obviously embarrassed that he'd given everything away.

"Cats?" I asked. I knew cats. An aggravation, and difficult to deal with, what with their claws and contrary way of thinking. But with this many Beings all in one place, cats couldn't be a problem.

"Not the cats you know," the Alpha said. He sat and scratched at an old collar around his neck, and I could hear the jingle of tags.

"What other cats are there?" I asked. Then I thought of the coyote. The dog who was not a dog. Could there be cats that were not cats? An unsettling thought.

"Humans call them cougars," the Alpha said. "Big, and mean. There are enough of us to keep them at bay, but you shouldn't be out by yourself." He stared at me. "Why *are* you out by yourself? You're a pet if I smell correctly. Aren't you?"

"I am," I said. "But I was told of this place and came to see it." I looked around. "Doesn't look like much."

The guard lifted a lip and growled, and I hung my head. I'd done it again.

"Sorry," I said.

"You should be," the Alpha growled. "We came here to get away from humans." He shook his head, and his tags jingled like a warning. "We found it here. If you don't think it's good enough for you, well, there's the road."

"Frisky, let it go," a voice echoed from somewhere in the dark. "He can stay, if he wants."

Frisky glared behind him, into the dark. "He's a tripod," he snapped. "He's no use to us whatsoever. And I told you not to call me that. Ever."

"Sorry," the voice said, but it did not sound sorry. It sounded distinctly Alpha-ish, and I wondered if perhaps I'd made a mistake guessing who ran this show.

The Being pushed its way through the undergrowth to stand by Frisky. It was small, with long matted hair that hung in its eyes and caught in the underbrush.

Then the small Being's scent came to me. Female, fixed. And something else—a stink that was familiar. Ear infection, I guessed, and shook my head again. Upright ears were so much better.

"My name is Lucky," the Being said.

"Slave name?" I asked, before I thought.

"It's the name my human gave me," Lucky replied. "If that's what you mean."

"It demeans you that you still keep that name," Frisky growled. He stepped toward her stiffly, like he was going to teach her a quick lesson in politeness, but Lucky turned on him all teeth and flashing eyes.

"I'm talking to the new guy," Lucky said. "Give me room."

Frisky snarled but backed off, taking his cohort of guard dogs with him to the other side of the human ruins. Soon, Lucky and I were alone.

"He likes to act like he runs the place," Lucky said. "Makes him feel like he's worth something." She sat and scratched forlornly at her matted ear hair. "So, tell me your story," she said. "Who are you and why are you here?"

I told her my names and what had happened. She nodded when I spoke of the stink of death still in the house, which had driven me out.

"I know that smell," she said. "It's hard to get that smell out of your nose."

"Exactly!" I exclaimed. "I couldn't stand it anymore and had to get away. So I made my break, and then the coyote told me about all of you, and—"

"A coyote?" she said, her eyes suddenly sharp.

"Yes," I said. "He told me where you were—well, not exactly where you were, but said that you were by the river, and that if I wanted to live, I should come here to be with you."

"So, they're trying to run everyone who is not a coyote or prey out of the parks," Lucky mumbled. "We'd heard rumblings, but this is proof." She looked past me to Frisky and his cohort of guards across the way.

"Oh, Great and Glorious leader," she called. "A word?"

I blinked and glanced at her.

"He likes it," she said. "Makes him feel like he's in control." She shrugged. "He was supposed to be a police dog, but he didn't have the stones for it. At least, that's what I heard."

"A police dog named Frisky?" I asked.

"That's the name his new family gave him," she said. "After he washed out of the Academy. He wasn't pleased. It's actually

168

better if you don't call him that."

"But you can?" I asked.

"I can," she said. Then the Great and Glorious leader, AKA Frisky, stalked up to her, and she focussed her considerable attention on him.

"The coyotes are taking over the parks," she said. "They're driving all Beings who are pets here. To us."

Frisky looked around, his eyes sliding over me like I was barely there. "We can't have many more here," he said. "You know that."

"I know," Lucky replied. "And I also know we can't turn them away. Looks like we have a conundrum now, doesn't it?"

Frisky blinked. "We can't have a conundrum," he said. "That's bad. Right?"

"It is," Lucky replied.

"So . . . what do we do?" He almost bowed to Lucky, then caught himself and looked around to make certain no one had seen him.

"Let me think on it," Lucky said. "Go be with your men. I think you should prepare them."

He blinked and grinned, afraid. "For war?" he asked.

"Maybe," Lucky replied.

Frisky licked his lips nervously but did as he was asked. Went back to his cohort, while Lucky turned to me.

"Walk with me," she said, and pushed through the undergrowth, the long hair of her tail and feet catching in the brambles. Once she yipped in pain, and I felt a moment of sympathy for her. Long hair that grows and mats. Definite disadvantage.

With so many disadvantages, why did Frisky see Lucky as the Alpha? And if she actually was the Alpha, why was she talking to me?

"We don't need a war," she said. "Not now. It's too cold, and there's not enough food." She shook her head, then sighed and sat so she could scratch her left ear, which seemed to be the worst for wear. "This frigging infection is driving me crazy," she muttered. "I can barely think."

"My—my old housemate Millie had the same ear issue," I said. "My Owners knew how to make it better for her. With the Vet and whatnot."

"A Vet would be nice," Lucky said. "I've got worms, too. Living rough is hard. You know?"

I did not know, but I nodded nonetheless. "Anything I can do to help?" I asked.

"Get me a Vet and a warm bed," Lucky said, and scratched her ear again, vigorously. "I'm so done with all this Queen of the Pirates crap. I want a warm bed. I want to be dewormed. I want my frigging ears fixed, and my nails trimmed. Can you help me with any of that?"

I was surprised, and so I asked the thing that was least important. "Queen of the Pirates?" I asked.

"Yeah," Lucky said. "That was the name I chose for myself, because I was the first one to find this place. It used to be a boat that humans used to find gold, back in the day. It was abandoned by the humans when the gold ran out."

"Gold?" I asked.

"A metal," Lucky said. "Humans can't get enough of it, apparently. But in the ruins of this boat were many hidey-holes, and I quickly made a life for myself. Then other Beings started showing up." She shook her head. "You wouldn't believe how many of us are turned loose by their Owners, every year. Coyotes hunted here originally, but they were easy enough to run off, once we had the numbers. They're afraid of everything."

She sighed and stretched. "It was good for a while, but then the cats came. The ones you know, and the cats who are not cats. Large, frightening beasts who don't care who they take. We fight them more and more every season."

"But what about the pirate thing?" I asked.

"Oh, my Human loved *Pirates of the Caribbean*," she said. "The movie. Have you seen it?"

"I'm not one for watching movies," I said. The Owner and my Chosen could stare at the television for hours every day, but me? I was glad I had my spot on the couch so I could dream of being outside and chasing rabbits. I'd done it once, and it had been glorious.

"I've seen those movies more times than I can say, and it felt like I was keeping my Human alive by calling myself a pirate when I came here," Lucky said. "Alive in my mind, anyhow." She sniffed. "I still miss her, and I've been here four seasons."

"But now?"

"Now, I'm tired, and sick," Lucky said. "The cats come most nights, picking off the weak, and now it looks like the coyotes are causing us problems as well. I'm so tired, sometimes I think it's almost time for me to walk alone into the bush. I thought that Frisky was going to be my replacement, but . . . he's not too bright. He can keep the perimeter, but he often doesn't remember that he must find food and keep everyone safe." She glanced at me. "You know?"

"I understand," I said. "A leader must look after everyone. Keep everyone safe and fed."

"I knew you'd get it," Lucky said. "You're smart. Perhaps you should take over my spot as Queen of the Pirates."

My Chosen always called me the smartest dog he'd ever known. "You could do my taxes," he always said every spring, when the Time of Stress and Crying took over the house.

I wasn't certain what taxes were, but I could figure things out, generally. And what I knew was, Frisky, AKA Great and Glorious, wasn't going to accept me. Not even as part of the pack. In his eyes, a tripod was the least dog, no matter how good the teeth and ears.

"I wouldn't make a good Queen of the Pirates," I said. "I'm male."

"Barely," Lucky said, with a snort of disdain. I was ready to take offence, until I realized she'd spoken that way because I'd disappointed her.

"A tripod will never be accepted as Alpha," I said. "And I don't think you're dying. Looks like you're stuck being queen."

"Yeah," Lucky said, and turned away from me, rather pointedly. "Lucky me."

FOR TWO DAYS, I hung around with the pack. I stayed out of Frisky's way, until the sun went down and we foraged. Frisky and his cohort found rabbits and tore them to shreds, sharing little with anyone who was not one of them. I went with the smaller dogs and found mice, which were plentiful. I made certain to bring one for Lucky every night. She took the mice in her little jaws, and though she didn't thank me, she seemed to enjoy the meals.

On the second night, the darkness became thick, cold glue, and we gathered together for warmth. Lucky wandered the outer perimeter with the guards, watching for owls and other predators. No wonder she was tired.

Then, someone called "Cat!" and it was as though a firecracker had been dropped in our midst. We scrambled away, and I got caught up in the terror before I really thought and turned back to help the guards and Lucky.

That was when I met the cat stalking the pack.

I've seen cats. A couple even had the temerity to wander through my backyard, but they were easy enough to chase off, because I am larger and have good teeth and a ferocious bark. But I'd never seen a cat like the one who came into the Place That Is Safe.

It stood at least thirty inches high, and by my guess it was seven feet long, nose to tail. It stopped at the edge of the settlement and growled. It sounded as terrifying as it looked, and to be honest, I was ready to leg it, when Frisky called for his guards to protect the pack.

Small and weak went to the middle, as was the way. The stronger Beings stood around the outer edge. I girded my loins and took my place with them, but Frisky took offence, as I knew he would.

"Get to safety, tripod!" he cried. "You're too weak for the fight."

He'd turned and stared at me, in an effort to drive me inside the ring of strength where the weak huddled, when a second cat, smaller than the first but not by much, hit him at the shoulder and bowled him over.

A second cat? Cats were independent souls. They did not work in a pack.

Unless we were wrong.

I bared my teeth and threw myself at the smaller cat, in an effort to drive it away from Frisky, who was squalling on the ground at the cat's feet. For a moment, I was the only one, but then the rest of the Beings on our side of the perimeter came to his aid, driving the cat away from him and deeper into the bush.

The large cat made a run at the other side of the perimeter, but we regrouped and snapped and snarled him back, too.

"Are you all right?" I called to Frisky. He pulled himself to his feet and shook the debris from his fur.

"I'll live," he grunted.

There was no more time for conversation, because the cats were back, circling us, looking for an opening. They finally found one, and the bigger cat grabbed a pup, who screamed in terror.

"Save my baby!" a female cried, and I jumped to action.

"Drop him!" I bellowed, my voice so deep and demanding I surprised even myself. "Drop him now or we will tear you to shreds."

The cat stared at me as though he could barely believe that a mere dog would make those demands on him, when the rest of the pack attacked.

Growls and flashing teeth and bites to back and tail and neck until the cat finally dropped the pup and backed away.

The guards took over then and chased him. We who were left tightened the perimeter and watched the smaller cat, who did not move, as the larger cat and the guards crashed and banged through the underbrush.

The smaller cat made one more half-hearted feint in an effort to get through the perimeter, but we were too much for her, and she finally turned away, slipping into the underbrush and disappearing, like smoke.

The guards didn't return for hours. And when they finally did come back, they threw themselves to the ground, panting. Frisky was with them, and I could see a small rivulet of blood running down his front right leg where the cat had hit him. He wasn't as good as he'd said.

I turned to Lucky. She was licking the smell of the cat from the pup, who looked none the worse for his adventure. "I think Great and Glorious is hurt," I said. "He should be checked."

"Thank you," she said, and checked Frisky's wound. It appeared to be minor. That was good.

"How often does this happen?" I asked Lucky. "With the cats and all?"

"The large one has been here before. But this is the first time they both came," she replied as she walked away from Frisky. "They're hungry. We may have to move."

"They should eat mice," I muttered. "There are more than enough of them."

Lucky shrugged. "Maybe they think they're above all that."

She sat, then groaned, and lay down.

"Were you hurt?" I asked, and sniffed her urgently.

"No," she said. "I'm just tired. That's all."

Frisky saw that she was down and trotted over to her, looking disconcerted. "What's wrong?" he asked. "We have to make plans."

She groaned and reached out a paw. "You're going to have to figure it out yourself this time," she muttered. "I just can't."

Frisky looked horrified and backed away from her. "We—we won't survive without your council," he whispered.

This admittance caused nervous grumbling through the pack. Frisky was the Alpha, at least in the pack's mind. He needed to act like it, for their good.

"Great and Glorious," I whispered. "Pull it together."

He grunted, like he was going to correct me. But I'd saved him from the cat and deserved at least a little respect. He shook his head, his tags clanking, and walked me away from Lucky, who was still lying on the ground, groaning.

"Lucky must be saved," he said. "We need her wisdom." He looked around, then bent his head close to mine. "I need her wisdom. I can't do this on my own."

"How can she be saved?" I asked.

He blinked, like he was thinking, and it was hard. "You still have a home, with the humans. Correct?"

"I do," I said.

"Take her there," Frisky whispered. "Take her to your humans. To your Vet. She needs to be healed, and then she can come back to us."

I sat back on my haunches and stared at him, even though I knew it was impolite to do so. "Why me?" I asked.

"Because Lucky thinks you're smart," Frisky said. "So, be smart. Get her to the Vet and then back to us without being caught and taken to the Place with the Smell. That's what we need. Now."

I scratched my belly though it was not itchy, so I had some time to think. I didn't know if I was ready to go back to the Owner, even though mice were not as good as my food and treats. The smell and the loneliness would still be there, in the house.

And there was a very good chance that the Owner would call the Place with the Smell, if I brought Lucky to them.

"How would I stop the Owner from turning Lucky over to the authorities?" I asked. "That is their way, you know."

"I know," Frisky said. "But you're smart. Think of something."

So, I thought. As the rest of the pack finally settled, I stared out at the frozen river and thought. And finally, just before the sun pushed its way over the horizon and turned the ice of the river pink and blue, I had the answer.

Owners are flighty. That is their way. A pet dies, and they get a new pet. Then the sorrow of loss goes, and life is good for them again. All I had to do was convince the Owners that I'd bonded with Lucky, and they could be convinced to keep her. For me.

If I played my cards right, she would be a dead tree gift, for me.

I told Frisky and Lucky my plan. Lucky struggled to her feet, and grinned. "I told you he's smart," she said. "That plan just might work."

Lucky seemed rejuvenated. I couldn't tell if it was because she'd slept for so long, or because of the plan, but she and Frisky spoke at length about next steps, which included moving the pack to the boat, for safety.

"Another boat?" I asked.

"The *Edmonton Queen*," Lucky replied. "Humans use it, when the river runs. It's closed for the winter, but there are good places to hide nearby, and I believe it's out of the cats' hunting range. They won't find the pack. I'm almost certain of it."

"And then we'll go to war?" Frisky asked. "When you come back?"

"We will discuss that, when I return," Lucky said. Then she turned to me. "We should leave soon. Are you ready?"

I nodded, and when Lucky walked away from the pack, I followed her. When we were out of sight of the pack, I took the lead, because I knew the way.

IT TOOK US longer to get back to the park beside my Owner's house than it had for me to find my way to the Place That Is Safe, because Lucky had short legs and bad ears, but we managed. And she was able to find better ways to travel when I was certain we had to chance it on the roads with the monsters. We barely saw any of them, or humans.

It bothered me that she'd been able to find paths that I couldn't, and thought aloud that perhaps I wasn't as smart as everyone thought, but Lucky shook her head. "I'm old," she said, "and I've been living rough for a long time. That's all."

We passed the Being jailed in the backyard of his Owner's home, and Lucky said we had to help him, because *that* was the way.

"The new way," she whispered, when I looked at her questioningly.

We helped him dig his way out, and Lucky told him where to find the pack, and he was so happy as he left that place that I felt bad for having left him.

"Don't worry," she said "You still have things to learn. When I'm well, I'll teach you. But first, take me home so I can heal."

Home. That word sounded nice. I thought of my couch, and my Chosen, and then had a flash of fear. What if they'd replaced me? I hadn't been gone long, but you never knew with humans. They were fickle beasts.

As we trotted along the sidewalks that lined the parks, I thought about this more and more, until Lucky finally turned on me, all teeth and flashing eyes.

"Stop the thinking!" she yelled. "You stink with it! Your humans will be happy to see you. Trust me."

I hung my head. "I'll try," I said.

"You and Frisky," she finally laughed. "He can't think enough, and you think too much. If only there was a way to blend you two. You'd be the perfect Being."

"Good enough to be the Queen of the Pirates?" I scoffed.

"Almost," she replied.

AT THE FAR edge of the park across from the Owner's house, I saw the coyote hanging around under a tree, and stiffened. He was watching us intently, and I could hear him sniffing the air with his good long snout.

"You," he finally huffed. "I thought I sent you away."

"You did," I replied. "But I'm back."

"Your companion smells sick," the Coyote said. "Want me to

take her off your hands?"

I snarled and bared my teeth, but Lucky surprised me by walking past me toward the rangy beast.

"I'm not to be played with," she said. "And when I'm well, you and I need to chat. There's a war coming, and you and yours should be prepared."

"A war?" the coyote huffed laughter, but I could see the hair on his neck bristle. "With your kind?"

Lucky didn't seem to see him stiffen, or didn't care. "No," she said. "With the cats. You may be good in a fight."

"We're not afraid of cats, and we're not fighting with you," the Coyote replied. "You can be absolutely sure of that." Then he walked out from under the tree, bristling, and I'd had just about all I could stand.

"That's it!" I cried, my voice deep and menacing. "Leave us! Now!"

And then, I charged at him.

He looked surprised, like he hadn't thought that tripods could run, but we could. I could, and I bared my teeth, snapping when I got close.

He yipped and jumped back, scrambling to safety under the tree. Then he turned and ran.

I followed him a few steps, to make certain he was actually on his way, then turned back to Lucky, who looked impressed.

"That was good," she said. "I'll have to tell Frisky, when I see him again. Now, take me home."

WHEN WE CAME to the crosswalk that would take us across the street to the house of my Owner and my Chosen, we waited for the street to be free of monsters. I could feel human eyes on us, and knew that two Beings on the street could cause a scene, so I hurried Lucky to my Owner's driveway, and then to the hole under the fence. Then we were in the backyard and safe from prying eyes.

"I can smell the death here," Lucky said. "It's very sad."

"It is," I replied. "But inside is warm and there will be food." I shrugged. "The Owner and my Chosen are actually not that bad."

"You miss them," Lucky said.

"I do," I replied. "But before I call them, there are a couple of things for you to remember. In this house, the couch is mine. And the toys, and treats, unless the Owner offers you one. And the Owner's husband is *my* Chosen. Always remember that."

"I will," she said. "You're the Alpha in this house. If that's what you want."

I almost laughed, because Millie had always thought of herself as the Alpha, when she was alive. I acquiesced to keep the peace, but now I would be at the top of the food chain. With Lucky's permission, of course.

"But when I am well," she continued, "and we go back to the river, I am the Queen."

"I understand," I said. I was Alpha here, and she was Queen of the Pirates out there on the river. I could live with that.

I demand-barked, and it was as though the Owner and my Chosen had been standing by the door, waiting for me to call. It slammed open, and they flew down the stairs, and then they hugged me, calling me "Buddy," over and over, as was their way.

Then they saw Lucky, and I watched as she transformed into a Pet before my very eyes. All big eyes and wiggling rump, and she even held a paw up, beseechingly. But she made very sure to cling to my side. To show them, without a doubt, that she was with me. I was her Chosen.

That was all it took. The Owner swept her up into her arms, and then we were both in the warmth of the house, where we were fed. And then we were washed, which Lucky enjoyed much more than me. And then the Vet was called, and the groomer, and Lucky did not look or smell like the same Being when she finally came back from their ministrations.

The Owner gave Lucky a new name, as was her way. And then she got Lucky a gift stocking, which she hung by the dead tree, beside mine. Treats would be deposited in both of them on the Day of the Grey Lights. As was the Owner's way.

But neither the Owner or my Chosen found the hole in the fence. It was still there, waiting for us to use again, when it was time to go to war. I just hoped the Owner would understand. It was not personal. It was just our way.

The Wolf You Feed

Melanie Marttila

BAZI KNEW IT was illegal, even as she thawed the meat, but one look at the emaciated wolf that had stepped out of the bush last night, and Bazi couldn't think of doing anything else.

The rump roast and four T-bone steaks were only lightly freezer burned. They'd been given to her by a well-meaning aunt, who couldn't have known Bazi had embraced vegetarianism, and wouldn't do the wolf any harm. Better than starving, in any case.

Feeding the wolf might also cut down on the predation of her chicken coop and beehives. If it was the wolf and not some other animal blitzing her little farm. Nothing had happened to the goats yet, but the ram was big enough to rout a skinny wolf. If there was only the one.

The neighbouring properties weren't so far away that they wouldn't see her tromping out through the snow-covered fields and out into the bush, so she waited until after supper. It would be well and truly dark by then. A waxing moon would light her way without exposing her to the hungry eyes of people who didn't know to keep their mouths shut.

She'd overheard the Wellstroms—next farm to the east—in the grocery store last week chuckling about "Crazy Bazi" as she'd turned into their aisle. They'd been speaking in stage whispers, and Bazi couldn't imagine they hadn't meant for her—and

179

everyone else—to hear them. Her gut felt punched, but she'd told herself that she didn't care what anyone thought, kept telling herself until she could stand straight again.

When the meat had thawed, Bazi removed the butcher paper and transferred it into a garden tote. The paper rinsed and stuffed in the compost bucket, she stowed the garden tote in the locked cabinet in the mud room. Duro, her lanky, shaggy deerhound cross, was already half mad over the smell.

She fed Duro and sat down to lentil stew by candlelight, listening to the faint sounds of the twilight howl and watching her neighbours' houses through the windows.

"GODDESS, BLESS THIS mission of mercy," Bazi said as she stepped out into the crisp December night.

Duro set up a racket, both because he was unused to being left behind and because she was taking the delicious-smelling meat away with her. She'd considered taking Duro, too, but couldn't imagine how she'd keep him away from the contents of the tote. Besides, he'd probably go bounding after the wolf again like he did last night. Leashing him would be even more problematic. Leaving him behind was the best option, even though it made her gut twist.

The cold penetrated her down parka. Each step made the snow crunch so loudly, Bazi expected the neighbours to hear. She stopped, scanned the area, and, seeing no figures in windows or outside lights turned on, resumed her journey into the bush.

The moon was only partly helpful. In her yard and the fields, the moonlight reflected off the snow, and her way was clear. Once she entered the trees, though, the pines and firs prevented the snow from covering the ground except in patches, and the bare-branched birches and poplars cast deceptive shadows.

Bazi jumped several times before taming her reaction. She should just set out her offering and leave. She didn't want the wolf to expose itself, though, and she didn't want anyone to find the evidence of her law-breaking. They wouldn't understand her altruistic intentions. People like the Wellstroms would accuse her of inviting the wolf to attack their livestock. It was exactly what she wanted to prevent.

A growl stopped Bazi in her tracks. Heart shooting into rabbit-mode. Not wanting to move, she shifted her gaze left to right. Nothing but trees and shadows and scant patches of snow. Her pulse fluttered in her throat.

The wolf—she hoped it was the skinny wolf and not one of a pack—took a breath, its growl hitching before rolling on. Behind her. To the left. She imagined what the wolf's teeth would feel like as they rended her calf, tore at her hamstring, sunk into the muscle at the back of her neck—*stop it!*

Her fear could set off the attack she wanted to avoid. Bazi breathed deeply, slowed her frantic heart, evicted the tension from every part of her body.

The growl grew softer.

Bazi focused on her mission and the compassion that had inspired it. She imagined her heart cracking open and those feelings flowing out.

The growling stopped, replaced by an anxious-sounding pant.

"I have something for you." Bazi ushered the words out on a breath, remaining still.

Panting yielded to sniffing. The wolf was right behind her. She quelled a surge of panic. "That's right. In here." She let one handle of the tote slide out of her gloved fingers.

Snow and dirt and pine needles scattered. Had the wolf startled? The sniffing started up again.

"Do you want it? Let me tip it out." She didn't want to spook the wolf, moved like a glacier; she felt a poke and tug on the tote before it settled on the ground. Then, trying not to flinch as the wolf dashed in with almost playful growls to yank the tote from her fingers, she kept lowering it until it lay on its side. "Just a little bit more."

With her next exhalation, Bazi dropped the remaining handle, stepped around behind the tote—in her peripheral vision, the grey form of the wolf danced back—grabbed the bottom of the tote, and dumped the contents. After the smooth, swift action, she crouched and waddled slowly backward, keeping her eyes focused on the ground.

"It's all yours. Have at, lovely."

OVER THE NEXT nights, Bazi repeated the ritual, walking further into the bush each time, slowly emptying her freezer of the meat she'd never eat. She walked Duro before supper and in a different direction, so he wouldn't be so upset when she left with the thawed meat later in the night.

The wolf didn't shed its guarded skittishness but seemed to understand that she didn't mean it harm. It ate all the meat, in any case. She cleaned up any uneaten bone she could find, returning to the scenes of her crimes to remove the evidence of them.

It was well past the full moon and nearly the new, nearly solstice, when Bazi took the last of the meat from her freezer. She was down to ground beef now and put two of the packages back. Best to set expectations. The wolf shouldn't become dependent on her handouts. It was one of the reasons feeding wild animals was illegal.

That night, Bazi didn't take the tote, just the hamburger in its blood-soaked butcher paper.

After that first, frightening, yet fascinating, meal delivery, the wolf hadn't approached Bazi or growled at her. It waited until the meat was out of the tote and Bazi had walked well away from it. The last couple of nights, though, she'd stayed to watch and didn't return home until the wolf had left, apparently satisfied with its snack. She wouldn't fool herself. A full-grown wolf likely ate more than she brought it, which was just as well. She just wanted to give the wolf enough of a boost to get it back to a healthy weight, if not back to its pack.

That night, Bazi continued her habit of walking further into the bush. It was stupid, really. There was a pack somewhere out there.

Instead of dumping the meat and backing away, she let the ground beef tumble out of its wrapping, wiped the blood off her gloves in the snow, and sat on a fallen tree a few metres away. She couldn't be sure, but the wolf had looked in her direction when she'd stayed to watch before. The idea that it knew she was there made Bazi unreasonably happy. Wanting the wolf to like her. Maybe she was a little crazy?

The wolf, when it came, edged forward and danced back several times.

Bazi held still, barely daring to breathe.

Eventually, it ate, practically swallowing the whole pound in one go, its dark eyes on her every second. It snuffled and licked the bloody snow and then dashed off into the bush.

She let out a shuddering breath, pulse making her eardrums flutter. There was nothing to clean up tonight except the crumpled butcher paper in her fist.

The subsequent two nights, Bazi divided the hamburger into thirds and placed each lump a little closer to where she watched.

On the first night: Gulp. Gulp. Gulp. And the wolf was gone.

On the second, it got close enough for Bazi to see that it was a she-wolf.

"There, lovely," she said, sending the words out on a breath. "That's the last of it, I'm afraid."

The wolf huffed once, dipped her head, and loped away.

She floated home on the verge of giggles, hugging her secret like a naughty child.

The day following was solstice eve day and Bazi had planned a ritual. Nothing elaborate. It would just be her and Duro in the backyard at dusk with some hurricane lanterns. A song, a dance, an offering to the mill of time that would usher in the return of the light, and they'd migrate indoors for a humble feast, after which she'd continue the candlelight vigil, reading and meditating, until dawn. Unless she fell asleep, which she usually did.

Still, as she set out her lanterns, Duro snuffling about, Bazi was suffused with a sense of well-being. She lit the candles against the coming of the longest night and stood at the centre of her circle, Duro leaning against her thigh in a dog hug. She stroked Duro's shaggy head and watched the sun set.

And then Duro was gone, barking and bounding beyond the lantern light.

"Duro, come." She couldn't see what he was after. "Duro, come."

She heard his play growl, his tags slapping against each other. "Duro!" Bazi was about to move outside the circle of lanterns—so she could see, damnit—when Duro's dark shadow came trotting back, panting, another pale, dog-like shape in tow. The wolf.

"Oh, lovely. You weren't meant to leave the bush." Her pulse throbbed in her temples. She looked around uselessly, unable to tell if anyone else was out. Her neighbours were hunters as well as farmers. They'd shoot the wolf and call it justified. "You need to go home, now."

The wolf sat just outside the ring of light. Duro finally returned to Bazi's side, tongue lolling.

What I need to do is repay your kindness.

Bazi's hand clutched Duro's fur, scanning the darkness frantically for— "Did you . . . speak?"

Silly woman.

The wolf's snout hadn't moved. Why should she expect it to waggle its jaw like some CGI creation? A laugh, near hysterical, burst out of her. What else should she expect from a magical night like this?

What can I do to repay you?

"I have everything I need." Her words were coloured with the vestiges of laughter.

I cannot be indebted to you.

It was like that, then. "Do you know what's been attacking my chickens?"

The wolf blinked. *A fox. I can kill her easily.*

Bazi put out her hands. "You don't have to do that. I just don't want to lose any more of my birds. Or their eggs."

The fox needs to eat. Your fowl are easy prey. It's been a lean year.

Right. Skinny wolf. "I'll just have to fox-proof the barn. And the hives. I should have done it after the first attack."

I cannot help you with that. How can I repay you?

"I don't know. What can you do that doesn't involve killing another animal?"

The wolf's head moved back like she'd been smacked on the nose. *I am not an animal.*

Every hair on Bazi's body stood. She didn't want to ask what the wolf was, if not an animal.

The wolf closed her eyes.

Bazi ran her hand through Duro's fur and tried to breathe.

Duro leaned into her. Dog hug.

Tension rose up in Bazi until she thought she'd either scream or suffocate.

I can give you a gift.

"Okay." It came out half-strangled.

The wolf stood and entered the circle of lanterns. *Kneel.*

Bazi dropped to her knees and Duro flumped against her.

Close your eyes.

She did and, moments later, felt the wolf's wet nose on her forehead and breath against her face. She expected something like dog breath. Maybe meatier. But the wolf's breath smelled sweet. The tension melted away from Bazi as she breathed the sweetness in.

It is done.

When she opened her eyes, the wolf had stepped back. "May I ask—?"

Peace.

The gift unfurled in her chest. "Thank you."

Bazi sat in her circle of lanterns watching the wolf walk away. Her visit had been enough magic for the night. Maybe for a lifetime. "Let's go in, D."

For the first time, Bazi stayed up through solstice night and watched the sunrise.

Apple Night

J. Y. T. Kennedy

VERDA TOOK A last quick look around her cottage to confirm everything was in order just as three raps bounced on the door.

"Coming!" She took a deep breath and swung the door open to reveal her visitor: young Linna, with a layer of snow caked over her shawl and rosy cheeks framing her irrepressibly cheerful smile.

"Good day, Grandmother!" Linna stamped the snow off her boots, then held out her basket as she stepped inside. Once Verda had set the basket on the table, and the snowy shawl had been hung up by the fire, they had a quick hug, and then Verda put the kettle on for tea while Linna sat on the bed. She had better manners than to take the only chair in the cottage of an elder, who was not actually her grandmother, but only called so out of respect. "The twins are doing much better, and Aunty says they have enough medicine for now," Linna reported, "but old Anjor says he wants to try what uncle's been taking, and Binny's cow is ailing again."

Verda nodded and took down the required items from the shelf, leaving off what was not wanted and adding the new requests to the usual items. She lifted the cloth from Linna's basket to unpack it, and was surprised by the vivid red of an apple. She picked it up appreciatively. She knew exactly what tree it was from: the only one whose fruit kept so well. The winter days had dwindled to their shortest, but the apple was still shiny and firm.

"Mother wanted you to have one for Apple Night. Will you come and toast the trees?"

"I don't know. I'm getting old and tired for hiking about in the snow."

"I don't believe you're all that old and tired. I saw the pile of wood you've got cut outside."

The kid did not miss much, that was for sure. "That's just the trouble. I got too ambitious and wore myself out."

"Well, I hope you'll come." Linna leaned forward, watching as Verda removed the carefully packed eggs from the basket. "Your hens still not laying?"

"I think they've about given up for the winter," Verda replied. "I'll be relying on you."

"It might be a Miskit," Linna suggested with perfect seriousness. "They can charm any sort of animal, you know. The hens will let them come and steal away the eggs and never even squawk. But if you put a mirror in the coop, then when the Miskit sees itself, it will go away."

"Why would it do that, do you think?"

"I'm not sure. Some people say it's because it thinks there's another Miskit there, and they're shy of each other. My cousin says the Miskit is afraid of getting caught in the mirror, because maybe they think there's another Miskit caught there and they'll get caught too, or maybe because they think they could fall into the mirror like a pool of water. Do you have a mirror? Maybe I could bring you one."

"I don't know if it's good luck to drive a forest spirit off that way. I think I'll try putting out some butter porridge for the Miskit so it won't want to eat so many eggs." There was butter in the basket too, but not as much as she wanted. And her supply of oats was getting low.

"Up to you." Linna's tone made it clear she did not endorse such coddling.

The two of them had tea and biscuits and talked over the news from the village and surrounding farms. The apple sat on the table between them all the while, its intense colour lending a festive brightness to the scene. At last, Linna was well warmed through and ready to return home with her basket full of Verda's concoctions. She practically skipped out the door, and bustled away homeward along the trail that she had trod down through the snow. From the pale sky, gentle flakes sifted down onto the trail, and the girl, and the woods all around.

Verda closed the door. "All right, she's gone."

The cellar door opened, and Fiko crawled out, stretching out the limbs that had been cramped in the space below. He was small and thin for his sixteen years, though lately he seemed to be getting stouter. Soon Verda might have to find him a new hiding place: perhaps she could rearrange the chicken house to fit him in, though she didn't want to disturb the hens too much or they might really stop laying.

Fiko's eyes were drawn immediately to the apple. He picked it up and turned it over in his hands.

"Handsome, isn't it?" Verda said.

Fiko gave a little twitch of acknowledgement, which was all she expected from him. He did not talk much, not since he had turned up on her doorstep a month before, anyway. He never talked about the army or the reason why he deserted, and Verda never asked. She did not ask about what he intended to do in the future either, beyond the understanding they had come to that he would stay until the spring. Most likely he would strike out through the forest to the coast, where there would be many shipmasters looking for sailors at that time of year, and not asking too many questions. In the meantime, absolute secrecy was essential. If he was discovered, both their lives would be forfeit, and anyone else who could be shown to have known about his presence and not reported it would be in peril as well. Verda's cottage was isolated enough to avoid periodic searches by the local garrison, so long as nothing aroused suspicion. Hopefully, Linna would not gossip too much about her woodpile.

Verda poured some more tea and passed a cup and a biscuit to Fiko, who set the apple back down in its place on the table. She got out her mortar and pestle and set about grinding up some herbs that she would need for the next batch of remedies to trade. She was getting short of a few ingredients, and her mind turned to how she could best make substitutions, so that she had almost forgotten Fiko was there when he surprised her by saying softly, "Maybe you should go."

"Go where?"

"Apple night. My mother and sisters ought to be there. You could see if they look all right."

"I expect Linna would have said something if they weren't all right." Verda had worried it might seem odd for her to ask after Fiko's family, with whom she was not especially friendly.

Fiko replied with another twitch and put the teacup up to his lips almost quickly enough to hide the way they twisted down at the corners. Verda returned to her mixing, but her mind was no longer on ingredients.

At last, she said, "Maybe we should both go."

Fiko looked up at her warily.

"We could go masked."

"People would wonder who I am," he murmured.

"Maybe, but they couldn't ask, could they? Bad luck to admit a masker on Apple Night is anything but what they're dressed up to be. And you know sometimes we get outsiders showing up." In truth, that was a good deal more rare now that there were few young men about to make a game of showing up at the celebration of an unsuspecting neighbouring village. But Verda had a good feeling about her plan, especially since there was not going to be another such chance that winter. And she could see hope rising in Fiko's eyes.

They set to work gathering their materials. It was not hard to find rags and straw to wrap about themselves and to cut a couple of masks from old cloth. They shaped some of the straw into two foxy ears and a bushy tail to make Fiko into a Miskit, and wove a crown of pine branches to transform Verda into an Eldenlaird. When all was done, they were quite confident that they were unrecognizable, especially considering that Fiko had grown a handsbreadth at least since his family had seen him last.

The sun was low by the time they set out, but the moon was up. It had stopped snowing, and the trail by which Linna had come and gone could be traced as a gentle furrow. At last, they knew they were nearing the orchard, because they could hear distant noises: voices raised in a chant to the time of makeshift instruments, accompanied by the barking and howling of the village dogs that had come along to join the excitement. The trail brought them to the top of a hill, and then they could also see the lights of torches and lanterns marking the procession that was already circling its way around the orchard, greeting each of the trees and calling upon them to bear well for the coming year.

The view did not last, as their way led back down the hill, but the sounds gradually became louder, until they could truly hear the words of the chants and not just imagine them. There was another hill right on the edge of the orchard, and as they walked up it, the noise sounded so close they almost expected to come out right in the midst of it.

This was not quite the case when they reached the top of the hill. The procession must have just passed by, because it was a short distance off and moving further away. They were close enough to recognize many familiar figures even from behind. There were masked figures scattered amongst the group: some in costumes similar to theirs, and some representing other forest spirits such as the Birkles, with their limbs wrapped in white bark. Most of the people were undisguised, but festively dressed in bright coloured scarves and shawls. Fiko's mother was easily recognized from behind by the shawl embroidered in red and green that she had worn on this night for many years. Verda thought she glimpsed at least one of his sisters dodging about amongst a group of youngsters who were adding further excitement to the event with a game of tag.

But then she looked toward the centre of the orchard, where there were fires burning and pots of cider mulling over them. A few people were needed to mind these, usually the elders who found getting to the orchard and back enough walking for an evening. But this time there was a larger crowd around the fires, and it consisted mostly of soldiers. They must have been given leave to come from the garrison. They were passing ladles of cider about in a chaotic way that suggested they had already had more than enough. Suddenly, Verda's confidence left her. She did not think anyone had seen them yet, still in the shadows of the forest edge. Perhaps it would be best to simply watch for a little while and then turn back. She guessed that Fiko was thinking the same, because he was standing as though frozen in place.

Then a shape broke away from the procession: a low-slung, shaggy shape that bounded over the snow with more enthusiasm than grace. It was a dog, light brown in colour with small folded ears and a great flag of a tail. It was coming directly toward them, and Verda could not think of a single thing to do. Some of the children had already turned to see where it was running. Now others, and adults too, turned to see where the children were looking. By the time the dog had reached Fiko and leapt up to put its paws on his chest and sniff at his chin, the whole procession had paused, and only a few odd voices continued to chant. Fiko could not resist scratching the dog about the shoulders even as he whispered, "Get down, Jomi. Down, girl."

The villagers came toward them, and since it was too late to do anything else, Fiko and Verda walked out into the orchard to meet them, with Jomi happily alongside. The chant had now stopped entirely. If all had gone as planned, somebody ought to have greeted them as forest spirits come to share the revel, but nobody spoke up. Verda thought to herself that they must realize who Fiko was. Jomi had given him away. Instead of being greeted, they would be denounced and handed over to the soldiers.

They stopped just a few feet away from the crowd of familiar faces. Verda wondered which of them would be the first, or whether it would be the soldiers that noticed something was wrong and started asking questions. Nobody old enough to understand the situation was smiling. The only movement was the enthusiastic wagging of Jomi's tail.

A child's shrill voice broke the silence: "That must be a real Miskit. Look how it has charmed the old dog!"

Magically, the faces changed. And then one voice after another called out the traditional greetings for outsiders. The next thing Verda knew she was being led toward the fires, right in among the soldiers, and then passed a ladle full of cider that was pungent and sweet and everything that hot cider should be on a cold night.

The soldiers paid little attention to them. Two of them were wrestling in the snow, and the others were far more interested in the outcome of that match than in two more wearers of quaint country costumes. As Fiko was drinking his share of cider, his mother reached out to touch his shoulder for just a moment and then moved away, but if anyone else noticed that small acknowledgement, they kept it to themself. One of his sisters quietly pulled Jomi aside and tied a scarf around the dog's neck for a leash. The procession resumed, with all its joyful noise, and the Miskit and the Eldenlaird slipped away into the forest.

When Linna came for her next visit, she brought plenty of oats and butter. "We figured you would want those for that butter porridge you were going to try," she said as Verda took them out of the basket. Then she pointed out a carefully wrapped package that had been stowed underneath. "Though some people insist that the best thing for Miskits is cake."

THE TEETH HAVE IT

Rebecca Brae

FLUFFY SNOWFLAKES COATED the windshield faster than the wipers could clear them. The weather report had been right, in a general sense, but a day off in timing. Alberta weather made fools of everyone.

Tess knew it was risky to set out for the cabin a day before a forecasted blizzard, but she was desperate. She needed time alone to decompress before the holiday rush of visiting and schmoozing and too-drunk relatives telling you way more than you ever wanted to know about gout. And, if she just happened to get snowed in and miss the festering-ivities . . . oh well. She was in no mood for any of it. Keeping a bright façade up so you didn't ruin other people's holiday cheer was exhausting at the best of times, and it had definitely not been the best of times lately.

The highway was bad, but at least she could mostly see where the road ended and the ditch began. She set herself up at a safe-ish distance from a truck—far enough away that she had some hope of stopping in an emergency, but not so far that their taillights disappeared behind the curtain of snow.

The truck cooperatively turned onto the same rural road she needed, but keeping the taillights in sight became increasingly hard. It was travelling faster than was safe for her sedan, despite

195

its winter tires, and the road was entirely notional. Her only visual point of reference was the fence posts peeking out of a snow drift to her right. Everything else was a sea of white.

She checked again to make sure her wipers were on the fastest speed. They were. Just like the hundred other times she checked. When she looked up again, the truck's lights flashed bright red and swerved. Tess hit the brakes and ground her teeth as she slid closer. She stopped at an angle in the road mere feet away from their tailgate. As she regained her breath, the truck took off, liberally coating the driver's side window and half her windshield with slush and gravel. Her wipers ground to a halt, unable to move the added weight.

"Fuck, fuck, fuckity-fuck!" She grabbed the snowbrush off the passenger seat and flung her door open. Encountering traffic on these backroads during a blizzard wasn't likely, but it wasn't exactly a comfortable spot to stay for long.

Thanks to the wind, the slush instantly froze solid, and she had to chip it off with the ice scraper. As she leaned across the hood to pry out the wiper blade, she saw a dark patch in the snow a few meters ahead. A small, pointed muzzle lifted for a second and then flopped down.

"Asshole!" She threw a chunk of ice into the storm where the truck had disappeared. "Who hits something and just takes off?" People were horrible.

Visibility was down to about a car length in any direction. What could she do? She wasn't a vet and there was no way she could drive the downed animal to one in this. There was also no way she could leave it to die, cold and alone. It was probably someone's dog. Once the weather improved, she could bring it to a clinic. If it was chipped, they would at least let the owners know that it had been cared for and safe in its last moments.

Tess dug her sleeping bag out from under the massive pile of groceries in the trunk and briefly panicked trying to find the dog again. It was already covered in snow.

Snowflakes hardened to ice pellets and assaulted her eyes as she brushed off its tawny fur and gently wrapped it in the sleeping bag. The dog felt thin for its size, but its chest was still rising and falling, so it was alive. The poor thing must have been lost for a while. She stared sadly at the pert black nose poking out of its cover. This wasn't how anyone wanted their companion found. A bright red spot steamed in the snow when she lifted the unconscious bundle, confirming it had just been hit. She swore again at the thoughtless truck driver. Hitting it had been unavoidable in this mess, no doubt. Leaving it injured to die was inexcusable.

She placed it on the backseat, sure that Reed would know what to do. She bred beautiful retrievers—helped them whelp, trained them, and took care of most of their medical needs. Tess slid into the driver's seat, pulled out her phone, and scrolled down to her contact. Her finger hovered over the call button before harsh reality crashed down. Reed was gone. It had been nearly two months. Fifty-three days filled with so many empty moments like this. She still couldn't bring herself to delete her number. Probably never would.

The whole year had sucked. Family, work, and other disgustingly adult responsibilities pulled her in a million directions to the point where she barely had space to breathe. And then Reed died. They were the same age and had been friends for half their lives. Suddenly, things that used to make sense and seem worthwhile just . . . didn't. Life, for everyone else, barrelled on like a laden train leaving her no time to process what had happened or grieve. Cancer. What a fucking travesty that it could end a life so vibrant.

Tears gathered at the base of her eyes and she swiped them away. Now was not the time to get blurry-eyed. The storm was treacherous enough. She shoved the phone back into her pocket, checked the GPS, and confirmed that she was, in theory, ten minutes from the cabin. She set off slowly as snow-hail pounded her car from the side. The drifts were now high enough that the fence posts were no longer a reliable guide. The truck's tire tracks were long gone, and the shreds of afternoon light able to penetrate the storm were rapidly fading. She turned on her headlights and immediately switched them off, blinking to clear the bright spots floating across her vision.

"Just get to the cabin. Then, we'll figure out what to do," she muttered to herself. "And have a good cry because this is some next level bullshit." If there were any gods, they surely had it out for her. She wanted time to deal with her grief, not acquire more . . . or die. She grimaced as the wind shifted and she momentarily lost sight of her hood.

She drove past the turnoff thanks to her GPS's sluggish refresh, got a tire stuck in the ditch while turning around, and eventually made it back to the cabin's winding driveway. Thankfully, the way was lined on both sides by fir trees, so there was no worry about accidentally bushwhacking. About halfway there, the car started making a deep grinding noise. The instrument panel had no warning lights and it wasn't a sound she'd heard before. She cocked her head, trying to figure out where it was coming from, and caught sight of movement in the rear-view mirror.

Her body tensed as two white orbs flashed in the reflected, low light. The sound she belatedly recognized as growling gained strength and a certain degree of angst. Her passenger was sitting up, leaned awkwardly against the seatback, lips curled around bloodied teeth. The sleeping bag slipped down, revealing long, thin legs and wide paws. This was most certainly not someone's dog. Tess clamped her mouth shut to trap a scream. She'd picked up a coyote. Yup. There was a coyote in her backseat.

She drove on, careful not to make any sudden moves or noises, dividing her attention between the driveway and rear-view mirror. If she stopped the car now, it would get stuck.

Tess hoped there was an afterlife so Reed could see this. Girl would be laughing her ass off. Why did this weird shit always happen? She didn't have the best track record with wildlife, going way back to the bat that got stuck in her hair at camp.

The cabin materialized out of the haze and she had to brake hard. The coyote slid forward, hitting the back of her seat with a loud grunt and a lot of scrabbling. She jammed the gearshift into park and leapt out, slamming the door shut behind her. The animal ran laps around the inside, scratching frantically at the windows, leaving smears of drool and blood over everything. Despite its injuries, it was still lively enough to rip the hanging Cheshire cat plushie off her rear-view in a fit of rage. The mirror succumbed as well, clanging against the dash before it fell into the footwell.

Leaving the coyote in the car was an option, but she couldn't keep the engine running all night. And, if she turned it off, the animal might freeze. She could open the door and let it run away. There was blood coming from its mouth, possibly from the cracked teeth she'd seen through the rear-view, which also meant it probably had a head injury. One of its front legs was crooked and it wasn't putting any weight on it even as it circumnavigated the car, viciously shaking the plushie. Releasing it now would be the safest course, for her. But what hope did a coyote with a broken leg have? Letting it go would be letting it die. Her stomach turned in on itself. She couldn't do it.

The problem of how to get a cranky, injured coyote from the car to the cabin mercifully solved itself. The animal lunged at the driver's side window and knocked itself out. Tess cringed, thinking that couldn't be good on top of whatever head injury it already had, and then realized her opportunity. She flung the door open, grabbed the unconscious canid and carried it like a baby to the cabin door. There was a significant amount of swearing when she realized her keys were still in the ignition. She trudged back, yanked them out while juggling her furry cargo, and then fumbled to find the right one to unlock the cabin door.

Once inside the frigid wooden structure, she laid the animal on the lone couch, a well-used futon that had lived its best life fifteen years ago while she was in university. As she leaned back to stand, the coyote bucked and its mouth clamped down on her forearm. She froze and stared at her arm as a detached "well, shit" feeling enveloped her.

There was no pain, only pressure. A thin rivulet of blood dripped onto the futon mattress. She couldn't tell if it was from the animal or her. An ache in her chest suggested she had been holding a breath in for too long and should probably try breathing again. Pain kicked in as she exhaled. Teeth had definitely broken through her jacket and skin. The coyote's golden eyes lazily opened and closed as if it was struggling to stay awake.

She tried slowly pulling away. It growled and increased the pressure on her arm. Tess wondered who one called when stuck in the middle of nowhere during a blizzard with a coyote gnawing on your arm. 911? She imagined the "hell no" look on the paramedics' faces. And what were the RCMP going to do? Shoot it? Not a comforting thought, for many reasons.

She glared at the coyote. It glared back between extended blinks, content to just hold her arm in its mouth.

Tess wrestled her phone out of her pocket with her free hand and put it on the floor beside where she knelt. Scrolling through her contacts, she came across the cell number her old vet had given when her geriatric pup was close to passing a couple years ago. She had been so kind and compassionate. And cute, but that never developed into anything because the vet had become inextricably bound up in the memory of her lost furry soulmate. Grief . . . what an absolute bastard.

It had only been a couple of years. She might still have the same number. Tess typed out a short message:

Tess >> Hey, been a while, but I need help with a bit of an emergency.

After a few minutes, her phone chirped with an incoming text, and the coyote clamped down again. Tess groaned and waited for her vision to refocus on the screen after the jolt of pain.

Hot Vet Amy << Ummm who is this

Right. She probably never saved me as a contact. Why would she? Or she deleted me. Or just has a new phone. Ugh. Who cares? Just focus on the problem at hand. LOL I punned and didn't even mean to. OMG FOCUS, WOMAN.

Tess >> Sorry. It's Tess. Gregs owner. He was the arthritic, allergic to everything, hound who howled for your liver treats

Hot Vet Amy << Oh yes. New dog? 24 hour emergency clinic is 555-230-6723

Tess >> It's more complicated. sorry but didn't know who else to contact. I remember you helped at some wild animal rehabs. I have an injured coyote

Hot Vet Amy << call RCMP if its a road hazard. Or animal services to report a sighting

Tess >> we're kinda attached,, via its teeth

Hot Vet Amy << ???

Tess >> long story. Someone hit it and I thought it was a dog so I picked it up. Guess that wasn't so long. Anyway, its at the cabin with me. Well, in the cabin, attached to my arm. Think its got a head injury and broken leg. Prob more. Also, how do I get it to let my arm go?

Hot Vet Amy << holy fuk. Are you for real?

Tess >> unfortunately. arms throbbing but doesn't feel like it bit too deep. just wont let go

Another few minutes passed. Tess watched the coyote watching her. Their faces were uncomfortably close, but it showed no sign of altering its toothy interest in her arm.

Hot Vet Amy << you need to call the police or something

Tess >> nobodys coming up here in this storm. I'm at old Joe's place. Bought it 5 or so ago. I'm on my own

Hot Vet Amy << It's a bad idea, but sometimes if you tickle a dogs tongue, it'll open its mouth and release

Tess >> you want me to tickle its tongue? With what?

Hot Vet Amy << a finger . . . one you aren't overly attached too. If you stick it far enough back, they sometimes gag and that can also help

Tess >> Are you serious

Hot Vet Amy << told you it was a bad idea

Tess studied the coyote. Its blinking was more lethargic. One of its eyes was almost swollen shut, but its breathing sounded clear, if fast. Then again, she had no idea how fast coyotes normally breathed.

Tess >> gonna wait a few. its calming down. Then I'll try your terrible finger idea

Hot Vet Amy << not sure I want to know what happens

Hot Vet Amy << no I do. Just please don't sue me if you lose a finger or hand or anything

Hot Vet Amy << for the record I think this is a bad idea and advise against it

Tess >> im wide open to other suggestions

Hot Vet Amy << got nothing. Sorry. I have some tranqs in my bag but cant get out to you

When the coyote's blinks regularly took ten seconds or more, Tess made her move. She slid her index finger in behind her arm and rubbed its tongue. The coyote's eyes shot open, and it let out a coughing growl as it clamped down harder. Against every instinct, she shoved her finger farther back and was rewarded with a sharp cough and head shake that loosened its grip. She shifted her weight and pulled back, finally free, minus half her jacket sleeve and a small strip of skin from her finger.

Tess scooted backward until she bumped against the door. The coyote shook the scrap of jacket, then went cross-eyed, groaned, and flopped its head down on its paws. She stood on shaking legs, turned the door handle behind her, and ducked outside, slamming the door without turning her back on the belligerent guest.

Ice pellets abraded her face and bare arm as she leaned

against the door and sank onto her butt. Cold seeped through her jeans and instantly numbed her nether regions. The storm did not look like it planned on letting up any time soon.

She laughed, then cried, then laugh-cried until she wasn't sure if this was all terribly funny or tragic. In the end, she decided it was both. She rubbed her arm with snow to clean off the blood. The coyote's teeth had only poked through the skin in a couple places. Most of the pain came from a lovely array of blooming bruises.

Sleeping in the car, turning it on occasionally to warm up, seemed the safest course. She probably had about a quarter tank to spare for heating. How much gas did starting the car repeatedly use? She'd have to make it work.

The cabin had no electricity and wasn't heated, but the walls were insulated. The coyote wouldn't freeze. It was the best she could do.

She reached into her jacket pocket and came up empty.

"Fuck." She checked around her butt in the snow and swore again. Her keys must have fallen out inside.

Tess hefted herself upright and laid her forehead against the door. "Please don't eat me."

She opened the door an inch and when nothing attacked, she opened it further and peeked inside. The coyote was lying on its side, still on the futon, eyes closed. Her phone lay on the floor beside the couch where she had forgotten it, and her keyring was near the halfway point. The animal let out a snore and twitched its nose in irritation.

The cabin was a one room structure with an antique wood-burning stove at its centre. There was a small kitchen and cold-hole pantry to her right, a creaky old double bed against the far wall, and the occupied futon was on her left. The car was still an option if she could retrieve her keys, but the gas situation was concerning.

What was probably the most ill-conceived plan of her life formed in her mind. Considering she'd just chauffeured a coyote around the countryside and stashed it in the only shelter within miles, that said a lot. She hoped it didn't become her last terrible life choice.

Tess kicked the door with a loud *bang*, ready to shut it if the animal made any aggressive moves. Its one good eye flew open and there was a slight lip curl, but nothing more. Eventually, it laid its head back down and the wary orb closed.

She slid inside, leaving the door open a crack, tiptoed to her keys, and picked them up without taking her eyes off the animal. The jingle of metal elicited a slit of a look and a disgruntled snort. She backed to the door and breathed a heavy sigh of relief when she stood safely out in the storm again.

It took three trips to grab all her supplies and toss them into the cabin. She left the meat in the trunk. The storm would ensure it didn't spoil. Each time she opened the cabin door she expected to be greeted by a flying coyote. Thankfully, each time it was still snoring away on its futon.

When she closed the door behind her for the last time, she heard her phone vibrating against the wooden floorboards and the coyote growling in its sleep. After a few seconds, it vibrated again, eliciting a louder feral remonstration.

Tess grabbed the hooked walking stick she kept by the door and cautiously approached. When she was within reach, she used the stick to slide the phone closer and retrieved it just in time to muffle another vibration. She stuffed it into her pocket and set about stocking the stove with wood.

Her fingers were numb and clumsy. It took a few tries to unlatch the handle on the heavy cast iron door. Lighting the matches she kept by the wood pile was beyond her dexterity, and she resorted to using the emergency fire starter flare from her hiking backpack. Bright orange flames burst to life in the stove's belly and she retreated to the kitchen, as far away from her cantankerous guest as she could get.

The phone vibrated against her leg and she belatedly pulled it out. There were five unread messages.

Hot Vet Amy << You okay?

Hot Vet Amy << This isn't funny. Im really worried

Hot Vet Amy << Please reply

Hot Vet Amy << I'm calling 911

Hot Vet Amy << They can do dick all right now. Plan B

Tess grimaced and fired off a quick text.

Tess >> Sorry. Everything good. Lost track of phone

She stared at the screen for a few minutes but there was no reply. Stifling her anxiety about actually talking to Amy, she tried a voice call. No answer. Twice.

The stove quickly heated the small cabin and feeling crept back into her fingers. Numbness turned into a dull throb but at least all her appendages were moveable again. The coyote's breaths became deeper and steadier, its snores long and drawn out. Occasionally, a whimper escaped as its broken leg jerked in the depths of some canid dream.

Tess set about dealing with the problems she could conceivably fix. It was now fully dark outside and she lit the antique oil lantern she had inherited from her grandma. Warm light embraced the room. The old brass lamp always filled the aching holes in her heart. Too many precious souls like her grandma and Reed and Greg were gone, but the beautiful moments shared in this light seemed alive once more in its dancing flame.

She pulled her mind back to the present and found the first aid kit she kept in the kitchen. The bruises on her arm were darker now. There was a clear outline of the coyote's jaw with deeper purple spots from longer teeth and several punctures near the front on the top and bottom.

She disinfected her arm with rubbing alcohol, relieved that nothing looked bad enough to warrant stitches. A rabies shot and antibiotics loomed on the horizon, but she'd received worse breaking up a fight at the dog park. Greg never could bring himself to back down. That was a trait they shared.

After adding a couple of period pads to cover the open wounds on top and bottom, she wrapped a whole roll of gauze around her arm. Not only did the pads provide absorbency for the newly reopened and bleeding spots, but they were great padding if the coyote decided to chomp down on her again. The chonky mass was as much a shield as a bandage.

Next, she rolled the five-gallon water jug from the door to the kitchen and hefted it onto the counter with considerable difficulty. Her adrenaline rush was long gone, leaving her muscles as useful as a pile of mush. She had started this ill-conceived adventure exhausted. Now she was far, far beyond that. She wanted to lie down on the floor and not move for a week. But that wasn't in the cards. The coyote would eat her.

She filled one of Greg's old bowls with water and carefully placed it on the end of the couch as near the coyote's head as she dared. Greg would be incensed to see his bowl offered to a howling nemesis. Whenever they had spent the night out here, he would launch into competitive howling contests with the area's coyotes. It was a good thing their closest neighbour was miles away. Gods, she missed that pup.

The coyote never even cracked an eye when the floorboard next to the futon creaked under her weight. Despite their tumultuous relationship, she felt sorry for the creature and was determined to help if she could. No. It was more than that. She was overly invested because she hadn't been able to do anything to help Reed. Nobody could. By the time they found the cancer, it had already spread too far. But, recognizing the futility of her motivation did nothing to change how she felt.

She didn't know if the coyote's deep sleep was a good or bad turn. It had to have a concussion. For a person with one, you were supposed to wake them up every so often. She decided to let it sleep for now, and then after an hour or so, from a distance, make a noise to see if it responded.

Tess grabbed her sleeping bag and laid down on the floor between the door and stove. She wasn't brave enough to risk the bed, which was farther from the exit. The bag smelt of musk and pee and blood, but she didn't care. It was dry-ish and warm. She set her phone alarm for an hour and closed her eyes.

Every hour, she got up, stoked the fire, and added another log. The first time, she had to clang the metal rod she used to open the stove against the chimney to wake the coyote up. It looked startled and grumpy, which she took as a good sign. The second time, she woke up to it lapping water from the bowl. It turned to glare at her before flopping its head back down and commencing snoring. Sometime within the next hour she rolled over to find it pressed against her side. Its breathing sounded more ragged and strained. She was so tired, she just accepted its presence and decided the fire had enough wood to last another hour.

TESS GROGGILY SHIFTED her legs, wondering how her sleeping bag always managed to get so twisted up on itself. And wet.

She levered herself up on an elbow and realized the coyote was sprawled across her thighs, head hung to one side and tail to the other. It was panting, shallow and fast. One golden eye stared out at nothing and showed no reaction to her movement. A wet spot spread under where its tongue lolled from its mouth.

She stared for a long moment. Then, something inside finally broke and tears burned down her cheeks. The damn thing was dying on her. A lifetime of grief crashed down like a tidal wave. It always ended the same. She was tired, oh so tired, of sitting with death. Just once, she wished she could beat the shit out of the relentless fiend and send it away, empty-handed.

Without realizing what she was doing, she ran a thumb over the velvet soft spot where its short ear fur met the coarse fur on its neck. When it didn't pull away, she sat up and gently stroked its head and back. She had never seen a coyote this close and couldn't get over how huge its pointy ears were. They looked like twin furry sails against the dark blue fabric of her sleeping bag.

Her tears sank into its thick ruff as she cradled it in her lap. She did her best to steady her chaotic breathing while she cried. She didn't want to shake it and cause more pain. It had almost made it through the night.

"I'm sorry," she whispered to the broken little body. "I'm so sorry."

Something approaching a whine came from it. Fur blurred and pinked, and there was suddenly a boy, maybe four years old, laying on her. Tess blinked, then looked away and back again. Still a kid.

Dazed blue eyes blinked at her. "Who're you?" He tried to sit up and winced, pulling his left arm closer to his chest. A yellow healing bruise surrounded one eye and part of his forehead. He looked hurt, but nowhere near as badly as the coyote.

His expression turned suspicious. "Where's Mommy and Daddy? I feel funny." And with that, he rolled on his side, spewed a massive torrent of vomit across the floor all the way to the door, and passed out.

Tess gazed around at the cabin, wondering if she was stuck in some kind of bizarre dream. There was no coyote hidden anywhere she could see. Just a tiny human contentedly snuggled in her lap.

Her overloaded brain ruefully hung up an "out of order" sign. Was she hallucinating the kid? Or had she hallucinated the coyote? Or did the coyote really become a kid? Were either of them real?

Not knowing what else to do, she folded her sleeping bag over the boy, who was now snoring louder than the coyote had. She was about to extricate herself when the cabin door burst open with a gust of winter air.

A vaguely human-shaped figure stood outlined against the storm, covered from head to toe in snow-encrusted winter gear. Two dark eyes peered out from a balaclava. A rifle muzzle swept the room and ended pointed at the floor in front of the interloper's boot-clad feet.

They pulled their balaclava and hood off, revealing a gorgeous round brown face and a long black braid that spilled halfway down their chest.

"Amy?" Tess choked out her name. She wasn't sure her brain would ever recover from the mental whiplash of tonight.

"Tess. Good Lord. Are you okay?" The vet kicked the door shut, deftly side-stepped the swath of vomit, and laid her rifle down. She unzipped the jacket portion of her one-piece snowsuit and let it hang around her waist. Underneath, she wore a black form-hugging woollen turtleneck. She looked like 007 transformed into a glorious alpine goddess.

Tess stared at her wide-eyed. "This is the hottest thing that's ever happened to me."

Amy blinked, obviously confused. "Did you hit your head?"

"No." Tess was sure there was a stupid grin plastered across her face but couldn't do anything about it. Her mental faculties were well and truly out of commission. "I'm fine. Physically, anyways. No rescue needed."

Amy sat back on her heels and raised an eyebrow. "I'm just here for the coyote, Ma'am." Her serious expression crumbled and she laughed. "Kidding. Maybe I jumped the gun a bit, but you didn't respond and . . . all I could think about was you up here bleeding to death after the coyote bit your finger off."

Tess wiggled her fingers at her. "All intact. Your plan worked perfectly. And I did text you back . . . and called. You never answered."

Amy dug around inside her snow pants, pulled out her phone, and sighed. "Sorry about that. I couldn't hear it ringing." She stood up. "I brought some supplies. You need a med kit or is it just the coyote that needs attention?"

"I'm good." She held up her bandaged arm. "I'm pretty self

sufficient. Just not with wild animals." Tess glanced down at the bundle in her lap. "And . . . that part has . . . changed." She sucked in a breath between clenched teeth and pulled the sleeping bag back, half expecting to see the coyote. The boy grumbled. "Hear me out. I swear I haven't been drinking or doing drugs. But . . . the coyote . . . is a kid. It didn't used to be."

Amy's eyebrows shot up as she looked between Tess and the boy. "Easton? What the hell?"

"Pretty much what I've been asking myself all night. Wait . . . you know him?"

She nodded and examined him more closely. "He's injured, but the switch probably mitigated the worst of it."

Tess tried to make sense of that and failed. "Huh?"

Anxiety etched a deep furrow across the vet's forehead. "You probably did or said something that made him switch back. Thank God. The young ones have a hard time remembering who they are, especially after a trauma like this. They need reminding. Poor little guy."

"Amy, I'm so very lost here. What the fuck is going on?"

"Sorry. I'm not explaining well. I'm just so damn glad you picked him up. If you hadn't been there . . ." She wrapped Tess in a firm embrace, then pulled back and whipped her phone out. "I gotta let his parents know." She retreated a short distance and gazed at the storm through the cabin's lone window as she talked to whoever answered her call.

Tess either couldn't hear or couldn't understand what was being said. Her brain was so frazzled she couldn't tell which. She gingerly extricated herself from the soiled sleeping bag. The kid slept on, snorting once as he yanked the sleeping bag over his head.

She sniffed her shirt and grimaced. Vomit and coyote piss was an eye-wateringly intense combination. She dragged a hand through her matted hair, suddenly self-conscious in the presence of the other woman's epic natural beauty and competence.

Amy came back shaking her head. "They had no idea he was even gone. They are so grateful to you . . ." She let out a long breath. "I have to get him to their healer. He needs to be seen by someone more knowledgeable about their anatomy."

Tess swallowed. "So, he was a coyote, but now he's a kid?"

Amy squeezed her arm. "This is a lot. Just know you did the

right thing and because of that, Easton is alive. Noal hooked up the cargo sled when I borrowed his snowmobile. I could use your help getting Easton bundled up and strapped into it." She squinted at the ceiling for a second, thinking. "Roundtrip will take about an hour and a half. Add in a bit for the handoff and random issues. I'll be back in just under two hours. Then, we can talk."

"You're going out again? In this?"

"I'm a rural vet. Give me a GPS and a snowmobile and I can get anywhere." She shrugged her jacket on.

"You promise you'll come back?"

Amy gently cupped Tess's face and looked directly into her eyes. "I promise."

IN HOPES OF getting in a nap while waiting, Tess dug through the previous owner's storage chest and retrieved some quilts that were probably older than her parents. There was no napping. Just a lot of cleaning, pacing, and snacking.

The intrepid vet was good to her word. She returned in exactly an hour and fifty minutes, looking cold and exhausted but infinitely less worried.

Amy shucked off her snowsuit and made a beeline for the bed.

Tess followed, sitting uncomfortably on the edge as Amy sprawled on her back with a satisfied groan. She held out a blanket, and Amy immediately tucked it up under her chin, asking, "Did I see BBQ chips over there?"

Tess nodded and retrieved the bag from the kitchen counter. "I have some questions."

"I thought you might." Amy's hand snaked out from under the blanket and snagged a chip. "I might have some answers." She popped the salty morsel into her mouth and reached for another.

Tess held out her bandaged arm. "Am I going to turn into a coyote? Or werewolf? Or furry?"

"I can't speak to the furry part, but I can unequivocally say the whole getting-bitten-by-a-shifter-turns-you-into-one is a total fallacy. I stumbled across the community the same way you did. More than one has sunk a tooth into me and I'm still just a boring old human. It's an inherited trait, not a communicable disease."

"Okaaay." That was one massive weight off. "But there's people out there, like Easton, who go from being people to coyotes? That's a thing?"

"Not just coyotes. There's different heritage lines." She paused. "Umm. You know not to talk to anyone else about this, right?"

Tess gave her an incredulous look. "Who would believe me?"

"You'd be surprised. The wizards have spies everywhere. I'm safe to talk to, obviously, and Easton's family. They're kind of set on me bringing you over tomorrow, by the way. Nothing to worry about. They just really want to thank you—"

"Wizards? What the . . ."

"Ugh," Amy scowled. "Don't get me started on those assholes."

Tess fell silent, trying to wrap her mind around the idea of shifters and wizards existing. She gave up. It was late. She was tired. And this whole night was beyond comprehension. "I don't know if I can handle visiting anyone tomorrow. How is Easton doing?"

"Just let me know how you feel in the morning. I'm sure I can put them off for another day. And the little rascal is sore, but he'll be okay. The healer said he'll be out of shifting commission for a couple weeks, but should be back to his naughty, escape artist self in no time. I hope you don't mind if I spend the rest of the night here. Don't think I've got another trip through this storm in me."

"I can't believe you made it up here the first time, let alone out and back again." Tess pulled another blanket from the pile at the end of the bed and laid down beside her. Sleep wouldn't come anytime soon, but she could at least go through the motions. Hopefully, her brain would take the hint and gear down.

"Just another night in the glamorous life of a country vet. I'll take you back to town after we visit Easton's family."

Tess groaned. "I was really hoping to get snowed in and miss Christmas dinner this year. I always end up ricocheting between one distant relative and the next, wishing they had brought their dogs so I could escape outside with them. But with your snowmobile . . . I guess that's out."

Amy turned to look at her, bringing their faces so close, Tess could smell the cinnamon gum she had been chewing.

"You were going to play hooky? Now there's an idea I can get behind. No horribly uncomfortable dinner. No politely telling

Uncle Ricky for the hundredth time to go fuck himself when he starts complaining about how I abandoned his blacksmith shop twenty years ago to follow my dreams. Maybe Noal's snowmobile ran out of gas and stranded us up here."

Tess sucked in a sharp breath and Amy patted her arm.

"It didn't. Don't worry. I've got two spare gas tanks that I topped up at the healer's, but only she knows that. And my practice is closed this week, notwithstanding the odd shifter emergency." Her eyes twinkled in the flickering lantern light and her expression suggested restrained glee . . . and possibly something more.

Maybe this was the start of a new friendship. Or something deeper. Tess had no idea what Amy's orientation was. Either way, it sounded wonderful, and she had many, many more questions about shifters and wizards. But . . .

"Here's the thing. I'd love to spend time with you, but I came up here to work through some shit that's going on in my life. I lost a friend a few months ago and I don't think I'm up to being a fun companion. I . . . am probably going to cry a lot." She was proud of herself for saying exactly what she was feeling. Old Tess would have pretended everything was fine, pushed her feelings and needs to the background, and fake-cheerfully invited her along for the week.

Amy slid an arm under Tess and pulled her in for a hug. "Reed. I heard. She used to bring her dogs in for their yearly shots . . . until she insisted I show her how to do them so she didn't have to pay the injection fee." She chuckled. "She was stubborn and quick as a whip. She should have been a vet."

Emotion clogged Tess's throat, so she just nodded. Reed would have been a fantastic vet. In another lifetime, maybe that would happen. She had never wanted to believe in reincarnation more. So many chances and choices had been taken out of her friend's hands. She did everything for everybody else, at huge personal cost. Tess had promised herself, and Reed, that she wouldn't do the same. That was partly why she was out here. To give herself the mental space to really think about what *she* wanted out of life, not just what everyone else expected her to want. For the most part, her friends and family meant well, but she could feel herself starting to suffocate under everyone else's needs.

Amy's warm brown eyes peered at her worriedly. "I'm sorry. Truly."

"Me too." Tess started to wipe away her gathering tears, then stopped and let them fall.

"I totally understand if you want to be alone. But, if you'd like someone to cry with, I'm your girl. There's some heavy stuff going down in my life, too. I don't want to encroach on your space or grief, but I'm here if you want a friend to share it with. And I rarely bite, unlike random wild animals you might pick up on the roadside." She snort-laughed. "I can't believe you did that."

"For the record, I really thought it was someone's dog. Poor Easton. I'm so glad he's okay." She wrapped an arm around Amy, returning her hug. "I think I'd like you to stay."

"If you need me to leave at some point, just tell me. I grew up with two sisters and a brother. I know how important alone time is." Amy leaned in and kissed a tear rolling down her cheek. Her lips were warm and soft and perfect.

AMY BURST INTO the cabin with the same gusto she always did. Tess's heart melted every single time. Their week had flown by in quiet companionship, heartfelt talks, and a very enlightening trip to visit Easton and his family.

Her world still wasn't right. Reed was gone and that cut to her heart would always be there. But this grief wasn't a weakness. It was a fire burning in her veins that carried her through a night of exhaustion and fear. She had been there to lend that strength to someone in the moment they most needed it. Even at the edge of death, Easton was able to transform and ease his pain. Maybe there was hope for her as well.

Despite Amy's declaration that she had time off, this was the second emergency the vet had attended. Once she stripped off her snowsuit, Tess handed her a glass of red wine and kissed her cheek. "Merry Christmas. How's the wolfdog doing?"

"Fine. It just had a piece of bone stuck between its teeth. They thought it might need surgery, but I got it out with the help of a distracting hunk of steak and a pair of pliers." Amy sipped her wine and sighed. "My little introverted heart has never looked forward to Christmas Eve so much." She held up a cloth bag. "I borrowed a couple steaks from the wolfdogs' freezer at the sanctuary and some cookies from the staff kitchen. I'll replace them next week."

Tess rubbed her hands together in delight and set the frying pan on the stovetop with a generous dollop of butter. "I didn't think I'd be able to face this Christmas at all, but thanks to the storm, it's the break I absolutely needed. Seclusion, steak, and wine. New holiday tradition?"

Amy laughed and slid her free arm around Tess's waist for a quick hug. "Don't forget hugs."

"Perfect." Tess pulled her over to the futon and snuggled up to her side. Life was weird. Far more so than she could ever have imagined. But, despite all the confusion, grief, and pain, the beautiful moments were worth fighting for.

"The Teeth Have It" is dedicated to Toby, forever in my heart. Her sarcasm, wit, and friendship are dearly missed. I hope you are free and running with your pack.

SHIFTING GEARS

V. F. LeSann

"HOLD UP . . . WHAT do you mean?" I asked, trying to swallow the rush of panic lodged in the back of my throat.

Cassie paused mid-swipe with her makeup brush, looking at me through the mirror, waiting for the punchline. She raised an eyebrow and repeated herself, slower this time. "I said: 'hey Luc, when we go to my parents' for their big dinner on Saturday, make sure you bring your green jacket'." She daubed the brush into another palette of powder. "Jodie and you can have your pub night another time this month."

"Sure, right, but I thought we were supposed to go over there for Christmas dinner?" I begged my voice not to crack.

"Mmhmm, and my family always does their dinner the Saturday before so my brother can work in the ER during the holidays." She sighed, again looking at me through the mirror. "I confirmed this with you the afternoon you helped me move my fridge from the apartment. Remember? You said you had the night off."

I scrubbed my sweating palms down the seams of my jeans. The vague ghost of a conversation burst into memory when I'd lifted the new fridge out of Cassie's old apartment, kicking along the flat-tired dolly that wasn't doing the trick. Absent *yups* and *no problems* while rushing and sneaking paranoid glances down

215

empty hallways, bare-knuckling a beast of Freon and mercury to the stairs. Obviously, I'd been lost in my own thoughts about the scary possibility of trying to move in with her for real and not paying as much attention as I should've been.

Indeed, I did have the night off, because of course I did. I had to.

She swivelled around fully to study me, her expression somewhere between amusement and—much worse—earnest hurt. "You actually forgot. You absolute jerk. My dad already thinks I'm making you up . . ."

My heart lurched, muscling through past my rising panic, and I took a knee next to her. (*Proposal pose,* my brain helpfully filled in. Definitely not the time.)

"No, I didn't," I said, infusing it with 100-proof sincerity. It was the truth. The mental Post-It note was clear in my mind, bright red and underlined: *First Christmas dinner with Cassie's family, do NOT fuck it up.* What I hadn't remembered was the exact date. "Believe me, this means a lot to me."

She eyed me, still dubious, but the tension was easing out of her shoulders. "Okay, so we're good?"

"Better than good," I said, tuning out the panic-screech echoing through the back of my mind and the big neon flashing *HERE COMES DISASTER* sign. "I'll be there. Green jacket, wine, in all my boyfriend-who-totally-exists glory."

Her expression broke into an excited smile, and she threw her arms around my neck, snuggling in to kiss me under the ear. All those big, bright disaster signs dissolved like spun sugar beneath the scent of her perfume. "You scared me, Luc."

"I guess I'd better make it up to you, huh?" I said, and pulled back just enough to kiss her properly, making it my personal mission to demolish the lipstick she'd just put on.

It was only later, walking home under the bright, accusing stars, it really became obvious that I couldn't exactly reschedule December's full moon.

"THIS IS WILDLY stupid," Jodie said. "Top of the list in the stupidest things you've done."

I gave a one-shouldered half-assed shrug. My smile felt dopey even to me while I was wearing it. "Cassie makes me a little brave."

"That girl makes you a doe-eyed moron." Jodie had her hand on her hip and jabbed me with a crescent wrench.

"Hey!" I stepped away from the assault to my stomach. Jodie was less than half my height, but filled her coveralls to the brim with muscle so I wasn't interested in letting her get carried away with that wrench. "I think it's still doable, if you're ready as my backup."

"El burro sabe más que tú," she muttered, eyeing me warily with an accompanied headshake that transformed her into her eighty-year-old grandmother before my eyes. Jodie's hands were on her hips, with the offending wrench still gripped tightly in her dominant hand—if I was a betting man, I'd wager that she was a few minutes of frustration from winging it at my head. "Listen, lobo loco, when people lose some brain-cells over a girl, we're usually talking shit like flash mobs and marriage proposals at live wrestling and, like, couples' yoga retreats, or matching tattoos. When guys like *you* get stupid, there's a potential body count."

It took some of the wind out of my sails, but the immovable bit of guts at the heart of me, the part of me that had always looked at life like it was something I could run down and devour, that part wasn't budging.

"I can make it work," I insisted. "It'll be safe. I'll swing in with a bottle of wine, make a little small talk, charm the parents, stay for a drink, and make my graceful escape when the appetizers come out. I'll be back here and locked up safe before the sun's even set."

"So, five o'clock?" Jodie said wryly.

"What?"

"It's December, loco. In a northern-ass latitude. Sunset's 'round five." Jodie folded her arms and leaned against the side of the van that had more parts outside than inside at this point. "Maybe do lunch instead?"

Something inside me howled at the unfairness of it all, before settling back into that red-hot determination to get this right. "Fuck. When's moonrise?"

"9:25 p.m.," Jodie answered without hesitation. She gave a shrug and turned back to the van, using her foot to pull the rolling creeper alongside her. "One of us has to give a shit about your well-being, hermano."

Guilt slithered through me. "I give a shit. I just . . ."

". . . want to do something crazy because you're crazy about her," Jodie finished for me, giving me a brief, sympathetic grin, and levered herself back down on the creeper, pushing back with her legs to disappear beneath the van again. "I get it, I do," she added, her voice muffled by the Frankensteined chassis. "I ever tell you I bought a backup ring before proposing, in case Sarah didn't like the first one? And you *know* I was living on ramen and discount macaroni."

I snorted, moving to poke through the mini-fridge. "That's cute."

"Yeah, it was until I couldn't return the second one, so I gave her two." Jodie sighed. "Five-eighths socket, and rear lift."

I retrieved the tool off the workbench and plopped it into her waiting hand, moving to the back of the van and lifting it a few inches higher than the jack was set.

"Good." She craned her neck to peek an eye out at me from under the bumper. "Look," she said, "I'd be three percent more comfortable if we had a backup plan. Do they have dogs? Like the small prissy ones people put in purses? Just shoot me a text SOS, like Code: Red October, if shit's bad, and I'll take a pass through the neighbourhood. Nothing gets suburban-folk riled up like spotting a bobcat in the Burbs, especially when they have those purse dogs!"

Laughing, I used my free hand to open the beer I'd taken from the fridge. "Jodie, you have one of those 'purse dogs'."

"Diablo? Bite your tongue! She's never been in a purse!"

"But she's a Yorkie . . ."

"Absolute garbage, dios mío!" Jodie hammered, drowning out her arguments under a clanking racket. "Drop," she said finally, as the offending rusted bolt skittered from under the van.

I lowered the vehicle frame back onto the jack and took a seat on the workbench nearby.

"You're charming when you want to be, and Cassie's pretty much got cartoon bluebirds fluttering around her head when she looks at you," Jodie offered, levering herself out from under the van to fix me with a serious look. "You'll knock their socks off. I just need you to remember that in the great rock-paper-scissors contest of the universe: wolf beats love. Every single time.

Promise you'll keep that in mind."

It was true. The wolf didn't stop because of wishes or hope or clean living. You couldn't bargain with it, couldn't bribe it, couldn't even slow it down. You'd have more luck arm wrestling the wind.

"I promise," I said, shooting her a reassuring grin as she slid back under the van.

And at the time, I really had meant it.

Jodie's phone started to ring and I moved to grab it from the workbench for her.

"Don't answer that," she warned.

"Why?"

"It's probably abuela calling to yell about your *dinner choices.*"

"What?! Bullshit," I leaned over the phone to see a picture of Jodie and her grandmother flash on the screen. "How does she know that?"

Jodie shrugged, wiping her hands and taking the phone. "Some questions we don't want the answers to, lobo."

Jodie answered the phone and rushed out of the room, her nervous voice disappearing with her. "No, he can't hear me right now, abuela."

"SORRY ABOUT BAXTER and Trixie," Cassie apologized, sliding a glance through the tempered glass of the front door that glittered with rainbows from the bright entryway chandelier. "They've never done that before."

The *they* in question were the two potato-sized attack dogs currently being jailed for bursting through the door and tearing at my pants with ferocious yips. The first impression I had of Cassie's father was a flash of a strained smile beneath a greying moustache as he scooped up two ferocious shih tzus and disappeared with one tucked under each arm. The door closed promptly behind them and Cassie and I were left waiting outside.

Giving Cassie a winning smile, I looped her in for a hug. "It's fine. You know dogs, they take a while to get used to new people. I don't mind."

Over her shoulder I watched the sky dive into molten hues giving way to night.

"Besides, we had to get the weirdness out of the way. There's always something and now that it's over, we can get to dinner."

I could feel her smile on my chest. "You're so stupid."

"I'd prefer cheesy."

The dusk barely lasted a blink in the winter months, and no matter how hard I wished, sunset always gave way to the full moon night. But it was still hours until moonrise, plenty of breathing room, and I tried to ignore the sound of a ticking clock my imagination kept feeding me.

When the door opened again, I could still hear the faint cacophony of whines and barks filtered through walls and closed doors. Cassie's father stood grinning and dusting off his hands like he'd slayed a dragon.

"Handled!" he announced, then stuck his hand out to shake mine, reeling me in to clap me on the shoulder when I took it. "Well, here's the guy!"

"Present and accounted for," I returned. His hands were about as callused as mine and I only had a couple inches on him, which was rare for me. He looked like a man who had worked, the edges only softening a little when work turned into dabbling as the grey hairs outnumbered the rest.

"Dad, Luc . . . Luc, Dad," Cassie introduced, pointing at each of us like we couldn't have figured it out. Her smile hovered somewhere in between amusement and serious nerves, and I suddenly realized—full moon or not—I was prepared to move heaven and earth to ensure I made a good impression.

"Call me Fred," he said, giving my shoulder another friendly whack before letting me go. "Come on in, come on in! Rita's been tearing up the kitchen all afternoon. Wouldn't let me taste-test a thing until you got here either, I'll have you know . . ."

We stepped into the front hall and were assailed by the scent of holiday dinner so thick it was like running into a particularly delicious wall, all roasting meat and spice, cloves and cinnamon, sage and rosemary. To my horror, the part of me that wasn't supposed to be on stage until much later tonight cracked a gleaming eye somewhere deep inside, raising a long toothy muzzle to steal a snoutful of that scent for itself, rumbling with interest. That wasn't a good sign. I tried to steady myself with a deep breath, which in retrospect was just about the worst possible thing I could've done. I didn't realize I'd grabbed hold of

Cassie's hand until she was shooting me a puzzled smile.

"You good?" she mouthed, following Fred further into the house.

The banister to the upstairs was wrapped in fake garland and glittering lights that set my head swimming like expensive drugs were kicking in.

"Totally," I mouthed back, with what I hoped was a reassuring nod.

An excited squeak interrupted the stern mental talk I was about to have with my feral side as a woman came rushing out of the kitchen, beaming up at me. If I had a couple inches on Fred, I must've had a solid foot and a half on the woman who was obviously Rita. She launched herself at Cassie, wrapping her in a tight hug that seemed to squeeze the laughter right out of her, then turned her attention to me. Her sweater was the cutest fashion disaster I'd ever seen, bright felt reindeer up on their hind legs decorating a sequin tree. The monster in the heart of me huffed a laugh.

Go back to sleep, I pleaded silently.

Funny prey, it rumbled back at me, coiling down into itself once more. I really hoped it was talking about the reindeer.

"Oh my goodness!" Rita exclaimed, "And this must be Luc. It's so good to meet you! Cassie's been talking my ear off about you."

I chuckled and glanced at Cassie to see if she was blushing, but she just grinned, unabashed, and I fell a little bit more in love right then and there.

"It's great to meet you guys too. I brought some wine. Wasn't really sure what went with what," I said, handing over the bottle casually like I hadn't spent far too long agonizing over the right amount to spend on it.

"It's wine," said the last person wandering out of the kitchen to bottle-neck the doorway a little further. "I'm pretty sure it pairs nicely with 'food'."

Though I was meeting him for the first time, I recognized Erik's voice from the nightly phone calls between him and Cassie. The ER tech out of med school, two years ahead of Cassie, and the one whose charitable scheduling was responsible for this meal ending up on the full moon. He stared at me like he could see through me, right to my organs and the pacing wolf between my ribs.

"Well," Rita said, cutting the tension with a chuckle, "at least Cassie brings her partner to dinner. Be damned if we'll ever meet Cameron."

"He's a pilot, mom. The holidays are busy, for both of us."

"Besides," Cassie smirked, "Cam got a chance to fly to Cancún this weekend. So, you know, choices were made."

"Erik-Justin, did you have a chance to take us to Cancún?" Fred piped up.

Erik was on the ropes now and the glare he shot Cassie reminded me so much of family dinner at Jodie's I almost laughed.

"I picked up a shift tomorrow," he protested weakly, "I don't have much seniority . . ."

"I think we might have to go over your head and deal with Cameron ourselves," Rita chided, beckoning us into the kitchen. "Sun-warm beaches in the middle of winter! What would a mother have to do to get a son that appreciated her?"

"What about you, Luc? What do you bring to the table?" Fred asked with a chuckle.

It was two beats before I even registered the question. My inner Lon Chaney Jr. was rushing centre stage before his cue, which left me scrambling to charm up a reasonable answer. "No free tropical vacations here, but I can fix most anything with a motor."

"Oh, wonderful! Hey Fred, tell him about the sound the Jeep's been making . . ."

"Mom!" Cassie pleaded.

"I'm teasing, baby," Rita said, adding a cheerful "mostly" under her breath. "Come on, everybody into the kitchen. I've also had to smell this all day with minimal snacking."

As soon as I stepped into the kitchen proper, I knew I was in trouble. If the smell of the meal had been distracting, the sight of it was torture. A massive picture-perfect turkey lay glistening and steaming on a tray on the counter, nestled around with roast vegetables, accompanied by a tureen of fluffy golden yams and an honest-to-God gravy boat. The wolf inside me opened both eyes, standing and stretching, nosing the air, and everything in the kitchen suddenly took on that crisp HDTV quality that meant he was looking out through my eyes. Which meant that, if anyone was looking at me, they'd be the wrong goddamn colour.

"Monster-mode", Jodie called it.

I whipped out my phone, staring at my screensaver with desperate concentration, gnawing on the inside of my cheek and scrambling for control, begging the wolf to settle.

Eat the bird, it taunted. *Sink your teeth in. One taste! Just one taste, quick while it's hot!*

The mental image of me hunkered on the countertop tearing into Christmas dinner with bare hands and teeth forced a horrible wonky noise from me. My sheer panic overwhelmed the grumbling wolf long enough for me to reclaim my eyes, the world fuzzing back to normal.

"I . . . I'm so sorry, but I can't actually stay for very long," I said, before I'd actually meant to.

Cassie's stunned "what?" was nearly lost under the chorus of "oh nos" and "why nots" from the others.

"This looks amazing," I said truthfully. "But . . . it's just that . . ."

I've got this little issue going on where I'm about to go Big Bad Wolf on your perfect Good Housekeeping centrefold spread. I don't trust myself, and I trust Mister Fuzzy running through my bloodstream even less.

Cassie's expression was flickering between confusion, betrayal, and disbelief like someone changing channels—all expressions demanding an answer.

"I'm . . . vegan," I blurted.

The wolf flopped onto its back, howling with laughter. Cassie's rapid-fire expressions landed solidly on "flabbergasted". Rita, who'd clearly spent all day in the kitchen putting together this picture-perfect meal, stopped scooping butter-glistening potatoes from a pot into a bowl, mustering an intake of breath, followed by an, "Oh? Cassie never mentioned that."

Fred slid a look from me to Cassie. "That would have been something worth warning your mother about."

"Cassie didn't know . . . I mean, it's a recent thing. I didn't want to be any trouble so I didn't mention it." The words were coming out fast, fuelled by the need to protect Cassie from the backsplash of my messy cover-up. "I just should probably go and get some . . . tofu . . ."

"No bother at all, honey," Rita reassured me, "I just would have portioned things differently had I known—more turkey sandwiches for Fred next week." She was already waving a hand at Fred and beckoning him to her. "To tell you the truth, I started making the change a month ago myself, a few days a week, so I made a few mushroom and yam side dishes to try out. How about I fix you a salad and some of those?"

I could feel Cassie staring daggers into the side of my head and Fred sliding suspicious glances between us. "Sounds great," I choked, trying to drown out the howling protest in my stomach.

"Looks like there's one less carnivore under this roof."

Veganism had failed me. Instead of getting out of the house, somehow I'd ended up closer to the danger-zone, three feet from a delicious hunk of meat I couldn't even eat, picking through what would have otherwise been a pretty amazing plate. It was hard to keep the flow of conversation. The wolf inside me was throwing a tantrum of epic proportions at getting screwed out of turkey dinner, every roiling howl and whine shuddering my bones, making the hair that wanted to grow into a brilliant pelt itch mercilessly. Time was ticking by too steadily and it was already past when I'd planned to leave.

External tension wasn't helping me find my inner peace either. My phone was buzzing with increasingly urgent check-ins from Jodie, and Fred and Rita were tag-teaming me with personal questions like they were trying out as Barbara Walters' understudies.

Though I didn't miss when Cassie gave my thigh a pinch under the table, catching my eye as the conversation shifted to some scientific chatter between Erik and Rita.

"What the hell, Luc? Since when?" Cassie muttered, cutting her eyes at my leaf-laden plate.

Lying to her hadn't been part of the plan. At least never this directly. It was part of the reason why I'd never really done the "serious relationship" thing before, the roiling nauseous feeling that swept through me when I had to lie to protect people from the not-quite-human part of me.

"Very recent," I said, which was the truth. "I was going to tell you."

"Recent like 'since breakfast'?" she countered. "You said you made bacon. And eggs. With *cheese*."

Luckily, like a knight on a horse, Rita saved me from the damning list of proteins.

"Now, no pressure at all, Luc, but we've got this family

tradition where we open a couple presents tonight after supper, since it's the only time we're all together for the holiday. Fred and I got you a little something, but you've got absolutely no obligations here," she said.

My cell buzz-buzzed into my pocket desperately like a trapped hornet. Cassie's stare was burning into the side of my face. Somewhere behind the jail cell bars of my sternum, the wolf was groaning and grumbling, antsy paws pacing. On an ordinary moon-night, we would've been safely secured in the garage half an hour ago. I was a ticking time bomb and needed to get as far away from these nice folks as I could.

"I'm so sorry . . ." my voice trailed off, scrambling again for a way out.

"You're either on call or a drug dealer," Erik said, cutting me off with a snort and gesturing to my pocket. "I mean, your phone's gone off non-stop. You have somewhere else to be?"

"Shut up," Cassie snapped, with a glare.

"Erik!" Fred warned. "Enough."

"I do . . . I mean, I usually do." My thoughts were fragmented, but I let my voice overtake the rising discord. "I'm sorry . . . The gifts . . . that's amazingly sweet and you've all been incredibly welcoming. It's just that usually by now . . . I'm at . . . church."

Cassie's jaw dropped like a cartoon, as she didn't even bother to disguise her confusion.

But sweet, cheerful, unflappable Rita was beaming with delight. My stomach sank with dread.

"Oh Fred, it's been decades since we've made it to a Mass. Christmas Mass! Wouldn't that be nice? I bet they're already doing the carols, and the candles were always so pretty with the stained-glass at the night-time services . . . Why don't we call this a new tradition and all of us can go with Luc?"

Just let me out, the wolf crooned. *At least it'd be quick.*

A kamikaze Mass was not what I'd pictured on the schedule, but here I was. Rita's eyes were sparkling at Fred and she left little room for argument.

If there was a Hell, I think I'd just guaranteed a first-class ticket down.

Angèle Gougeon
A Furtastic Gathering

Angèle Gougeon is a Canadian speculative author and artist with a love of fantasy and all things canid. Her work has been seen in literary magazines and anthologies, as well as having a dark Gothic paranormal, *Sticks and Stones*, published through EDGE Science Fiction and Fantasy Publishing.

Sarah Hersman
Yule Moon

Sarah Hersman has a PhD in Neuroscience, and is currently working as a scientist in the biotech industry. She published her first novel, *The Night's Gift*, with Mischievous Muse Press in 2018. In her spare time, (such as it is), she reads voraciously, sings opera, and writes. She lives in Boston with her husband JJ and her dog Jackson.

Rhonda Parrish
Two Loyal Dogs (And a Hornhead in an Apple Tree)

Like a magpie, Rhonda Parrish is constantly distracted by shiny things. She's the editor of many anthologies and author of plenty of books, stories, and poems. She lives with her husband and cats in Edmonton, Alberta, and she can often be found there playing Dungeons and Dragons, bingeing crime dramas, making blankets, or cheering on the Oilers.

Her website, updated regularly, is at rhondaparrish.com and her Patreon, updated even more regularly, is at patreon.com/RhondaParrish.

JB Riley
Playing the Odds

JB Riley writes and edits technical healthcare proposals for a major US-based corporation, but has loved reading and writing speculative fiction ever since discovering *The Chronicles of Narnia* at Age 8. When not trawling the shelves at the local bookstore, she enjoys travel, hockey, beer, and cooking. JB lives in Chicago with her family; which currently includes an 80-pound dog, a puppy the size of a bathtub who thinks he's a lapdog, a 15-pound cat, and a 5-pound cat that scares the hell out of everyone.

Louis B. Rosenberg
The Curse of Christmas Present

Louis B. Rosenberg is the author of three sci-fi graphic novels (*Eons, Upgrade,* and *Monkey Room*) from Outland Publishing and an award-winning web series (*Lab Rats*) from Frostbite Pictures. He is also the author of two surreal picture books on artificial intelligence (*Arrival Mind* and *One of Us*). His short fiction and poetry have appeared in *Time & Space Magazine, Abyss & Apex, Andromeda Spaceways Magazine, Dark Matter Magazine, Sci-Fi Lampoon,* the *Tales to Terrify* podcast, and various anthologies.

Robert W. Easton
Rex Invictis

Robert W. Easton is a long-time writer of short stories, poetry and roleplaying adventures for his friends and family. Rob is currently living in the environ of Calgary, Alberta, Canada, with his wife, daughter, and a varying number of black cats.

Rob has been previously published in *Strangely Funny III,* the online poetry anthology *VAMPoetry, Enigma Front: The Monster Within, The 30 Day Collective Vol. 1: The End, Strange Behaviours: An Anthology of Absolute Luridity, Anthology Askew 005: Fantastically Askew, 100 Word Horrors: An Anthology of Horror Drabbles, Hyper-tomb: Crypt of the Cyber-Mummy,* and *100 Word Horrors Part 2: An Anthology of Horror Drabbles.* In 2018, Rob published his first novel *Fortress of the Heart.*

Jennifer Lee Rossman
O Howly Night

Jennifer Lee Rossman (she/they) is a queer, disabled, and autistic author and editor from Binghamton, New York. Follow her on Twitter @JenLRossman and read more of her work on her website jenniferleerossman.blogspot.com.

Lisa Timpf
Where the Hearth Is

Lisa Timpf is a retired HR and communications professional who lives in Simcoe, Ontario. Her speculative fiction has appeared in *New Myths, Third Flatiron, Future Days, From a*

Cat's View, and other venues. Lisa's Russian Blue cat, Smokey, and her border collie, Emma, provided the inspiration for the characters Quicksilver and Pepper. You can learn more about Lisa's writing at lisatimpf.blogspot.com.

Rachel Sharp
All Bark

After a decade of touring the country, Rachel Sharp now lives in Vermont with several plants and her questionable sense of humour. She is the author of the *Phaethon* and *Planetary Tarantella* trilogies. She also lives with chronic illness, plays ukulele, and tries to save the planet.

Sarah L. Johnson and Robert Bose
Corn Dogs

Sarah L. Johnson and Robert Bose lurk in Calgary, Canada where they're co-dreaditors at The Seventh Terrace, a small press for dark/horror/weird fiction. They write stories together and on their own, have been published widely, and share a fondness for whisky, tentacles, and running insane distances over dangerous terrain. You can check out their misdeeds at the-seventh-terrace.com.

Krista D. Ball
The Twelve Days of Dating

Krista D. Ball is an Edmonton author of over twenty books, including the popular *What Kings Ate and Wizards Drank.*

Rebecca M. Senese
The Yule Wolf

Based in Toronto, Canada, Rebecca M. Senese survives the frigid blasts of winter and boiling steams of summer by weaving words of mystery, horror, science fiction, and contemporary fantasy.

She is the author of the contemporary fantasy series, the *Noel Kringle Chronicles* featuring the son of Santa Claus working as a private detective in Toronto. Garnering an Honorable Mention in "The Year's Best Science Fiction," she has been nominated for numerous Aurora Awards. Her work has appeared in *Bitter Mountain Moonlight: A Cave Creek Anthology, Promise in the*

Gold: A Cave Creek Anthology, Unmasked: Tales of Risk and Revelation, the *Obsessions Anthology*, *Fiction River: Superpowers, Fiction River: Visions of the Apocalypse, Fiction River: Sparks, Fiction River: Recycled Pulp, Tesseracts 16: Parnassus Unbound, Ride the Moon, Tesseracts 15: A Case of Quite Curious Tales, TransVersions, Future Syndicate*, and *Storyteller*, amongst others.

Find out more about Rebecca at: rebeccasenese.com.

Lizz Donnelly
Bark! The Harold Angels Sing

Lizz Donnelly is a writer, knitter, and owner/dyer of Dark Sea Yarn from upstate, New York. Her writing has appeared recently in the Aurora Award-nominated *Swashbuckling Cats: Nine Lives on the Seven Seas, Space Opera Libretti*, and *Grimm, Grit, and Gasoline*. She can be found talking mostly about yarn and 80s crime dramas on Twitter @LizzDonnelly.

Adam Israel
In Anticipation of Their First Transformation

Adam Israel is a writer and software engineer living in Ontario, Canada with his wife, two dogs, and several cats. He can be found online at adamisrael.com.

E.C. Bell
The Dead Tree Gift

E.C. Bell is the author of the award-winning paranormal Marie Jenner Mystery series. She lives in Alberta, Canada, and when she's not writing, she's scouting out new locations for her upcoming novels or renovating her round house where she lives with her husband and their rescue dog, Buddy.

That's right. Her house is round.

Melanie Marttila
The Wolf You Feed

Eyes on the skies, head in the clouds, Melanie Marttila writes poetry and speculative tales of hope in the face of adversity. She lives and writes in Sudbury, Ontario, in the house where three generations of her family have lived, on the street that bears her surname, with her spouse and their dog.

J. Y. T. Kennedy
Apple Night

J. Y. T. Kennedy is an Alberta based writer, focusing on speculative fiction and poetry. Other anthologies that have featured her work include *Stellar Evolutions, Alice Unbound: Beyond Wonderland*, and *Danse Macabre: Close Encounters with the Reaper*. She also performs as a storyteller, with a particular interest in folktales and historical tales.

Rebecca Brae
The Teeth Have It

Rebecca Brae lives in Alberta, Canada with her partner, daughter, and growing pack of animal companions. She has co-authored two urban fantasy novels, *Chaos Bound* and *Curse Bound*, published a fantasy novel, *The Witch's Diary*, and has short stories in several fun anthologies. Connect on Twitter @RebeccaBrae and at www.braevitae.com.

V.F. LeSann
Shifting Gears

V.F. LeSann is the co-writing team of Leslie Van Zwol and Megan Fennell, united for greater power like Captain Planet, sworn to tread the wobbly line between grit and whimsy. Already huge fans of all things wolves (were-variety and otherwise), they were stunned to realize that although they've written about everything from sentient spaceships to dragon-riders to maudlin party-gods, this is their first published story with an actual werewolf in it.

CPSIA information can be obtained
at www.ICGtesting.com
Printed in the USA
BVHW070217251121
622490BV00001B/9